LIST

This

All Happened

Michael Winter

A Fictional Memoir

LIST

This edition published in 2013 by
House of Anansi Press Inc.
110 Spadina Avenue, Suite 801
Toronto, ON, M5V 2K4
Tel. 416-363-4343
Fax 416-363-1017
www.houseofanansi.com

Distributed in Canada by
HarperCollins Canada Ltd.
1995 Markham Road
Scarborough, ON, M1B 5M8
Toll free tel. 1-800-387-0117

Distributed in the United States by
Publishers Group West
1700 Fourth Street
Berkeley, CA 94710
Toll free tel. 1-800-788-3123

House of Anansi Press is committed to protecting our natural environment. As part of our efforts, the interior of this book is printed on paper that contains 30% post-consumer recycled fibres, is acid-free, and is processed chlorine-free.

17 16 15 14 13   1 2 3 4 5

Library and Archives Canada Cataloguing in Publication

Winter, Michael, 1965–
This all happened : a fictional memoir / Michael Winter ; introduction by Lisa Moore.

Originally published: Toronto : House of Anansi Press, 2000.
With new introduction.

Issued in print and electronic formats.
ISBN: 978-1-77089-372-6 (pbk.). ISBN: 978-1-77089-377-1 (html)

I. Title.

PS8595.I624T45 2013   C813'.54   C2013-902777-7
                             C2013-902778-5

Library of Congress Control Number: 2013938670

Cover design: Brian Morgan
Cover illustration: Jillian Tamaki
Text design and typesetting: Brian Panhuyzen

Canada Council   Conseil des Arts   ONTARIO ARTS COUNCIL
for the Arts   du Canada   CONSEIL DES ARTS DE L'ONTARIO

We acknowledge for their financial support of our publishing program the Canada Council for the Arts, the Ontario Arts Council, and the Government of Canada through the Canada Book Fund.

Printed and bound in Canada

MIX
Paper from
responsible sources
FSC
www.fsc.org   FSC® C107923

This

All Happened

Introduction by Lisa Moore

Gabriel English, the narrator of Michael Winter's *This All Happened*, has a lot in common with the writer Michael Winter. For instance, Gabriel is writing a novel based on the American artist Rockwell Kent. Michael Winter wrote the novel *The Big Why*, based on Rockwell Kent, soon after the publication of *This All Happened*.

Gabriel lives with roommates in a creaky downtown St. John's house with raspberries growing in the garden. Michael Winter, for a time, lived with roommates in a house downtown very like Gabriel's. When a visitor ate raspberries out of Michael's garden, she could smell them, later, on her fingers, just as Gabriel does.

And Gabriel has fallen dangerously in love with a gorgeous, much-sought- after filmmaker girlfriend who is full of errant desire and equivocation, ambivalence, ambition, joyousness, and insight. A girlfriend who, when she throws back her head in laughter, at the New Year's party that opens Winter's startlingly beautiful and spare novel, has a taut white throat, and lips in a crescent of broken apple.

But who knows for sure if it can be said that the same thing happened to Michael Winter? We are given a caveat: "This is a work of fiction. Any resemblance to people living or dead is intentional and encouraged."

Much of *This All Happened* is an interrogation of what is true, or how the stories we tell help the truth to shape-shift and transform. The chasm between truth and how we try to capture it with words (that ever-warping medium) has always been a preoccupation for Michael Winter, one that makes us aware of our subjectivity, causes us to question our beliefs, and jostles our understanding of what, exactly, happened.

Winter invents; no two of his novels are alike. Here the form is a record of a full year, unfolding day by day in an urgent, charging present tense. *This All Happened* is a log, noting the course of a turbulent love affair, each entry in chronological order, marked by the date.

Some entries are as brief as a koan: "There are white flowers on the raspberry bushes."

Some are aphoristic: "Life is a battle between attaining comfort and rebelling against it."

There is unabashed poetry: "The cod are full of capelin, Max says. They are little purses full of silver coins."

Some entries contain maxims about writing: "One of my key tenets: if you know what the next scene is you've already written it."

And there are elongated entries about moments: "I'm writing honest moments and people who are themselves and people who make fun of themselves and are silly and childish and unsophisticated and warm and generous and loving and full of toughness too and original and sexy and rough and animalish and playful and have guts and a red red tender heart bursting crying at small wonderful irrational things at moments at hot moments that steam and penetrate our brains and sizzle like a branding iron into the marrow and make us horny and I like trying to put words to these moments give particulars and hand them delicately to people..."

On January 2, Gabriel tells us his girlfriend, Lydia, has these words for life: want, crave, desire, yearn.

He says: "And who wouldn't want these words, but they do frighten me."

In this way, Winter differs entirely from Gabriel English, because in this novel the author's very pulse and breath is full of want, craving, and desire—and though there's the boiling-over engine of jealousy, this prose is fearless.

Here is what I crave in any novel: surety.

An authority of voice that allows the reader that singular and intense pleasure: the suspension of disbelief.

This All Happened is bursting with that kind of authority. Also, there is humour, lust, jealousy, landscape so accurately rendered the reader looks up and sees the boulders and scrubby spruce and churning ocean as though she had never seen them before.

There is talk of writing, of style and form, infidelity, drunkenness, community, friendship, canoeing, and anguish-inspiring, crazy-making, meaning-of-life-provoking love.

Love that burns so very hot and bright, it is destined not to last.

But one thing of which we may be certain: the record of the moment will endure.

Gabriel writes in his last entry: "A moment winks like

a black locomotive, harnessed fire, sitting impatiently on its haunches, forever primed to lurch and devour."

What this means is that if this has *not* really all happened, it will, and will again and again, for every reader.

to, for,
and because of
MARY

Gabriel English was the protagonist in a book of stories I wrote entitled *One Last Good Look*. Let me tell you about Gabriel English. He is a writer. He's supposed to be writing a novel. Instead, he writes a collection of daily vignettes over a full calendar year. These small windows onto moments follow the evolving passion and anguish Gabriel feels for Lydia Murphy. The vignettes also document the desperate relationships that blossom and fail around him. Gabriel discusses his friends, confesses his failings, copies overheard drunken conversations, declares his dreams, reports gossip, and charts the ebb and flow of his love affair with the people and geography of Newfoundland — in particular, the port city of St John's. The result of this daily examination is the book youre holding. *This All Happened* is a literary tableau of Newfoundland life, for better or for worse, seen from within.

Caveat: This is a work of fiction. Any resemblance to people living or dead is intentional and encouraged. Fictional characters and experience come to life when we compare them with the people and places we know. New experience is always a comparison to the known.

— *M. W.*

Contents

January

1 Lydia leans back to laugh at something Wilf Jardine says. Her breasts are the closest thing to Wilf, and he is looking down her taut white throat. Lydia's teeth and lips a crescent of broken apple. Offering up her breasts and throat to Wilf. She wants to go elsewhere after the midnight fireworks, and that ambition to persist, I have decided, is drawing me to her.

A toast! and Max Wareham hands me a brandy. Max is naked under a pale raglan. I steady myself against the back of a chair. I love Max. This year I must confess all to Max. And in the periphery Lydia is still entranced by Wilf. Can I love a woman who is so entranced? Wilf lurches to me, kisses me, and I want to smack Wilf for being powerful in Lydia's eyes. I want to make sure my forearm catches his chin in the follow-through. Wilf Jardine's short white hair and suit jacket are doused in peppermint schnapps. He's apologizing for wolfing down Lydia. That's what he is, a wolf. Wilf the white-haired, ravenous wolf. He clinks my glass when the clock hands meet at twelve, and Max cries out, To Old Year's Night! I watch pearls of liquor spinning out before my brandy snifter smashes on the hardwood. Wet splinters across all the shoes. All Shoes Night. And Alex, our hostess, says, Nobody move.

Alex Fleming, in a black sleeveless number, brushes our feet with a straw broom. She pushes flakes of wet glass into a yellow pan. She sweeps the toes of my black shoes a little extra, first act of the new year. Swipes at my knees, brush handle between my legs, and Max my dear friend Max is dancing barefoot in a raincoat.

Alex, just minutes before, had fingered the dust on the windowsill and said, drunkenly, Gabriel, you shagger. She pressed a thigh against the outside of my knee and I could see down the entire front of her black number. Imagine, she's all of twenty-six and pressing me. She said, If I could get my claws into you. She gave me her entire eye. What I mean is she threw herself at me with one eye. And while I did not lurch, I did not decline.

Maisie Pye grabs my elbow and steers me back to Lydia.

Lydia leans on my shoulder. Wilf, she says. Wilf said, Any chance of a Christmas fling?

Me: Wilf said that?

Make you jealous?

Wilf Wilf fuck you Wilf.

Lydia and I rock against the fridge, Max opening the door for the last few beers. There's a garbage bucket full of ice cubes and broken beer bottles, and Max Wareham, when he spoke to me almost naked, spreading lapels to show his fat nipples, Max had a sliver of brown glass hanging from his lip the size of a number-fourteen wet fly. He says, I know youre the apple of someone's eye, Gabe.

I love you, man.

Max: I love you too, man. He pauses, almost in deep sorrow. He says, Hard to say I love you without adding man.

Me: You love me?

Max considers this.

I'm talking to Lydia, Max.

I love you anyway, man. I love you unconditionally, and you can leave off the man. Pretend I never said it.

I'm thinking, Never ask the one you love: Do you love me?

Lydia: I love you, darling.

The ghost of burnt fireworks hovers over the water.

Max, as we wait for a cab, makes angel's wings in the garden. His shaved head in the snow. Lydia pulls up the collar of her astrakhan, holds me tight. I want her head to sink deep inside my chest.

2　Words Lydia has for life are want, crave, desire, yearn, and who wouldnt want these words, but they do frighten me. The appetites. They are good for an actor to possess. Lydia is a good actor and a filmmaker, though she is not meticulous in her technique. The frame is full of life and love. In life she cares for colour, quality of fabric, but if there's a rent under the arm, she hardly notices. I have seen her orchestrate the actions of a hundred crew and cast. Giving direction is her normal bent. It's what attracts and detracts.

I woke up in my own bed, alone. The cab dropped Lydia off and I went home alone and walked down the pathway to my little house on the cusp of downtown. I made new footprints in the snow, the first prints of the new year. Iris and Helmut were in the kitchen dancing to the radio. I didnt even brush my teeth. Stripped, that felt good, and being alone was good, too. I love a cold bedroom. And in the morning I turned on the space heater and boiled the kettle and ate buttered toast and tea. All New Year's Day I sat in my room and stared at the frozen harbour. I thought about marrying Lydia Murphy. I have two New Year's resolutions: to decide on Lydia and to finish a novel.

I love this room. I love the huge windows that meet at the corner of the house. I watched the snow patiently accumulate over surfaces. I called Lydia, but we took the day off from each other, exhausted.

I called Max. He'd gone to emerge with frostbite on his ears.

I wrote off the first of the new year. I heard Iris say to Helmut, I will meet you in Brazil. That phrase could have melted a snowman.

3   I call Lydia. She'd gone to Maisie and Oliver's last night (I declined, so hung over). Wilf was there. Wilf played a game with them at supper. Of putting a word on the forehead of someone else. Lydia stuck CHARM on Wilf's head. And he put TRUTH on hers.

Not jealous of her time with Wilf. Because of her tone of voice. The loving.

Maybe we should get married, I say.

Maybe.

Can I define Lydia's hesitation? Perhaps it's that I blurted out the marriage offer. Her tone was warm, trepidatious, scared of the prospect rather than of me. A good sign. Of course, I've been hinting at marriage for eighteen months. Am I that pathetic, that I wanted to marry her after our first date?

4   I walk down Long's Hill to Lydia's. Lydia's house is of better material than mine, but she has no view and the house is attached. There is a wooden banister and hardwood floors and exposed beams and a funky bathroom sink and tub. My house is the windows, the eyes that study the downtown and the harbour, that witness the marine traffic and the weather accumulating over the Grand Banks.

Lydia says she has met this woman, Daphne Yarn, and thinks she's perfect for Max. Daphne's a nurse, she has land in Brigus where she grows herbs and goats. I say, What makes you think of her and Max? Lydia: Max is a man who can appreciate nature. And Daphne has a serene beauty.

I find the term serene beauty insulting. Words like grace, serenity, harmony, peace. They all connote some kind of composure. How some people adopt a tone. The cultured poise that unnerves me. A measured evenness.

Lydia: Sure, youre like that when you leave a message on the phone to anyone.

And she mimics me. She may be right.

I dont know, though, if I'd wish Max on any woman. He's a hard case. I love him, but I'm not a woman.

How did she note this in Max — this need for a solid fixture at home? It's true, and perhaps wildness desires a measure of calm. I know that I desire to spend some time outside of town. On my own. I tell Lydia I may ask Maisie and Oliver about their house in Heart's Desire. To spend a week or two there. Lydia says, It might be good for your writing.

5   I sleep at Lydia's and we cook poached eggs (I watch her add a drop of vinegar to the water) and we lie around the fire with Tinker Bumbo and then we walk over to Maisie and Oliver's. Before we leave Lydia's, she looks at the electric meter. It's winging around too fast, so she steps back inside to flick something off.

We buy beer at Theatre Pharmacy. You can buy bandages, a lady's purse, a car battery, and beer at this place. I get light beer to please Lydia. There's a dogberry that still has fruit, snow capping the berries like patriotic Canadian desserts. Little Una in the porch hands us slippers and I say, That's a very European thing to do, Una. Is she nine?

Maisie Pye folds her glasses by her plate. Ten years ago I went out with Maisie. Sometimes I think of this. I think, I could be married with a nine-year-old daughter. And so could Lydia. Lydia's ex, Earl, has a son now. Earl lives two streets away. Once, when we were walking home from the Ship, Lydia told me to shush. We were talking about Earl, under his window.

There is salsa and blue corn chips. Russian cold bean salad. Scalloped potatoes. Ham and pineapple. What a feed.

I ask if I can borrow their house in Heart's Desire. Oliver Squires dunks a cold shrimp into a hot sauce. That house is too cold for you.

Lydia: It's too cold and too far to drive.

Oliver: Are you both going out?

Me: It'll just be me.

Oliver: Put antifreeze in the toilet when you leave.

Maisie says she lived out in Heart's for one winter with Una. While Oliver finished his law degree at Dal.

What she doesnt say is, When Oliver and I were going through a hard time.

6 Snowstorm, the city closed down on Old Christmas Day — but from my windows it's nothing compared with childhood storms. Lydia has stayed over, though she doesnt like it here. There's no privacy from Iris and Helmut. There's a grain of aggravation in Lydia that I can't make a go of it without a roommate. And then there's the fact that I owe twenty thousand dollars in student loans. Lydia is solvent whereas I'm scraping by. The bedroom doors have an inch gap at the floor, so it's hard to be intimate. At least I could replace the doors. We wax up (waxes have lovely names: orange klister) and ski downtown, dropping off Lydia's last mortgage cheque. She owns her house. It'll be nineteen years before I own a house. Driveway shovellers encourage us by wagging their aluminum shovels. There's a new, wider shovel called a push.

Discarded Christmas trees are blown in wide arcs down the hill, clumps of silver tinsel attempting to make the trees respectful. Lydia slips by me on the road, crouched and silent, plunging into the downtown. Just a whirr from her skis. Her strength is sexy.

All day the snow piles on. Towers of snow teetering towards houses. We buy split peas at Hallidays to make soup, and ski past the video store that glows against the twilight, the snow on the sills is fluorescent, a cat asleep by the cash register. We ski along Gower Street, to Lydia's little two-storey clapboard house. She's left lights on and it's like a pumpkin house. How soft the city is, silent, in the snow.

7   Snowbound in St John's. I sit by the fire at Lydia's with Tinker Bumbo. He is fifteen, arthritic, snores, and farts. His balls flop out of his hindquarters like a purse. Lydia's doorbell rings. She's in the shower, so Tinker and I get it. Tinker wags and moans, his balls swaying from knee to knee, a scrotum pendulum.

A short man pushes past me.

Hello, I say.

He sits on a chair and slips off his overshoes. He lifts an elbow to me. I take it. He wears a blue suit, is in his fifties. His eyes blink, then open wide. And I see now, he's blind. Short silver hair. Portly, with sausage fingers. He takes a dog biscuit from his breast pocket and Tinker sits to receive it. He leads me to the piano by the Christmas tree.

Youre new, he says.

Yes, I say.

I've been tuning this piano for thirty years.

He is wrenching off the small nuts in the back of the stand-up. It's a fair model, he says.

I ask if he'd like some coffee.

I rarely have anything between meals.

I bring coffee up to Lydia.

The piano tuner is here.

Mr O'Brien. Oh, good.

She is leaning over, rolling her wet hair in a towel.

He must have walked, blind, through the drifts to the front door.

8   I meet Alex Fleming for dim sum. I havent seen her since New Year's. She wants help with an art project that deals with passion. She says, Did I reach between your legs with a broom? Did I?

She reaches into her purse. I dont picture you as a man who is quiet, she says. Who doesnt talk much.

Alex has thin skin on a strongly defined face, long bleached hair, twenty-six. She has big eyes. Her eyes, I imagine, will get bigger. The eyes are slightly crazy. Or, she has come through craziness.

We are paying the bill. I notice she has a passport in her purse. You were born in seventy-three, I say.

I am trying to be a customs agent, or prescient. I am formal but flirting. Alex Fleming pulls out the passport, numerous ports of entry. I see her photo and birthdate. Her full name:

Marie Alexandra Fleming.

I was born in October, Officer.

She says officer in a tone that is courageously sexual. This tone lingers for a moment. I am supposed to be a border guard considering her credentials. Then the word and its tone disappear. Flirting is such a delicious act. I show her a photo of Lydia when she was five.

Alex: Youre a sentimental guy.

Her knuckle touches my hand. She has sophisticated fingers, the slight cool of a silver ring. Alex is not asking about the photo — if she asked I'd say it reminds me that Lydia is crazy, mad, sexy, brilliant, funny. And that being with her, I lack regret. But that would bore the hell out of flirtation.

Dim sum means small heart, Alex says, or appetizers.

She turns her cup over and twists it clockwise three times.

I lift her cup and read her fortune.

I see a beach, and bright skies. There is a window with louvres. A man is bringing you something.

Alex: Is the man good to me?

Me: He has tender hands.

You love the word louvres, dont you?

I confess I am a lover of louvres.

Alex: Did you know there are no muscles in the fingers?

We examine each other's fingers. It's an excuse to touch. Then she reads my cup. It involves two quiet sailboats. Meeting at a boom.

Alex: It is meeting someone else. Briefly.

Me: Do they have an affair?

An affair of the heart, she says. And there's a successful career too, a well-earned one.

Pluck rather than luck, I say.

Alex: Although youre very lucky.

Outside a fat snow falling.

And this too seems shocking.

I can smell cologne.

Alex Fleming is a woman who wears cologne.

There is a figure riding a bicycle, leaning hard over the handlebars, and I recognize the bicycle. It's Lydia.

Lydia: Oh hi!

Alex opens a lavender umbrella to the snow and three nude women pop out, dancing across its ribs. And I cannot see Lydia for the umbrella.

9 Me: She wants me to write some prose poems on passion.

Lydia: Youre sure she doesnt want more than poems.

It's a collaboration. I'm going to do the seven deadly sins. I've remembered them with an acronym: scalp egg. Except there's only one G.

What?

The first letters: sloth, covetousness, anger, lust, pride, envy, gluttony.

Babe, you won't fall for Alex, will you?

It's work is all.

I show her the key to Heart's Desire. Imagine, Lydia says, writing a novel there. Who would believe it. Too corny for words.

But I want, this year, to write a historical novel, set in Brigus, where the painter Rockwell Kent and the northern explorer Bob Bartlett both lived. I want a boy who is fourteen to meet them. To have these men inform the boy of the outside world. The boy will be the last person born in the nineteenth century.

I shove a piece of cardboard between Jethro's radiator and grill, to help keep his engine warm. I drive by to pick up Tinker Bumbo. I hold Lydia by the shoulders and we kiss and I love her shoulders. She almost decides to come.

Well, visit me.

I will, babe.

10 There is a moose on the highway. I wake up Tinker Bumbo, and a youthful transformation slips over his frame. He sniffs at the lip of the window. The cow stares at me in the snow, waiting, patient. And then a grown calf emerges from the woods. They trot off together, wedge open the spruce, and are gone.

Heart's Desire. A Catholic town nestled between two Protestant ones (Heart's Content and Heart's Delight). The fishery closed. I pass a man pulling logs out with an all-terrain vehicle. He waves and I honk.

Maisie and Oliver's little red house is beyond the bridge. The key will not work, so I have to force the side door. There are boys on cold bicycles hauling sleds, watching me. There's no water.

I lug in wood from the shed and get the stove going. I

open the vent and hear the fire roar. I turn on a radio. It's less desolate with a radio. The same radio voices you'd hear in St John's. There's a distant rush of water, under the house. A frantic sound. I turn on a tap and get the hollow sound of air.

11 Heart's Desire is not a pretty town. The modern bungalows clutch the road, the abandoned saltboxes are pilfered for lumber. The church was torn down and relocated in a complex that includes a bingo hall and the mayor's office. There's no vista here; a bare inlet, a spruce backyard, and flat land. I phone Maisie to ask about the water. She says, Look under the house. But a storm has begun, and I decide to ignore it. Gallons of water are escaping somewhere under the floorboards. The faucets are all dry. I sit in the living room, near the woodstove. The walls and windows buffer the wind, but you can still feel it. There's a slight current of cold, wet air. The sky darkens and I peer outside. I have no flashlight. The storm is so thick I can't see the lights across Trinity Bay. The wind whips the porch door from my hands, smacks it against the house so hard it is wrenched off its hinges. I step down off the porch and crouch into the crawl space. I feel around, I feel water charging through the kitchen drainpipe. A boy comes by on his bicycle and I tell him.

Light a kerosene lamp, he says.

I go inside and light one. But when I bring it to the door, it douses in the wind.

He says, Light it when we're under.

The lamp coats a false, cheerily maniacal face to the vicious

13

pipes, the fall of water — ice forming savage stalactites around the main sewer line. I am in awe at nature's lack of shock. That a process will not stop when a situation becomes horrendous. There is no fairness, no honour. I break off chunks of smooth ice from the mad clown. I find a tap and turn it until the water ceases.

I'm Josh.

I'm Gabe.

Josh: No one stays in this house over winter. Drafts and whatnot, the water freezing up on you. Though it's never good, he says, to have a house empty.

12 I drive to a grocery store in Heart's Content. Bright aisles and surprising sales. A fresh plump chicken, the whole plucked bird, for three dollars. I snatch it up. It's true I dont feel right about owning a whole chicken. I have a problem with my own deserving. There's fresh horseradish and ripe mangosteens. The cashier doesnt know what to charge me for the mangosteens. She looks at them as if I might have snuck them into the store under my coat.

I've never eaten a mangosteen. But I want to support the idea that a little place in Trinity Bay will import them. I want to encourage the mind that brought them here. Let the accounting show that three mangosteens were purchased on the road to Heart's Desire.

13 Lydia phones. She is spending a lazy day, loving me. She went downstairs and saw my photograph on the fridge and knew.

She says, Sometimes I feel shy.

Come and visit me.

I'll try.

Want to live together?

We'll see.

What else can I say? I cut short the call and brood around the house. I want to live with Lydia. I'm tired of separate places, and as it stands I dont even have a key to Lydia's. I want to rent her place and have her move in with me. Or the other way around, though I'd miss the view.

I thaw the freezer and get impatient. I lay a hammer to the ice and crack the freon tubing so I shut the door on it. I read one of Oliver's crime novels. I e-mail Alex and Max and Maisie. Each, I realize, encourages a different e-mail voice. For instance, Alex told me of a naked eye she's building. When you look at it, the pupil grows larger. She wrote: The pupil is not a thing but the absence of iris. It's the iris shrinking that makes the pupil grow. That's eros allowing in more light from the object in question.

When you abandon love, flirtation increases.

Max writes spoonerisms: All guns and fame until someone oozes a lie. And Maisie is literary. About the problems a novel presents over a short story. She wrote: A good story should be a door opening onto a scene already begun and closed before the last word said. A novel should be told by the voice of an authority, yet a voice that is still discovering the meaning of what the story is. There should be wonder. And all traces of the technical problem a novel delivers (that is, how do you keep the story afloat for three hundred pages?) should be erased or masked.

14 Two boys on their bikes knock at the door. It's Josh and his buddy Toby. They have a good laugh at Tinker Bumbo.

Toby: Tha's a town dog.

How can you tell.

He got a collar and a dog tag.

I tell them it's my girlfriend's dog. And they are curious about Lydia. I remember Maisie had said that when she was out here, she'd never done any writing. She was a woman with a child and no occupation. You could drop in on her. When she said she needed time to write, they couldnt comprehend it. They invited themselves over. She gave into it.

Josh: So what's your girlfriend do?

She's an actor. And she makes films.

Josh: That's healthy. And what about you?

I try to capture people by their actions. By quick glimpses of how they do or say things. Moments.

Josh says he does that all the time. Except he'd call it gossip.

Me: Let's do a project together. You tell me who lives in Heart's Desire, and I'll write it all down.

Josh and Toby look at each other and sit on the couch.

All right then.

They stretch their necks to look out the window. We'll start across the road. Madge is in the green house; she's a nun.

Josh: She's not.

Toby: No, but close to it. Next to her is closed up, but Et Coombs, she used to live there.

Josh: Lives in the graveyard now.

Toby: The Rumboldts, they got a little tiny house and a little tiny car. Tom Rumboldt we calls him Tommy Ginger, cause he's always crooked.

The boys rhyme off fifty-four families that live along the road. They are like old men in their depictions and knowledge. They are far more knowledgeable of the people they love than I am of my own.

15 I've asked Lydia Murphy to marry me. I've called her and asked her. On the phone her voice was little. Yes, she said, I think so.

When I responded that she sounded dubious, she said, nervous and excited, Okay, I'll marry you. I said, Are you sure. I said it as a statement rather than as a question. She hesitated. She had to go. She'd call me back. I waited for two hours. Then the phone rang. Maybe we should talk about it tomorrow, she said.

I e-mailed Maisie to tell her about the burst water pipe. And then I got into the issue of marriage. I felt a woman would be closer to another woman's ambivalence.

Maisie wrote back, You never meet hesitation with hesitation. That only fosters doubt. When Lydia says no, you say okay. When she says yes, I think so, you say okay. When she says no, you say okay. When she says yes, you say, again, okay. When she says no again, you say okay. And when she finally says yes, you say okay. And then you get married.

This, apparently, is how everyone gets married.

16 I watch Josh and Toby run from the school bus straight to my door. They want to pet down Tinker the town dog and tell me who lives on the Head. They are flaked out on the couch with Tinker between them as I type this. I close up my novel file and open the Heart's Desire one. I am going to use these boys in the novel. What they tell me I'll inject into the story.

I read what they told me yesterday and they crack up.

Jamie Groves just west of us, Josh says, he paints cars. And has a beautiful wife. Toby's grandmother died of a fluke. Renee Critch has a butt so big she walks through a door sideways. Smooth Jude drives the bus and he's so fat his car can barely carry him. There's Uncle Mary, who looks and acts and talks just like a man. Joey Langer couldnt walk before, then he had a operation and he walks perfect now.

John St George was captain of the SS *Eilleen*, a boat they blew the motor in her and smoke went flying everywhere and gas. Then it's Harld Powr.

Me: Why do you say it like that?

Josh: Cause he talks so fast and he walks so fast you can't pass him on bike.

They both laugh and slap each other's legs.

17 I've laid some snares and Tinker finds a dead grouse. It startles me (the snares are set for rabbits). Its long neck rubbed

down to a red hose, brass wire wrapped several times around the branch. Feathers in the moss. A struggle, a large, long battle to get free. But now lifeless. His chest flattened a little to the moss. I set the snare again instinctively. I set the snare even as I feel shame.

I show the white grouse to Josh. He says it looks healthy. Let's go clean him, he says.

I've never cleaned a bird before. Cutting off the head and feet and wings. Beautiful plumage. Prying the beak open to see its perfect mouth. The feathers peel off like a pelt. Coiled black entrails flop out and stink. The heart solid and big, the fresh liver. The chunky flesh of the breast.

Tomorrow I'm taking those snares up.

The ruffled whirr as the birds ascend and disperse. In Peterson's guidebook: at a distance the grouse's muffled thumping is so hollow that sometimes it hardly registers as an exterior sound, but seems rather to be a disturbing series of vibrations within the ear itself.

The strongest socket is in the wing. The legs are like the front legs of a rabbit, no ball joint. The eye sunken but brown.

Josh says, With the cold, the meat should be healthy. He says Franky Langer was once lost in the woods and had to eat his dog. He was gone four days, Josh says. I mean, four days. He couldnt last longer than that before eating his dog?

18 I miss Lydia. When youre used to holding someone, a physical habit, you miss it. Is it habit to miss a voice too, to miss a response to your thought? I do no writing. There is nothing in

Heart's Desire to fill the absence of Lydia. I stare at the road and wait for the school bus. Josh says, in an accusing tone, You wasnt up by lunchtime.

How do you know? You were in school.

My parents said at noontime there was no smoke coming out of your chimley.

Toby: What happened to Maisie's fridge?

I broke it trying to thaw the freezer.

Josh: You laid a hammer to it.

Yes, I went at it with a hammer.

Trying to break out chunks of ice.

Yes.

They both shake their heads.

Josh: Dad got a old fridge in the basement.

Well, I'd love to have it.

Josh: I'll see what I can do.

They take the axe and go out to the shed to cleave up some junks of wood.

19 Josh's father, Cyril Harnum, stands up on the grey flat-bed truck, the garbage truck. With two men helping. The flatbed has a fridge roped to it.

The young driver, with a screwdriver, pops out the hinge bolts on the side door.

I can smell coffee, the other man says. You want her plugged in or thaw her out?

I should have kept the plug out of her last night, Cyril Harnum says.

I have paid fifty dollars for this fridge. The fat, heavy enamelled door that opens onto a salmon pink interior with two chrome shelves that swivel out. There is a pair of lightbulbs sunk into the bottom so the shine strikes up on your food, floorlights on a stage. It makes the food seem solid, planted, stars of the grocery world. The corners of the milk carton lit in a gold aureole, the spout silhouetted. I e-mail Alex about it and she responds that it was built in a time when kitchen appliances were treated as art.

All night I leave my work to go open the fridge door and admire the rich pink interior.

Cyril Harnum: Come over to supper tomorrow.

20 I call Lydia and beg her to come out. She says, I thought you wanted time on your own? I have no response. I miss watching her do things. She doesnt do things the way I do them. She makes a lot of ice cubes. I'm a man who forgets to make ice cubes. She makes sure there's air in her bag of lettuce. She sprinkles talcum powder in her hair if it's greasy.

Josh comes by on his bike with no handlebars. You like fish? He is steering with a set of vice grips clamped to the front fork.

I eat nine pieces of fish with slices of hot homemade bread. The fish is served from the stove. On the table are jars of tomato and rippled pickle slices. I have a mug of boiled water in which I can put a tea bag or a spoonful of instant coffee. There's a can of evaporated milk.

Josh's mom, Doreen, is rolling cigarettes at the table. There's a patch in the varnish at the end of the table faded from cups of tea. I've told them my decision to lift my slips and Josh thinks it's foolish but his dad can see how it's cruel.

Cyril: There used to be no grouse out here. Now the woods is thick with em. Theyre easier to pick than turre. With turre you got to dip em in boiling water first.

There is a big hook in the ceiling that I ask about. Doreen laughs. Cyril has a sore back, she says, from working in the woods. It's all right in the summer, it's in the winter it acts up. So he put a screw in the ceiling beam with a rope through tied to his waist. He hoists himself off the floor with the rope. He won't go see a doctor.

Doreen hands me a fresh loaf as I leave. The snow just wisping over the ground. The loaf is warm in my hand.

21 I tie on my snowshoes and venture into the woods. Tinker wades in a few feet, then sits down. I do love solitude. I am a simple man when it comes to being satisfied by the natural world. The sun poking through in patches, lighting up a knoll here, a dip there. Tinker begins to bawl when he's had enough. I can still see the roof of the house.

A man at the store says, I'll give you twenty dollars for that dog.

You want my dog?

Sure, he looks like he got one more winter in him. He's full of bird dog.

Tinker wags and smells the man's hand.

He's not my dog, I say. I dont want to explain the absence of Lydia, so I leave it at that.

I've got the woodstove vent opened wide, but still I'm cold. Didnt write at all today. I forced myself to read fifty pages of Proust. Maisie and Oliver have great books. But there's no hot water. My hair is greasy. I sweep the floor and visit the Heart's Content grocery. Lydia comes tomorrow. I will hear her catalytic converter.

22 When I opened the door we were shy. We were relieved that Tinker Bumbo was a diversion, but we were awkward together. Twelve days apart and all that we've formed together has burned off, grease on a stove element. We are two individuals again. We do not act in concert. We are not convinced by the prospect of living as a couple. We were brought together by Maisie, and we still feel unnatural. It wasnt our idea to be together but someone else's, and both of us resent that intrusion into domestic affairs. Lydia circles me like an animal, inspecting. And I feel judged.

But I've been told that I have a critical eye. Some people mistake my gaze for judgement. When all I'm doing is looking into your eye. I have an open eye, I admit. This can unnerve some people. Make them uneasy. But it's their insecurity that is exposed. However, I admire the skill Max has for making a person feel comfortable. Max lives in his skin, completely, whereas I float within my body. Not quite filling my frame.

And right now, with Lydia in the kitchen, adding to the fridge with some city groceries, I'm dreading having to make conversation. We've been together eighteen months, and still I have this black, boggy fear creeping into my joints.

Nice fridge, she says.

She has a blemished finery about her. Her good looks only heightened by the small scars incurred from reckless behaviour, when she has hit the corner of a kitchen cabinet or smacked into a cement wall.

23 Josh and Toby are impressed with Lydia. That she's been on television and she owns Tinker. She makes them cookies. I explain our system to Lydia. I unfold the laptop and they begin. There's Rosy Langer with four youngsters and they havent got the same father, and Fail Burden they got a song made up about him about a cigarette or a power saw, and France Clarke lives in a small house, not bad but not very big. About the same size as this one.

They look around.

Same size. France he's after losing a nice bit of weight. He has a car brought up solid on a rock and he got out and the car rised up about three foot. Next is Leonard, he wears pork chop grease to keep his hair down and puts his cap on squish. Then there's Pat Whelan, who got a glass eye.

Lydia: How did he lose his eye?

Toby: I thought it was a hook at the wharf.

Josh: No, he was foolin around and got stuck in the eye with a prong.

Sure, that's what I said.

John Harris is up to the store every day. He uses his trike for a car. Next is Killer Sean; he's married. His wedding was only half an hour long cause they havent got any money.

And that's it for half the harbour.

With the presence of Lydia they cut it short. Josh says, So are you two married or what?

Lydia: No, we're not married.

Me: We're entertaining the prospect.

You guys should get married and come out and live here.

Lydia: We'll think about it.

24 I'm telling Lydia about the novel, how Max Wareham will be the model for Rockwell Kent, how I'm stuffing the novel with facts from the present, stuffing garlic and sage into a leg of lamb, when her body suddenly tenses, her leg lifts off the couch. She wants to interrupt. But rests again. As if her entire body is full of the words she wants to say, have coursed through her and stalled before sputtering out.

Me: What is it.

Lydia: Nothing. It's unrelated.

Me: You may as well say it.

She releases her censor. She says, Do you call Max a friend of yours?

Why.

He was talking about you. He had questions, but the questions were leading.

What did he ask?

He asked what I thought of you. If I thought you were aloof.

And you said.

That I loved you, and yes, you are aloof.

And he said.

That youre obviously attracted to me. He said that I'm too good for you.

He's said that about all my girlfriends.

He wanted to take on Wilf in the basement. He wanted to wrestle. He wanted to wrestle naked.

Was serene Daphne Yarn there for that?

They left together.

You got them together?

I introduced them.

Max has been single a long time.

It was the kind of party where everyone was hitting off everyone else.

I won't even ask.

Wouldnt it be fun to have a party like that? Everyone naked except for trenchcoats.

Me: I think it would be silly.

You think it would.

I think it's funny to think about, but not to go ahead with.

It's fun to laugh, dont you think?

Yes, it's fun to laugh.

25 We load up the cars. I pull the plug on the fridge, prop the freezer door open with a piece of cardboard. I fill the toilet with antifreeze. I stoke up the woodstove one last time, then lock the front door. The boys are in school. I look back to see a puff of pure blue smoke. I follow Lydia as we drive back to town. We pass a harbour seal lying in the snow by the side of

the road. His skin is so full of meat, like a forced sausage. I can see the instinct behind clubbing and sculping.

Lydia says her father thinks we're getting married. She had asked him what he thought of me. And then she had to tell him that we're still thinking about it.

26 Back home on Long's Hill. Helmut Rehm is studying the plans of the racer, *Sailsoft*. He says he will lose about fifteen pounds on the final leg of the race. They will begin in Boston in June and sail to a small port near São Paulo. The next leg has them cross to Namibia. This is the toughest section. Some racers like to veer to an extreme southern latitude, where higher winds exist and therefore greater sailing speed. But there's the danger of shoals, hurricanes, ice, and brutally cold temperatures. They'll lay up in Africa for a month and begin again around the cape to Bombay. Head southeast to Sydney and north again to Hawaii and over to San Francisco. Thread the needle at Panama and then boot it to Boston. A five-month race. Their boat is sponsored by a software company.

Helmut says he can sit in our living room all day and be entertained by the fronts combining to make weather. He has never seen weather like it.

27 Lydia's cousin is getting married to a man who studies geology. He has shown me a series of maps that shave plates of rock off the island, as though it were an anatomy lesson, revealing pockets of magma and oil and natural gas, seams of coal. A network of veins stripped away to expose muscle groups, then these

lifted to display skeletal structure. You understand, from the rock, that the island is chunks of three continents fused together.

In the church, an aunt two pews ahead turns around and mouths to me, Congratulations. I frown. She mouths it again, five distinct syllables.

Lydia: That we're getting married.

Lydia leans over the pew to tell her the difference.

At the reception Lydia spills punch over her blue tulle dress. She says, I guess I'll have to walk around all night like this: one hand on her belly, laughing. The stain between her hand and her laugh. She kisses the groom on the shoulders. She kisses her cousin on the eyelids. The aunt who whispered to me says to Lydia, I can see your bra strap.

Lydia lifts a shoulder, bends an elbow, and slips off her bra. She pulls the bra from her dress like a rabbit. She stuffs it in my jacket pocket.

On the way home with her parents, Lydia in back with her mother, her father dropping me off. We kiss across the seats as he pulls the handbrake against the steep hill. Her parents are disappointed. Mr Murphy had said to me, I hear there's been a proposal. And I had to say to him, We're still negotiating. I hand back her bra, cupped in my fist. The crisp rustle of that blue tulle dress.

I've known her now for eighteen months, but even this one night informs me. I can love her way. But I can't love her if she doesnt love me.

28 Max introduces me to Daphne Yarn. I was expecting

someone quiet, but she has a story. She's taller than Max, but then Max is short. I remind Daphne of her brother. And when I talk she laughs, because we talk about the same things. She says the way I say things is occasionally impossible to follow. She has to wait for more information. And I understand that Lydia is right about me. That I sometimes make people uncomfortable because I'm not clear. I'm confident but obtuse. And they dont want to hurt my feelings. So they laugh good-naturedly. Usually it's a joke that I make where the leap is too large.

Daphne's hair is tied back in two pigtails, and this forces her face to be intense when she laughs. The laugh is something that is not serene beauty. There's a gruff undertone that means she's game for anything.

29 I meet Maisie Pye to discuss our novels. She's making a novel about what's happening now. It's thinly veiled autobiography. Except she's pushing it. The Oliver character has an affair, and her friends, when they read it, think Oliver's cheating on her. He's not, she says. People believe if you write from a tone of honesty, conviction, and sincerity, if you capture that correctly, then readers will be convinced it all happened that way.

I said I'm having great fun with my characters. Because it's all set in the past. I describe Josh and Toby and Heart's Desire. About the research I've done on the American painter and of Bob Bartlett's trips to the North Pole. I'm using Max and Lydia and others as these historical characters. Max is going to

be my Rockwell Kent. My father might be Bob Bartlett. That
way, I can be present in the past.

Maisie says, So who am I?

I havent used you. Yet.

And she's disappointed.

30 The harbour is caught over with a thin ice sheet. A transport vessel, the ASL *Sanderling*, slices through the ice on its way
to Montreal. It leaves a cold blue strip of linoleum behind it.
It'll be back in six days. The *Astron* left yesterday and the *Cabot*
will arrive tomorrow. Cold days, the heater on behind me. The
light is marbled, you see the current of the harbour. Gulls
standing on the ice as the raw sewage surfaces. Sewage melts
the ice.

Through the Narrows a thin line of open Atlantic. The hills
that pinch the horizon have been trying for ten thousand years to
accumulate topsoil. I love how you can see an entire afternoon's
walk. The sweep of one topographical map playing itself out.
Enough variety to keep me busy with a pair of binoculars. When
Grenfell, a hundred years ago, first entered this port the entire
city was still smouldering, burnt to the ground, only chimneys
left standing, the sides of churches. These same churches.

Iris is downstairs. She's making coffee for Helmut. Helmut
has large hands and his longest finger is his ring finger. You notice the ring fingers when he's gesturing. It's an attractive gesture.

31 Lydia's off to Halifax for a week. So we spend the day together. We sharpen our skates and drive to the Punchbowl.

Max and Oliver and some kids have cleared the ice. There's a hockey game and there's a loop ploughed off the ice. I watch Oliver lean into a turn and cross his skates. A fluid hockey player, a product of the minor leagues. I never played hockey, except in the backyard on a rink made out of water from a hose. I skate behind Lydia, tuck down and hold on to her hips, and she leans ahead and tows me.

Max has a fire going in the woods beside the pond. He's having a boil-up, hot dogs and coffee. He's brought birch junks from home. Life is good.

February

1 Lydia left this morning for Halifax to work on a script. It's not her script, but the money is good and she feels better when she's working. I am at the Ship, having a drink with Max and Maisie. Max is holding his shaved head. The stubble is coming through and right now there is the outline of a cat's ears at his temples, so it's like he's stroking a cat. It gives him a devilish look, as though faded horns are burning through his scalp and he is trying to tame them. Max is building cabinets for Oliver and Maisie. But he is articulating one of his dreams, his hands up, gesturing wildly. He wants to make moulds of men's asses and hang the moulds in a row in a gallery.

Max: Also, I want to bolt a giant erect fibreglass cock onto the Royal Trust building. The cock would be a sundial.

Maisie: That's funny. I just wrote today that the protagonist acts as a gnomon for the action.

Me: All over town, little strips of snow are hiding in the shadows of chimney stacks. The white strip angled north away from the sun. The chimney is a gnomon.

Maisie: When the world is a sundial, everything looks like a gnomon.

Max: Can I take a mould of your ass, Gabe?

You can have my ass, Max. And that's my limit.

2   I should be writing the novel, but instead I concentrate on Lydia. Remembering how she smelled a pair of gloves and knew who owned them. How can I turn that into a historical moment? Moments never attenuate. Moments are compressed into the dissolve of real time. I will never forget how she looked when she smelled those gloves. They were Wilf's gloves. She could smell cigarettes, she said. Mixed in with an indefinable personal scent, unmistakably Wilf's. I will have Rockwell Kent's wife have this ability. But Kathleen Kent is nothing like Lydia. Lydia is firmly planted, no-nonsense, strong clavicles and shoulders. She is attractive because of her mixture of gumption and beauty. Whereas Kathleen has a silent, introspective quality. She is serene. Lydia would never have thought that identifying an owner of gloves by smelling them was a special gift, unless I told her so. Kathleen Kent would know it was a skill worth prizing.

3   From my bedroom window I can watch Maisie walk down Parade Street with groceries. She's wearing a yellow raincoat. Una skids down the ice ahead of her. On the southside, skiffs

are bunched together, hiding from the weather behind a rusting trawler. Two coast guard vessels, the *Henry Larson* and the *Sir Wilfred Grenfell*, are nose to nose, having a conversation about the cold.

I wait until Maisie is in her porch. I can see her run for the phone.

You should close your front door, missus.

Who is this.

I've frightened her. It's Gabe, I say.

Jeez, boy.

I tell her I'm reading about the barber who noticed Midas had big ears. The barber has to tell someone, though he has sworn to Midas that he will keep the secret. He digs a hole and whispers the gossip into the hole and buries it. But when the wind rustles through the grass, it is saying Midas has big ears. This is the story of all good fiction. A good story whispers whenever there's a breeze. You can dig a hole and bury your story, but the words will emerge from the undergrowth. Let the story whisper down the reader's backbone.

Maisie says I'm getting a little too poetic for her taste.

4   I pick up Lydia at the airport. She is full of people she met in Halifax. She tells me details of people I do not know. She tells me who she's attracted to. She says, You should have taken a left there. I say to her, I like going this way. She says, That way is shorter. This makes me tight. Lydia believes there is a right way and I believe there are many ways. This is a truth about our personalities. I was thinking this while I watched her plane

pivot over the airport. I saw it, bright on a wing over chopped acres of Newfoundland winter — Lydia said it looked like a thousand white sandwiches at a funeral. I walk in to stand by the luggage carousel. There's a crowd. I hear an attendant say, St John's is unique. The number of locals that come to greet the landed. I see Lydia. Her funky glasses and the angle of her jawline. At a distance, she's always smaller. Perhaps I judge size only from a distance. We hug and we are strangers, smiling a little too energetically. She avoids kissing me on the lips. It depresses me. We climb into Jethro, a cold air between us. As I'm driving I watch her wrist twist the rear-view mirror and apply lipstick. This makes the sadness melt.

I say, Youre a fashion cougar. And she laughs.

She says, When you travel, time rushes at you and past you and then you come home and — bang! — time stands still and you have to walk through it again.

It's like that optical illusion you get in a car that's been speeding all day and you stop for gas and the earth slowly slinks away as if youre in reverse. That's how Lydia has felt over the last few days. As if St John's is slowly moving away from her, she can't really get into it again.

Me: Or want to get into it.

Maybe that's it. When I'm alone I think of men who live in other cities. Whereas you think of women you'll see today.

I nod agreement to this.

She says, Arent you going to ask if I had an affair?

I say, I know you.

Oh, she says, there's lots I get by you.

5   There's an old woman in lane one with a white bathing cap. She's doing little push-away strokes and a few slow crawl strokes, neck arched way back.

It has taken me thirty-six days of the new year to begin exercising. I will do forty laps. I'm not in bad shape.

When she gets out it's slow up the chrome steps. She barely hauls herself out. A large savannah mammal. She finds her walking cane by the steps. Her knock knees. Thin legs and wide back. I think, if Lydia is like this at seventy-four I can still love her. Then I see she's one of the two slender, well-dressed ladies who shop at Coleman's. So careful to get to her chair. Where there's a bag and towel. She drapes the white towel over her shoulder, like angel's wings. I finish my laps. Twelve then twenty then eight, but I'm not tired (except my neck) and it's more the monotony. I catch up to her as she's still carefully reaching the women's showers, but she doesnt recognize me. For I am disguised as well in bathing trunks.

6   Max Wareham says he fell for Daphne Yarn because her eyes watered whenever it was windy. He noticed an inner light in her eyes that mirrored her external being. I said, Are you saying she has a serene beauty? No, he says, she has a deep laugh that undercuts the composure. But I've found a connective force, some adhesion, and this force pushed me to commit.

Max says, I'm crazy enough for two people. I need someone anchored.

He says his mother married his father after he asked her to dance to Hank Williams. They waltzed and he told her of his dog opening doors with its teeth, and she laughed.

He says, Now you with Lydia. I've never seen a man so cuntstruck.

I thought about that word all day. Cuntstruck. I had to go out for a walk with it. It was a little dog that I put on a leash and let wander ahead of me. It was one oclock, the night's first puny hour. I stepped outside, preparing for it to feel like the furthest thing from summer. But a wind from the Gulf of Mexico had drifted in off course. You could smell the heat. Redolent and cuntstruck. It's true. Tonight should have been the coldest night on earth, and yet the soft wind reminded me of summer. I thought of the wind in sexual terms. That this wind was having an affair with my little dog.

7 I write three pages on an old man who lives in Frogmarsh, near Brigus. I'm calling him the remittance man and I'm basing him on Wilf. He's done a bad deed in England and fled to the colony. A novel needs evil men. While driving, the remittance man sees a car broken down, a couple, and stops. He gives the man a lift to the nearest gas station. The man's wife stays with the car. At the station, the man says he can find his way back. But the remittance man, instead of continuing on, doubles back. He picks up the wife. He says, Your husband asked me to bring you to the gas station. She gets in, but the remittance man drives past the station. He pulls in to a dirt road that leads to a salvage yard.

This is all plot and action. And invented. It doesnt interest me.

8   When I think of God I think of a voice in my chest I tell promises to. I will not lie. I will give away a hundred dollars this month. I will not read Lydia's journal. I will praise others and not myself. I will steal only from corporations. I will not fool myself about the truth of my actions.

This type of promise builds you. It is the moral foundation.

I do not want to write another word on couples. On the words they tell each other. On detail. I have no interest in this. I want insight. So often my interests are prurient and carnal. I want to leap, rather than be hemmed by the drudgery of copying down rote event. There is nothing wrong with deluding yourself. I must pinpoint motive and repercussion.

9   Lydia calls and she's full of love, but I'm irritated. She was inviting me to come down for supper, but I declined. I said I'd already eaten when I hadnt. I declined because she had thought of me at the last minute. But that's her nature. Lydia lives with the evidence that surrounds her. She was oblivious to my existence right up until the moment she called me.

I walk to the pizza joint and order a slice. I have made a date with Max to play racquetball. I realize I've been volatile all week. I've been tight in the shoulders. I understand it has to do with the marriage proposal, how the proposal has been stored away in a cupboard behind Lydia's ear while she prepares for roles and a film this summer. The word that best describes my plight is anguish. The word comes to me while I'm whacking a racquetball. Max is exasperated. Anguish, he says, is something most people cannot afford to have (he smacks a low shot into the back corner). It is a self-made dilemma. Most people are dealing with forces beyond their control. Anguish implies a position of your own doing.

But what's wrong with suffering from your own hand?

Everyone, he says, gets into moods and it's no big deal.

But there is no room for me to have a bit of a mood. Lydia gets angry at me.

Just tell her youre in a bit of a mood.

I dont always know I'm in a mood. Small things build when they should stop. Mood should not feed on mood.

Max can offer me no solution to this one.

10 Helmut Rehm is on his way to Boston for ten days. The company boat, *Sailsoft*, needs a new boom. I ask Helmut if sailboats, when they cross the Atlantic, take the Gulf Stream.

No. It doesnt go north now.

He says the Gulf Stream is a river in the ocean. It's about ten or fifteen miles wide and sailors use it all the way up the seaboard. It is a mechanical stair, he says. You just coast. But to cross the ocean you must wean yourself off it.

Everything in nature is a comparison to the human state. There is a stream in relationships, a highway of water you can take that is the easiest route to destinations. But you both must be in that route.

11 I meet Lydia at the Ship. The bar has a different light to it. Directly behind Lydia there are strings of white pins of light taped to the ceiling beams. White taffeta trailing from the posts

in anticipation of Valentine's. The white taffeta and white pins seem to bloom out of Lydia's head. As though she is of pure thought.

Oliver Squires puts on his coat and waves goodbye to us. He is still dressed in his court clothes, so I know he's been here since five. It's evident there's a large block of frost between him and Maisie.

I tell Maisie I dreamt she read a version of my novel and said, You can't write it like that, it's too much like my style. And I realized the style that I wanted was Maisie's. I had no style of my own. That I've never had personal style, but instead adopted the styles that I admire. The fear of being derivative.

Maisie nods and Lydia says being derivative is a fear we all have. The white taffeta lends a weight of truth to her statement.

12 I drop off the first few pages of the novel to Maisie. I put them in her mailbox. As I turn I see Oliver Squires walking towards me. He's just breaking for lunch at legal aid. He's loosened his black tie. His neck is too big for his shirt. He says, Have you been eating and defecating in my house again?

He invites me in. Welcome to the hellhole.

He asks what my place is like; he has never been up there. We are at the window and look up the hill. You can see my bedroom window from there.

I've always admired that house, he says.

Oliver seems to be in a mood for confession. He appears exhausted. He fixes himself a sandwich and I decline. He keeps the fridge door open with one foot. He says, One thing I miss about being single is sleeping in my own bed. Maisie, she nudges me over to the edge of the bed. It's like she's pushing me out. Like I'm a piece of grit in her shell. There's this acre of bed in front of her. We have this joke that she's cultivating a national park. I ask if any animals were poached last night.

He is telling me this story because he knows I'm a writer. He is telling me this so I'll write it down. It's as though he knows Maisie is writing about him and he wants me to have a piece of the action.

Oliver: One time, I dreamt I was in that park. I was tiny, on the duvet, like one of those fairground moonwalks. Puffy. Maisie was a mountain range in the distance, and I had to make my way across this desert. But the animals, of course.

Me: You didnt make it.

Oliver: No.

So it's good the way you are.

I suppose so.

Stick with what you got is what youre saying.

Is that what it all means?

Everything he says is tinged with the possibility he's having an affair.

13 Wind shudders the telephone poles, the cold churches. I pick up Lydia and we walk over to Max and Daphne's Valentine's party. Oliver in his speckled bow tie, his ginger-grey curly hair, and Wilf Jardine in that wool jacket and jeans discussing Spinoza. We try putting Oliver in the fridge as he's fetching a beer, but Maisie saves him. Or she's saving the fridge

from injury. Part of Oliver wants to go in the fridge. But then he decides on two Jockey Club in one hand and a bottle of red Chianti in the other. His breath hot with alcohol.

Oliver: Show us your tits, Alex.

Alex leans back and flashes her tits at us. Just long enough for her nipples to register on the retina.

Oliver: What a gorgeous girl you are.

Max walks in with two dozen fresh ones. The tips of his ears red. Generous Max.

Max says, Oliver tries to be sophisticated. But I once saw him make instant coffee with hot water from a tap.

Daphne stands behind Max. She will use Max as a shield to get through this night.

Oliver: Those were my years in the wilderness.

Max: Sure, youre only at an oasis. And youre some vain with your ginger hair.

Oliver: At least I have hair.

Max: You seem to have more hair now than you did then.

Oliver: Back then. When I was with a Hobbesian woman: nasty, brutish, and short.

Alex, to me: How do you prepare oysters?

The oysters lie fiercely shut on a plate and I take them to the sink and ask Daphne for a strong, small knife.

Alex makes her way over. She is flagrant and I am drawn.

She tells me of her short infatuation with Wilf Jardine. Wilf is showing Lydia the chords to his song. They talked on a bird count. Wilf wrote Alex a letter. She found herself watching him play guitar down at the Spur. He sang his one good song.

Then, during a break, he sat in front of her and she studied the back of his neck, the grizzled white hair. She bought him a beer. He said, Alex. But in a frozen way. She knew then it was a mistake, but she slept with him. Sleeping with him got him out of her system.

Me: And he was your age when you were born.

Alex: He's just a sexy guy. Or he had a moment of sexiness.

I am prying at the crimped, ceramic mouth.

What was the moment when Wilf became human?

When he got irritated, she says. We were driving through town in his old Valiant and I suggested we take a route and he was irritated.

I sever the muscle, wring a lemon. The lemon spurts over my hand. I lick the crevices of my hand. I hand Alex the opened oyster. She lays its ceramic mouth on her bottom lip. She leans back. I watch her white throat swallow. Her nipples, in the periphery, just show through her top. Then she stares straight into my eye. She says, Theyre delicious.

14 We're at an erotic reading in a room above the St John's curling club. Both Maisie and I are reading. When you go to the bar you can watch the curlers sweep down the rink. Wilf Jardine, at one point, leans to me and says, I think she likes you. Meaning Alex Fleming. And then he says, I wouldnt mind finding a blonde here tonight — one with a great set of assets.

Wilf leans back and straightens his grey wool jacket lapels. Sometimes his face relaxes and you see that he is fifty-two. He

has large eyes and a broad face. One of those faces that has got
thicker over the years. He stares at the helium balloons framing
the room-wide window that looks down on six lanes of curlers
casting rocks. The tray of desserts being wheeled out, like a
sweet patient.

Wilf: I like this set-up because you know you won't be
talking to a load of drunks.

Lydia: Unlike last night.

It's hard to feel anything erotic as the poets whisper up
their attempts at arousal. When it's my turn I realize the problem: eroticism rests on intimacy, and a roomful of people
destroys this intimacy.

We eat dessert. We plough into the sweet patient.

The speaker system is accidentally attached to the downstairs intercom, so the curlers hear every word.

Wilf says, The problem with the word erotic is that it has
the word rot in the middle of it.

15 There is no colour in the hills now. Whatever quality
affords colour in colour film is no longer in those hills. Below
the hills in dry dock is the trawler *Wilfred Templeman*. It looks
like a part of the sentinel fishery. Hauled up alongside the
Beothuk park, deep in the shipyard.

You must listen to your heart of hearts. You must know
there is a cable of love that connects, that carries an undertow,
that tugs and anchors you during the white storm. When I
look into Lydia's blue eye I want to see that cable. The storm
can shave away all bindings, but the silver cable persists.

The roofs are white. But the roads have melted to black. All the windows are black or a very dark green. Windows allow light but offer darkness. If you are attracted to windows you probably like looking out through them. Otherwise, you like looking at yourself in them, as darkness allows a reflection.

Iris says there's a new prison in the mountains of Germany. Helmut was telling her. And the only windows are slits, like a glowing envelope on edge. And Helmut wonders if you can see an entire mountain through a slit. This is the project we all undertake, she says. Isnt it. To accept everything if you love a piece of everything.

16 Lydia tries on clothes at the Value Village. A green wool suit made in Dublin. It fits her like stretched fabric over wood. Her thin chest and full thighs. She cocks her hips, pulls up a shoulder.

What do you think?

I think youve rescued it.

Then it's a wine V-neck sweater that hugs her little tits. I am in the change booth with her. I run a hand over her pubic hair. I can't help it. What about this, she says. A black number with white stitching. I am learning to choose clothing for her. At first it seemed anything would look good on her. I was astonished at how small a top could be. The size of children's clothing.

She says, Youre some chummy with Alex.

Me: Youre one to talk.

17 Forty laps in a thirty-metre pool. I love swimming in winter.

But I'm winded after ten laps. The water playing off plexiglass like starfish made from sunlight. Moving a plate of light around the room off your watch.

Lane one, a man, about forty-two, with a bald spot and a small pot and tufts of hair at his nipples and belly button. A young guy with him learning to shallow dive, tattoos on his shoulders, something meek. I practise the crawl, blowing under water, sucking under my arm. I take it easy. Lane three, a sleek woman ploughing through lengths like she's churning cream.

Some people you care for, some you dont, just from their look.

That man and the younger man could be lovers, except I see that it's my neighbour, Boyd Coady.

I drive home and there's a message on the machine: Lydia's out for a run and she's going to come over. Then I see her walking down the path. She is carrying a bouquet of carnations.

How did you run with flowers?

I held them behind my back.

When I hug her, her body is hot and steamy.

18 Maisie Pye and I get drunk. We havent been drunk together in ages. It's so good, she says, to get drunk with you.

She pulls on a lock of her brown hair and nibbles it.

She says she can be direct with me. She can utter anything and it won't be misconstrued. She says, The fact that we've slept together avoids all that sexual tension bullshit.

That was ten years ago.

Doesnt matter. Does it matter to you? I mean, do you have any sexual feelings for me?

I guess not. But I didnt know it was because we'd slept together.

Well, thanks a lot.

That's not what I meant.

Maisie: With most men I have to watch it. Or they watch it. But with you I'm perfectly comfortable.

So youre saying —

I'm saying you should watch out for Alex.

We're only ever flirting.

I think she's interested in you.

We leave it at that. She asks how things are with Lydia.

Me: We were thinking about getting married.

Maisie nods at this. Maisie got us together in the first place, and now I can see she's having doubts.

Maisie: My flaw is I'm convincing. I can convince people to do things, even if theyre the wrong things to do.

You dont think we should get married.

I'm not saying anything. I'm just worried that the right thing gets done.

Well, how do we look from the outside? From your angle?

You look infatuated. Which beauty can drug you on. You have to work through infatuation.

And how do you know if youre infatuated?

Your work suffers.

Maisie says you have to watch yourself in any relationship, or you'll end up in torment.

I ask how she's doing with Oliver.

Well, she says, I speak of torment. You can't run a relationship solely on flair and conversation and desire for life.

I say: It's warming yourself at a fire. When it dies down youre cold.

Maisie: It's like watching a movie of the one you love.

What do you mean?

It's like when you enter a movie and youre absorbed. But it's the world of a movie, separate from you. After two hours you'll leave, entertained, but you return to your own world. And the movie knows nothing of your life.

We both silently gauge ourselves by this.

19 Yearning. I want a real love and a woman fully mine and I am fully hers. A deeply entrenched togetherness in some kind of alchemical bond that is inseparable and you change and become a different person because of that woman. You would almost die, yes you probably would die, a shell or a core of you would wither, if that woman left you or you left her. Something else always blooms in the aftermath, but deep chunks would be ripped out and isnt that fear part of a deep love? A thing that we are all desperately craving and searching, smelling, listening for, even when we arent conscious of it. And any other arrangement or agreement is fine for the time but is always susceptible to outside forces that will gnaw on the hawsers and dissolve you like sugar in liquid. I know Lydia has gone through this type of deep love with Earl, a love where she craved him all day long and then came

49

home to him almost lunging and yes she was shocked and hurt by this kind of love and maybe what she has now is a nurtured and careful and indeed beautiful thing and maybe that's good for her, who am I to say. But I want to caution her against this separation of self from me, if that's what she is doing or trying to maintain. Give me a rooted thing that is fierce and dedicated and incredibly powerful in head heart and animal.

20 I'm at Maisie's and she's on the phone, so I'm talking to Una. She says, Dad only recently discovered the drive-you-thru. He didnt know how to talk to the man on the intercom.

She is making a birthday card and puts in nine dollars. Andrea is nine, Una says. It's a makeup party.

The invitation reads Don't Blush! and I ask her if she catches the double meaning. Yes, she says.

When she writes Happy Birthday on the card I ask her if she knows how to excite and jazz up sentences.

Put an exclamation mark, she says.

She says this in a declarative way.

Some kids end a sentence with a raised, doubting tone. And here Una is adding an exclamation mark, sure of herself.

She says, A question mark is like half a heart.

I say, Sometimes questions are asked half-heartedly.

21 I've invited Lydia up for supper. Helmut is back from Boston. Iris and I will team up to cook. We sit in the kitchen and dig up Helmut's life story. How he was adopted and found

his sister only last year. As he's telling us, a big man with a cast on his arm walks in with a summons.

Gabriel English?

Lydia, Iris, and Helmut look at me.

You guys, I say, know nothing about deception.

I confess I'm Gabriel English.

Man with cast: You owe the government twenty thousand dollars, and change.

I look at the summons. The Cast says, Youre a hard one to track down. Dont you ever vote?

I vote, but I swear an oath to where I live.

The Cast is puzzled.

I lie, I say, about where I live.

The Cast is very polite, says he has been around a few times but got no answer at the door. He says he can let himself out.

I can see Lydia looking at the summons with disapproval.

I'm going to talk to Oliver. I'll lay ten thousand in cash on the government table. That's what I borrowed from student loans ten years ago. The rest is 12 percent interest. The rest, I say in a righteous tone, is usury. If they accept it, I'll take you to lunch.

Lydia: Last of the big spenders.

They won't turn down ten grand.

Lydia: Not when they see the likes of you.

22 Oliver says it's worth a try. I will do this generous monetary transaction on my birthday. It will clear the slate to begin my thirty-fifth year. I could declare bankruptcy, but that taints the

future. Also, integrity tells me to pay what I owe but be stubborn on the interest. Also, bankruptcy is not an attractive trait. I can see Lydia wants me to clear this up without it coming to that.

Mom called. She wants to visit, but she'll come on the bus. She misses me because I dont come back for Christmas. She calls it a pagan holiday. The only ceremonies she celebrates are marriages and Easter. She doesnt even raise her glass to a toast.

23 I wrote a passion poem for Lydia. I left it in her mailbox: Send me an ounce of cinnamon, it said, wrapped in paper and string. Send my love's own grain. An ounce will do, an ounce of cinnamon. For apples, you said. My mouth that eats apples. Tied in paper and string. Eat my mouth in green apples that have been given to him, stapled and pinned. An ounce of cinnamon; send it, given to him who has no cinnamon, save himself. For love's own grain. Send me this in a cloth so fine and wire so hard it will prove our own forgiveness.

I am wired into an insane part of me.

24 Lydia says the poem was appreciated. Her tone implies she didnt, no one could, understand it. I said it was a nonsense poem, just read it for the intent. There's intent behind it.

She wants to paint her study. So I drive down and pick her up and we zoom over to Matchless Paints and choose a colour I call avocado green. Lydia says there are a lot of greens in avocado.

The centre yellow, closest to the pit.

We get the man to add one fraction of green. It's the green of unripe banana.

The man lifts his arms and slips a finger under the tight short sleeves of his shirt, as if his biceps need room.

A fraction is the minimum amount of paint that can drip from the beaker. It's enough paint to cover your fingernail. Enough to change considerably the hue of a gallon of avocado. The power of pigment.

With all the pictures off the walls her study looks relaxed. We've stacked Lydia's paintings and lamps in between the legs of upended chairs in the hall. I expect a caravan to be hauled up outside, a thin horse, ruts in the road from wagon wheels. There is a primitive, European feeling of exodus, of imminent rush and migrant behaviour, hanging around Lydia's stairwell.

25 Stories are all about meeting someone, Maisie says. You have the narrator. Then you are introduced to a character. And how does that person shape the protagonist? That's all a story ever is. Your protagonist meeting someone. That's how my novel begins, I say. Little Leo Percy (Josh) meeting Rockwell Kent (Max) at the train station.

I want to write a kid's book for Una. Have a whale meet a shark and discuss his time on land. How his tail is flat now and he has to return, always, to the surface to breathe. A story about returning home, but how the experience away changes you permanently.

26 I wake up on the couch cushions on the living-room floor. The rain sounds like plastic bubbling off the walls. Mom is directly above in my bed. I picked her up last night at the bus

station. I watched her guide her feet down the steep hammered-metal steps.

She had her bags on the chair by the phone. She said, Is that okay?

Yes, I said. We can bring them up to your room later.

Oh, there's a limit, she said.

What?

They only go that far for now — it's a joke.

She asks about commitment, and I explain that Lydia and I are considering the question. She says, You should give yourself a deadline.

I say, I've never been in love before.

She says, Well, it's good to have your heart broken.

27 I introduce Mom to Iris and Helmut, and they look at her with little grins on, as though she explains certain aspects of who I am. Mom tells them I was a quiet child and I went through a time when I said even less. I would stay in my room. But she wouldnt investigate. I was conscientious and reliable. My brother, Junior, would come home from school and sprawl in the porch. I've just got to rest, he'd say. My mother told him people were waiting for their newspapers. When I took over the route, I was an obedient paperboy.

She mixes brewer's yeast in orange juice for her breakfast. She says she can run on that all morning.

She notices I have a hole in my shoe. She says, You take after your grandad. He wore starched shirts and wingtip shoes, very grand. But the shirt cuffs were frayed and the soles of the shoes had holes.

28 Lydia wants to take us out for lunch. She chooses a table against the wall. There are fresh flowers and Mom admires them.

We order the specials.

Mom says money is just after sex for problems in a marriage. Then she clarifies: Money never came between us in an irreconcilable way. We had differences but worked through it. And as for the first thing, the same can be said.

When the waitress arrives my mother asks: Are you having a wedding, or do you always have flowers?

Waitress: We always have them.

Mom: It's like having fruit when youre not sick.

Simple pleasures, and Lydia's happy to have her out. Mom thoroughly enjoys a meal cooked by someone else.

March

1 I convinced Mom to fly back to Corner Brook. And she called to say it was terrific, so fast, and Dad sort of enjoyed picking her up at the airport. The only drawback was that she missed having a bowl of soup in Gander.

No snow. Cold, though. Strange but acceptable to have the city so bare. I hate frozen slush. When I was seven I thought Newfoundland was attached to Britain. And with Confederation they floated the island over.

So often I wake up and the fog, the blizzards, living here is like being on a barge, adrift in the Atlantic. There is no buffer to weather. We're forced to take the brunt of it. I love it.

Admission: I love choosing hard times. The not being able to choose is what frightens me. And that's what scares me most about having kids. It's true I dont care for surroundings. As long as the roof is solid, the fridge stocked, and you dont see your breath. But wallpaper and matching dinner plates and a brand-new car make my neck tight.

I have a gut feeling that Newfoundland can float. It's not inconceivable to haul up anchor and drift into the Gulf Stream. Any thought is possible.

2   I've found only two dots of snow in the crags of southside hills. Old man's beard, they call it.

I am incorporating a proposal of marriage into the novel. One of my key tenets: if you know what the next scene is, youve already written it. The novel is full of contemporary events. Lydia says, Be present in the past. But what I'm doing is being present, then infusing this into the past.

At the Ship the pussy willows, cut three weeks ago for Valentine's, have begun to bloom in their demi-litre jars. Fresh green shoots, seal fur, in the dark bar. The pussy willows know nothing of winter.

3   I was about to call Lydia when I pictured her phone and I thought about what she had to say about being present in the past and how impossible it is but instead I'm writing honest moments and people who are themselves and people who make fun of themselves and are silly and childish and unsophisticated and warm and generous and loving and full of toughness too and original and sexy and rough and animalish and playful and have guts and a red red tender heart bursting crying at small wonderful irrational things at moments at hot moments that steam and penetrate our brains and sizzle like a

branding iron into the marrow and make us horny and I like trying to put words to these moments give particulars and hand them delicately to people like Lydia and I want them from her too that is my only demand on anyone because that is life that is all life is is moments doesnt she think and I think she does and she does among other things when the moment's right.

4   It's after badminton, on the only day of the year that is a command, march forth. Let's have a small drinky-poo, Lydia says. Maisie Pye and Max Wareham and Lydia Murphy.

At the Ship there's a little whiff of grass.

Maisie says they are moving to a house on Lemarchant Road.

Max: When?

I've got the keys now. It's a little three-bedroom. Yes, I have to move.

I'm thinking they can't pay the mortgage. Or maybe they were renting. Maybe Oliver has lost his job. But then we realize it's only Maisie and Una. No one can speak.

I say, So what's going on?

I'm leaving Oliver. I have to leave.

Maisie says it with finality. Her hands on the table edge pushing her shoulders back, her eyes closed.

Me: Do you want to say anything else about it?

Just that it's something I have to do.

Well. It's good that youve managed to reach a decision.

She puts an arm, briefly, to my shoulder.

Lydia says, I'm so sad.

Maisie: It has been two hurdles. To decide, and then to actually do it. To find a place. To think about getting beds.

And how is Oliver?

He doesnt want me to go.

Shouldnt he be the one leaving?

He says he can't leave.

Is he having an affair?

I found condoms. We dont use condoms.

Oh, Maisie.

Then he told me about this paralegal woman.

Are you capable of calling someone if you do need help?

Yes, Gabriel. Thanks.

In bed. Me: It made me afraid to be with you.

What do you mean?

If it can't work out between them.

Baby, does it make you not want to be with me?

Oliver's a legal-aid lawyer and Maisie's a writer and I thought, That's a good balance.

Lydia: And Maisie said it so simply, yet their life is so substantial. I wanted to say to her, Have you given this a lot of thought?

Me: She has given it a lot of thought. Both families, Oliver, everyone is probably saying to her, I hope youve given this a lot of thought. Do you think I was a little too direct?

I think she appreciated it. I didnt know what to say. I thought you were good.

I felt strange.

You like her.

Yes. But I wish they were together. I like it better that way.

Does it make you nervous?

I guess I was uncomfortable.

I think she likes you too.

But we've gone out. And she's that way with everyone.

That's true.

But we do seem to understand each other well.

I think she likes you. Dont you?

I guess so.

5   I'm sitting with Helmut, reading, when the room is suddenly painted with revolving blue, hungry light. There is the beep of something big going in reverse. Out on the end of Young Street, a cul de sac, a rogue city tractor piles snow against our fence. The attached houses are cast in fluorescence as the cab light spins. The snow is eight feet high stacked against the fence. I open the screen door. Youre nudging the fence, I say. The driver leaning out his door: If I knock it down, call city hall.

He reverses. Chains on the fat industrial tires smack against the pavement, sending up sparks. Kids are huddled behind a car, watching. They have made igloos out of the snow. I notice other neighbours are at their screen doors, calling in their children. The driver revs and shifts into first. The nose of the tractor rears. Headlights jerkily bear down on the mound. He races into the snow, stretches the tractor's hydraulic neck up, and the fence buckles. Six steel posts bend. The pickets lean and splinter, buttons on a fat man's gut. Three pickets burst and shoot off into the trees. The dark fence cracks and a raw new light is exposed from deep in the wood. The driver lifts the shovel and retreats, halts. Then roars towards the pile again. The steel posts groan, nails pulled from a board. The palings snap. A mound of heavy, dirty snow tumbles across the path. He retreats, studies the cul de sac. This time he pivots and heads back to the depot.

6 I look up from writing to watch the dying sun turn the snow on Signal Hill pink. The bottoms of clouds another pink. I can distinguish between pinks. There's a pigeon cooing, and it sounds like a rope pulled taut.

I walk down to Lydia's. Tinker Bumbo, asleep, is a balloon losing air. The flame in Lydia's fireplace sounds like a finger rubbing grit off a record needle.

We eat supper and walk down to the Ship. Lydia pulls down her tights to imitate Oliver. She is so quick and apt with imitation. Maisie, disgusted, throws away the chalk after scratching on the break. How funny is that. Can you weigh funniness. How long does an image stay with you. I think now that it was so funny. Yet I didnt laugh when Maisie threw the chalk. It's a funniness that lingers. Maisie threw the chalk out of not blind disgust but a self-conscious look-at-how-shitty-that-shot-was disgust.

The cue ball hops over the cushion. It hits a beer bottle. I dont mind, for this moment, if Lydia sleeps with Wilf. She wants to go to the Spur, where he probably is. How I love Lydia gossiping with Maisie about men.

Somehow the world is more intimate and loving and I am generous with what I love. All love is displayed on an embroidered white cloth on long grass beneath a sycamore and generosity is running towards it from a ball field, both teams at once, running, throwing their gloves in the air.

7   Heartache is something you can have without ever having your heart broken.

Sometimes. In Lydia's kitchen. When she's mixing ingredients for a cake in front of a sunny window. Sometimes, like in photographs of swimmers in the distance, standing on sailboats, the sun cuts through the bodies so the knees and ankles and elbows have light coming through them. Bodies are cut into segments. Sometimes I see that happening to Lydia, so thin. When she's sideways. At the mixer churning a cold block of butter. And slowly the silver egg beaters mangle.

In the closet: the sleeves of my coat tucked into Lydia's coat pockets. The toes of her boots nudging into mine.

8   Max picks me up in his truck and we head down to Maisie's. She has put yellow sticky notes on the bits of furniture she's taking. There are garbage bags with bedding. A cardboard box stuffed with cutlery. She has dresses and shirts still on their hangers draped over a full-length mirror. She says, I just want to take one truckload and no more.

Her house on Lemarchant is little but solid. She has spent

the weekend scouring it. I realize I havent been helping her.

But when we get the furniture in, and we've had a beer (the only thing in her fridge is a box of beer), she says, Thanks, boys. Now I want to be on my own.

Max says, Can we do your ass now?

I am leaning against the bathroom sink, my pants down. I've washed myself and spread vaseline from my hips to my thighs. Lucky youre not very hairy, Max says. Some people I ask to shave.

He is slapping patches of cold plaster over my ass. It's nice to have a set of confident hands moulding my ass.

He fires up a blow dryer.

He begins by prying from my left hip. It reminds me of peeling dead skin off my brother's sunburned back. Wet blisters of skin. Except this is an entire dry shell. And I see the form of my ass, I'm surprised how curved it is. It's a pretty ass. Max offers no criticism of it. He makes off with the mould in the fashion of a thief.

9   Lots of fat snow. We drive to Churchill Square for a bouquet of irises and carnations and a bottle of port. For Maisie. This encouragement of spring. I am in love with fresh flowers. They are a lavish and outrageous fact of living here. If nothing else, you can get fresh flowers at the start of March in Newfoundland. Lydia picks up some fat-free cookies and ultra-violet lotion.

On the way to Maisie's Lydia says, There arent enough storytelling songs.

I say, It's time Wilf Jardine wrote some love songs.

But he hasnt experienced that. He's experienced yearning. And break-up.

That's what love songs are all about, I say. The before and after.

But we are both absorbed in the here and now.

10 A trait in Lydia: to begin feeling guilty, then guilt transforms into resentment and anger. In the morning, when I'm leaving Lydia's and she doesnt want me to go.

I say, You want me to go, though. Youve said enough times you want more time alone.

Yes, Lydia says. I should work.

But she holds me, doesnt want me to go. I carry her to the couch. Then she's rigid. I've got so much to do, she says.

Okay.

I clap my hands and say, All right, let's get to it. Lydia pauses, then jumps up stiffly.

Okay, she says.

Me: What just happened?

Nothing.

Why are you being stiff?

Oh, it just sounds like youre talking to Tinker Bumbo. Come on and get up, clap your hands.

I'm not talking to you like youre Tinker Bumbo. I dont even talk to him like that.

Well, it felt like it.

I'm just trying to get us both started. If you want to work

— if youre resenting not having worked yesterday — then let's get at it.

She says, Are you upset that we're not hanging out?

I say, Not upset, just disappointed.

It's a little fuse of anger that Lydia focuses on time spent with me as the thing to cut back on in order to get her work done — and I'm trying to cut through the lingering and so she resents it.

Okay then, I'll see you.

And I leave, both of us angry.

Lydia will often say, What's wrong, baby? and when I tell her what's wrong, involving her in blame a little, she'll accept it for a minute, be sorry, then retaliate. She'll become defensive. If she could absorb it and leave it, without feeling that she has to defend. That she's in the right. It's as if she holds a club behind her back, asks what's the matter, and when I tell her, agrees, then gives me a quick dash on the head.

11 It's a sunny day and I'm thirty-four. When youre sad, events take on symbolic importance. Sadness connotes lacking, a want for something. Lydia brings over a Gabriel doll she's made for my birthday and I cry laughing. The black leather coat and stuffed body, stitched face. A rose corsage blooming, not that I wear a rose, but it's indicative of my joy — at least what used to be my happiness. And it strikes me that this image is no longer who I am. Somehow, other emotions not my own have crept in. I'm no longer a romantic figure. I have grown wise.

The clothesline is frozen in a shaded bank of snow. I have decided to settle my student loan. I phone the loans officer, Fabian Durdle. It's my birthday. He says, Do you think that'll impress Ottawa?

I get a bank draft for nine thousand dollars, and fifteen hundred in cash. I grab an elevator and knock on Fabian Durdle's office door.

That's half what you owe.

The rest, I say, is outrageous interest.

He calls Ottawa. Fabian is nodding in a bored way into the phone and then pauses.

Yes, he says. Gabriel English is here in front of me. With ten-five on the table. He says take it or he'll go bankrupt.

Fabian puts the phone down.

Sign here.

Theyre taking it?

He nods.

I say, I'd like a witness, as it's a lot of cash.

Fabian: Gabriel, youve got to trust people more often.

But he's been dealing with me for ten years, and knows my idiosyncrasies. In fact, I know he respects them. No, I dont know that. But he is the perfect man for this job. Fabian Durdle holds no grudges. He calls in a secretary. As we're waiting Fabian studies the bank draft. He's not familiar with bank drafts.

He says, I'll have to call your bank to verify this.

As he's tapping the number I say, Fabian, youve got to trust people more often.

Touché, he says.

And now I owe a penny to no one.

Nor do I own a penny.

Ah, details.

12 Lydia is working on her script. She wants me to read the scenes and see if it flows.

I've been avoiding Jethro, trying to walk. I see a woman in a wheelchair in the melting road up against the sidewalk curb. I say, Do you need a hand? And she yells out, straining her neck around me to a tailor's shop, Kevin, I wants you now!

I'm wearing a pair of linen pants that I bought at the Sally Ann two days ago and dropped the cuffs an inch and they flop with a lazy southern wind over the rim of my cranberry leather shoes. They are quite out of place for March. On Mom's advice I've had my shoes resoled at Modern Shoe Hospital. When I look down what I see are the pants and the shoes and I feel very lavish.

Lydia's door is locked and I have no key, which I resent but am silent about. Lydia has my key. She keeps meaning to get around to it, but she hasnt.

I'm surprised when Wilf opens the door. He says, in Lydia's voice: It's me, transformed into Wilf's body!

He tries to kiss me.

Bonus, I say.

13 I call Max. Want to see a movie?

When?

In fifteen minutes.

Pause. Let me check with Daphne.

Pause.

Okay!

I pick him up and he chuckles on Elizabeth Avenue. He slaps his thighs.

He looks out his window, enjoying this.

So what's the big delight?

Daphne's pregnant.

Max.

It's a good thing. She's moving in.

Youre a fast worker.

I'm a potent man. And speaking of which, your ass will be on display next month. Alex is giving me a wall.

The movie has one good image: a peeled, steaming eel wriggling on a set of tongs. Then we drive to Burger King.

This reminds me, Max says, of twenty years ago.

I say, You have to go back twenty years to be reminded?

Of this particular moment, yes.

We watch the girl serving us lean towards the milkshake station, one hand on the waxy cup and the other pressing the chunky white button. She holds the cup near her waist and she looks down, and she is looking down past her own body, at the work.

She shovels fries into cardboard pockets. The golden yellow lights of the fry stations on her forearms and hands. She's wearing white shoes. I used to work at Burger King. I used to date girls like this.

We drive to a bar that has chessboards. A drawn-out win for Max. Then I drive him home. He has filled my tank with a credit card. He had tipped the card out his half-open window. Make it twenty bucks, he'd said.

The whole night Max is revelling in his luck, his night out, my ass, his child-to-be.

14 I train my binoculars on the southside hills. On the shadows and snow-capped mansard roof windows. The detail. I tell this to Lydia, about using the binoculars as a device in painting.

I watch a crow on a pole. It looks around until its beak is hidden. Its furtive eye flashing grey, a pure grey I would never see with my naked eye. So binoculars make colour appear. A claw clamped on the edge of the pole's top rim. As the crow lifts it plunges to the left, raising its breast slightly to the side to catch wind. It caws three times and lunges from the shoulders, swooping as it caws. I can hear the caw through the window.

I wouldnt have heard it if I wasnt seeing it. So binoculars create sound.

But looking at things up close — for instance, spruce inside a copse of hardwood — can inform you of the colours in a smear. Magnification breaks down smears to components (blue and grey and yellow and pink, instead of a smudgy green). Enlarging encourages colour to show itself. Lydia says Monet has become an adjective, describing something that, close up, breaks into fragments.

15 I see Max and Daphne peering through the rippled glass of my porch. Daphne with a bottle of raspberry wine and a silver pendant with agate that the light shines through. These are Daphne touches. A tardy birthday gift. She holds the pendant up to demonstrate. Why would a stone appreciate light? What would be the advantage?

We speak of mulberry trees and ginko leaves and selling oak and hawthorn to local nurseries and all sorts of farm things to do on crown land at a hundred dollars an acre.

Daphne wants, eventually, to give up nursing and farm full time. And Max looks like a man who has considered this avenue his entire life.

I've always thought berry liqueurs were a way to go.

Daphne: If you make them I will cover them in chocolate.

And suddenly I'm hooked.

She has grafted apple plants and divided sucker seedlings and boiled down extracts, and has other assorted technical skills I would have to learn. If I'm serious.

If I plan on getting into the tree-farm business.

Do I plan on that?

I realize I have been convinced.

Who would love an Avalon farmer? Drop this literary crap.

We eat a crisp salad in the living room with sun drenching the rooftops and catching the avocado leaves and making the dressing of mustard garlic with cilantro — which Daphne says is coriander — glow.

I am so affected by the passions of others. There is nothing more I want right now than to be an Avalon farmer.

16 I bump into Oliver Squires at the Honda lot on Kenmount Road. I'm picking up a wiper motor. He is with his paralegal student. She is young and thin and silent. Oliver's dressed like the lawyer he is, but it surprises me as I never see him when he's practising. He wants my advice because my brother is a mechanic. He's not uncomfortable at all.

But I'm not my brother, Oliver.

Oliver makes a hand motion that implies I'm splitting hairs. There are new models in the showroom.

I say, Cars inside buildings is a strange image.

Yes, he says. Those cars they raffle in the mall.

Mass-produced things are harder to replicate, in appearance, than natural things. It is easier to draw a tree than a telephone.

Oliver is buying a car. To replace Maisie, he says. And laughs. And his paralegal student smiles. How people laugh when they are in pain. Oliver is getting on with things. And really, all this chatter is about not losing me as a friend.

17 Lydia doesnt feel free to see other men, feels that I'm uncomfortable whenever she's around a man. We were drinking cognac on my bed. She said she just wants it fair on both sides. I'm free to have lunch with someone I've had an erotic dream about (Alex) or share writing with Maisie, I live with Iris, but Lydia doesnt have the same freedom.

I want to bring up dinner and rehearsals with Wilf, but this is too obvious.

I said, I want you to do what you feel like. It's true, I've felt jealous. Not all the time, just sometimes.

Kissing me, she tells me a crewneck will get me laid before a turtleneck. How I like her making sure my shirt front is done up while my sleeves are unbuttoned.

Lydia: If you find your cuffs are still buttoned, do you feel sad that I havent released you?

Yes.

18 I love Lydia. I love all her harbours and coastlines and high tides and contour lines and all four compass points of her body and the interior landscape of her brain and how the trail blazes through her and I want to thread her needle and sew up a life together and be scared with her and silly and stupid and profound and come to some understanding some kind of substantial truth on this shaky ground of living near the middle of our lives.

19 Maisie Pye has pressed her nose to the window in my porch door. She is wearing a blue-and-orange silk blouse buttoned loose to her chest. It's freezing out. I often forget to look at her. I talk to her but never look at her. But now that she's not with Oliver I give her a look. She is small, a little awkward in her elbows and knees. Sometimes her smile slides up the side of her face.

We have a drink in the living room.

Maisie's confidence makes me shy. She's intellectual and she's a good laugh. I must gather evidence on how she tries to express herself, her kindness, her appreciation of other people, not confrontational but sharing.

We have another drink.

Maisie: What happened to us, Gabe?

And I know she is talking about ten years ago. When everything was different.

We were both seeing other people, Maisie.

Maisie: I'm thinking now that it was a mistake. You should have been bold.

Me: And hang the consequences.

Maisie: We should not have been devoted to the idea of fidelity.

Her face, a strong personal beauty. When I first met her, she had plump cheeks. But these have gone. As has her time with Oliver. Maisie is remembering her life prior to Oliver.

20 Lydia suspects I've been drinking, but I'm just loose. I want to run at the mouth, I want to be free to do anything, say anything, have anything happen, accept all consequences, embrace possibility, ramble on into the night. Lydia is wrapped up in a red tam and scarf and gloves. She has left the car running and says, Youre late. I decide to ignore things that usually irritate me. I try not to be sensitive. I want to be big.

I try coaxing her.

I ask, just to be provocative, Am I inside you? In here?

Heart.

She says, I dont know.

This does not stun me. It makes me even more relaxed. Honesty. Lydia feels distant, asks if I feel it. I'm thinking she means do I feel distant too, and I dont, I feel the immediacy of life ticking on around me — she means do I feel her distance. Yes. She hasnt felt connected to me.

She doesnt feel as sexual as she usually does, and this has never happened to her before, not to this extent. A general lack of sexiness.

Me: Is it related to me directly, or do you feel sexual to others?

Lydia: I havent let myself do that, so I wouldnt know.

She wants to be good for me but feels she doesnt know what I want.

I tell her how Maisie understands me, and I know her. We instinctively understand and accept each other. This, of course, saddens Lydia.

Sometimes, I say, it feels like you dont understand me. You dont like how I behave. You wish I were another way.

Yes, she says. I agree with that. But I also resent that you compare me with others.

I say, I should be cherished every day.

Lydia suddenly laughs, agreeing. And there is a melt between us.

21 E-mail from Maisie: she woke up last night to singing. She went downstairs and found three sailors in her Lemarchant Road kitchen, with jugs of liquor and food. They cheered her. They were Portuguese. She had to yell at them and they were confused. She pointed to the door, but they would not go. So she called the police.

Today, in court, she found out that the house she has rented used to be a brothel. The Portuguese come every year. They didnt know. Their ship was leaving port today and Oliver, who represented them, asked her to drop the charges. She did, on one condition: they make a plaque that says, in three languages, This House Is Not a Brothel. The men agreed.

22 If I could hand deliver on this first day of spring. From my hand to Lydia's. Hold her shoulder as I give her a simple message. If I could roll it into a thread and slip it in her ear as she sleeps in her bed. My last line would be . . . No, I would have no last line. There would be an ellipsis. There are no last words. Only words that belong in no last line. There are end words such as possibility and promise.

23 Called Maisie to get a book. She says she admires Max because he persists in doing what he thinks is right (integrity) whereas Oliver does what people seem to expect.

Me: People expected he'd stay with you.

Maisie comes from a deep-seated philosophy, you can depend on her to say a point of view. And I realize I dont come from there, I'm too sceptical of a truth. I argue not from a position, but from an example.

A sheet of thick plastic is wrapped in the bare oak on Long's Hill. Max says the denser the wood, the harder it is for leaves to unfurl. Oak are the last to bloom. Beyond the oak the brick church steeple with green copper peak. I like looking at this spire while I write. I'm going to look up the kirk's style. Squinches in spires.

24 Maisie says she was washing dishes one day. And she slipped the ice cubes from a whisky glass into the dishwater. It was Oliver's glass, from when he was on the phone with his brilliant paralegal student. Maisie held those cubes of ice under the warm water, held them fiercely, and noticed her wedding ring on the windowsill. That's when she decided to leave Oliver.

25 Lydia offers me the dental floss. She brings me coffee and sliced oranges to bed. I love the way she pours coffee. She sits on my lap while on the phone to Daphne. Daphne says the rumour is Oliver got his student pregnant.

Where did you hear that?

Daphne: You hear everything in social services.

Lydia, to Daphne: Craig Regular is in town. I saw him last night. He's looking great.

When she hangs up the phone, I say, You never told me that Craig was in town, or that you saw him.

She says, All your best friends are women.

I say, All your best friends are men.

That's not true, she says.

Me: Well, maybe women are easier to be best friends with.

26 I'm crouched at Lydia's car door in the dark, having thanked Max and Daphne for the rhubarb pie and coffee. Lydia says I love you and I say, But I can't get your door shut. She drives home with my arm across her midriff holding the door handle and she asks if I'm loving her a little more today.

I say, Every day that happens.

Tell me something you love about me.

I love it when you wear your red kimono and sit on your kitchen counter to read a recipe book with your goggly glasses on.

At the lights a fire truck screams past us and we follow it to my place.

Daphne had confessed to eating things in grocery stores. She will not buy an orange before she pokes her finger through one to taste it. Lydia says she does the same with peaches.

Lydia had asked Max for a light. And for a second I am jealous. But also, in as brief a moment, I am assured she is committed. I realize jealousy knows no bound. That I could think of a moment when Lydia and Max were sexual.

What I love of Lydia is that her head is full of new, unfinished thought. No complete ideas, always renovating opinion. She has conviction, yet she can be converted, if she believes your evidence.

Daphne tells us a story of a horse she had as a child that got into the grain — grain that hadnt been watered.

Daphne: I had to pull that mare off the ground. And walk it around Brigus. The field arcing up and the sky bending down, tugging this horse around to save it.

I'm going to use this detail in the novel.

Talking about the past, Max says. It's like sewing a fabric and pushing the needle through two thicknesses, through both sides of the cloth. His father, Noel Wareham, is going blind.

When Max visits, his dad asks him to thread all the needles.

27 Snow is melting under mounds like sudden child pee. Bold shadows thrown onto things, firm and sure of themselves.

The southside hills wear a mist that makes them look gigantic. Patches of snow in the dips. Fog and the sea beyond. I like watching weather work in the distance.

28 I lay a tray of frozen chicken in the fridge to thaw. I am a fervent believer in letting nature do work for you. And conserving energy. I've left a casserole dish to soak in the sink overnight, so it's easy to clean now. I am a patient man.

The harbour a cold deep marble blue, blue of blood in the veins, starved of oxygen, water so cold and dense the oxygen is squeezed out, the blue of hydrogen.

I walk to the library. I choose microfiche film of newspapers from March, 1914. Knowing what the news will be. That the preliminary reports are optimistic. There are hints to the disaster. A novelist uses foreshadow. Whereas a newspaper's reports are never infused with such prophecy. The sealers are missing. Now the sealers are dead. On a day like today.

29 Oliver Squires invites me to play snooker. I'm so surprised that I agree. He'll meet me there at nine.

It's hard to talk around a snooker table. It's five dollars an hour, so we spend about two dollars of time just talking. Oliver holding his pint carefully, the blue tip of his pool cue leaning on his shoulder. He says, I called Maisie but she's out.

Hadnt heard from her. I see her walking to her car and she calls out, she's friendly, but I'm low-key. And she pounces on this. She's had a hard day, not a second to call me. About Una.

Oliver says, I know youre Maisie's friend, but I appreciate your listening.

Maisie, when she found Oliver low-key, started to yell. Why dont you go fuck yourself. That's what she yelled. I dont want to have to deal with that kind of attitude.

Me: I'm thinking how lucky I am. This morning I was served a peeled banana and coffee in bed. A nice lingering kiss. And Lydia called me to say I never did tell you, but it's great that you paid off your student loan.

Oliver: I never did get that kind of appreciation.

She's upset at you.

Maisie's upset it didnt work out.

She's upset about the rumours.

I can't stop rumours.

Me: Let's call her now.

You think so?

Yes, let's do it.

Oliver calls and says hi, expectantly. I'm leaning against the wall, holding our pints. He says, Maisie, do you think we'll get along okay? Youve forgiven me?

He nods at me.

How am I? Well, I'm just startled at the ferocity of your anger.

No, no, no, I mouth, and spill the pints. But by now the

phone is a foot away from Oliver's ear and even then you can hear her.

30 Oliver Squires, Lydia says, is a cynic. Yet he's a purveyor of honesty. He has a way of using phrases that are not cliché but are found in phrase books, a conversational gambol using more intelligent clichés. He likes the word peccadillos. He uses words like malfeasance and anomie and confesses to lacking secular connections.

Lydia: He has a wicked tongue. If you hurt him he will betray you.

Me: I left him still pacing the snooker table. Bewildered that Maisie has left him. And then, almost in the same breath, he's perplexed that the Canadiens can't seem to score goals in March. There is no variation in the weight he puts on problems.

Lydia: Men are like that.

31 Sometimes, to be squeezed shoulder to shoulder in a kitchen party, the frenetic energy of bodies, the physical pull and tug and unanimous decision to be frenzied and fun and enjoy being incarnate. Earl Quigley is back from a conference in Santa Fe, and he is telling me about the true size of the universe. This is the man Lydia spent four years of her life with. I've had a few, so I can relax and almost pretend I am Lydia. There is something enjoyable in being Lydia in her past life, something revealing. Then Iris interrupts to say the caplin are so small these days and they used to come in June but now

they roll in July. Maisie Pye, who has decided to appear and I'm glad of that, says Random House is interested and Wilf Jardine is being encouraged to play an original. Wilf is drinking tequila, lime soda, and ice. He says, you know how they say there's a fork in the woods or you walk down the road less travelled or you can't see the woods for the trees. Well I'm saying I just went bombing down the road and never saw any woods at all.

By two the party dwindles to a fortress of stalwarts in my kitchen. I have begged Lydia not to go but she has a meeting in the morning, so I kiss her goodnight and she is sharing a cab with Maisie Pye and Craig Regular. I have watched her look at Craig Regular all night and, because he is so tall, her look can be mistaken for admiration. I return to Earl's attention. Earl is on the phone to Casino taxi, ordering rye whisky.

There are just the four of us left — Earl, Max, Iris, and me — with this twenty-six-ouncer of rye and excuse me I must piss in the garden oh what a night the double daylight breaking over Cabot Tower.

While I'm pissing Iris sits on the steps. She says an old boyfriend of hers, a marine biologist, buried a dolphin under a rose bush. This boyfriend used to bring her flowers he'd stolen from cemeteries.

I wake at noon on the living-room couch. Upstairs in my bedroom Earl and Max are snoring hard. Iris makes me a hot cup of tea with lots of canned milk and two slices of toast with butter.

April

1 Lydia had spilled wax on the sleeve of her astrakhan. She lays the coat on the floor, takes a piece of butcher paper, and irons it to the sleeve. Kneeling over the coat, sun shining branches into solids and shadows over her head. The wax melts into the butcher paper, the grease of an animal.

2 There has been an absence of wind for more than a day. How rested the trees look, the harbour. Like horses. Patient horses.

We meet Maisie down at Alex and Max's opening. Maisie is staring into the pupil of Alex's eye. The pupil dilates. Flaccid, Maisie says, should be pronounced flax-sed. And, turning to the wall of bums, says, The only two descriptions are for a penis or for prose.

She shows us a copy of the letter she sent to Michael

Ondaatje. Do you think he gets many letters?

Lydia: A hundred a year.

That many?

They won't be as good as this, Maisie, but he's read all over the world.

Me: Yeah. He's bound to get a lot of mail.

Maisie's depressed by her first royalty cheque. She sold 214 books. In the letter she says to Ondaatje: My mother has a lot of friends.

She is trying to figure out how many strangers have bought her book.

We walk to the bums and try to pick out mine. There are twelve plaster moulds of bums hanging on the wall. Lydia points out mine. I see Wilf Jardine studying them, and then I know Wilf's bum is up on the wall too. It is right beside my own.

Wilf stares at his own bum. It has a taut carriage. He is sucking on a hard candy. He holds his elbow and wrist in a gay posture. He is oblivious to this.

Some tight ass on you, Wilf.

Yours is pretty nice too, Gabe.

Which is it?

Isnt it this one?

And Wilf picks out his own bum. Or is it.

3   Supper at Max's. He's blanched and roasted an entire seal carcass that his father, Noel, has sent him from Arnold's Cove. We all stare at the beast. Even Daphne.

The seal's massive, coffee-brown, steaming torso dominates the table. It's daunting to approach it with a knife.

I've never had anything but flipper pie, Lydia says.

The rib cage has thin strips of meat and the flippers are tender. It's a boiled dinner: turnip, carrot, potato, cabbage, and pease pudding. Max is delighted. He grew up sealing, and he has a set of sealing tools: a sculping knife, which separates carcass from pelt, and a flensing knife, which is used on the pelt to carve blubber from fur.

4   I study the city with binoculars. The southside hills have gone grey overnight. Like a black dog will go white around the mouth as he gets older. The toes, the tip of tail. As if the cold exhalations of winter freeze the fur white. I think it's a frost in the scalp of the hill and the sun is shining deep into it.

The wet trims on all the mansard roofs glint like shining gifts, like metal boxes that hold new hardware. Fresh hinges. Uncollected garbage. A mattress sags against a boarding house. Broken vinyl siding exposes styrofoam and the faded paint on rotting clapboard. Inside a window two men sunk in a floral couch roll cigarettes while an astonished parakeet swings in its cage. Children toss a bicycle tire over cold telephone wires. A man in a wool cap pedals up the street with a towering load of bent aluminum balanced over his front wheel, secured with rough yellow rope. He exhales over the aluminum and his breath looks like aluminum vapour.

The aluminum flashes in the sun, and the streets are bone dry. Thirsty streets, salt stinging the sidewalks. When dogs begin to hunker down and chew their paws.

I open the window and smell boiling fat. A slow, glacial grease slips down the sidewalk from the backs of fish-and-chips shops. Liquid copper slides out of the eavestroughs on Gower Street United. Staining the sidewalk green.

A light dry snow wafting. With the shadows sitting under their objects.

Mere description.

5 Max stalks around the snooker table, analyzing percentages. His forearms toned from constant heavy carpentry work. He has an exquisite long shot. The quiet green acre of snooker cloth. He is reverting to a former life. He has made money shooting pool. He wipes the palms of his hands on the stubble of his scalp. His jeans have a hole worn in the back pocket that reveals a corner of his black wallet.

His firm bridge on the nap. The puny pool tables have an eerie blue cloth in comparison, and it seems classy to pot balls that have no numbers.

6 Remembering how Max had said, The body is the only motor that doesnt make noise. And these furnaces of heat inside us (he points to his rib cage) — if we didnt give off heat, it would seem magical for a body to be warm. All the senses are quite mysterious inventions. Max once lost his sense of smell for a few weeks after a roofing truss fell on his head.

Max: Name me the things you love about Lydia.

Her face. She has a face like a beautiful shoehorn.

Max: I wouldnt tell her that.

She laughs from her solar plexus.

Yes.

Lydia is always right and I am always wrong.

That's something to love.

It allows us to step away from argument.

What else.

She has tremendous legs, legs that will serve her well when she's ninety.

Gabe, I got to tell you.

No. I know. You think I'm being unkind. Okay. I made cabbage rolls and soup and she picked out the cinnamon and the cardamom. She nailed seven distinct ingredients. And she makes these little movements of her hands to remind me to flick off all the lights.

Max: That's good. When mannerisms annoy, you know youre in trouble.

She's animated, Max. I've been seeing her for almost two years now.

Max: She says she's been seeing you just over a year.

Well, that's true. I was going out with Lydia for six months before she started going out with me.

Max: That's pretty funny. But aint it the way.

7   First iceberg of the year, drifting across the mouth of the harbour. Lydia had said, Let's play cards this Easter. Okay, I said. Nickel ante and five dollars to the table. Lydia: And the most you can raise is the Lord.

This morning I had Una up to blow eggs through pin-holes. I blew my cheeks purple on the first one. Una, brandishing a brush, ready to dive on the egg, says, You sure it's empty?

Yes.

Maybe we should crack it open first and check.

8 Got home this morning and the sky was turning blue. Out with Max and Maisie. Where's Lydia, they say, and I explain she's rehearsing lines with Wilf. We end up at the after-hours boozecan, avoiding fights with a guy who wants to shove something up someone else's ass.

We tackle Max in the street until he has to tell halted taxis that it's okay, just horsing around. Wilf passes us and nods.

Fiction writers, he says. Theyre a tough crowd.

Where's Lydia?

Left her with Craig Regular, he says.

We pick up Alex at the foot of Solomon's Lane. She is fresh from the Ship, wearing a long yellow trenchcoat. She has a bunch of carnations and daisies she stole from a vase, and she's slipping them into my jacket pocket. It's a free-booze night, some ceremony, some stand on principle, and everyone who is anyone is out crawling the mild, wet streets, a bit like Dublin folded into a Paris. Europe of the twenties, when everyone is walking home with a person they shouldnt be walking with, people going home with the wrong people for one night only. Alex leans into me and we kiss against the coarse clapboard of a house (I scrape my knuckles).

Max and Maisie say, Break it up. Maisie in particular is rough with me.

Goodbye, Alex.

She slips another flower in my pocket.

And Maisie and Max haul me away.

Max walks me home. He knows which route will save us valuable steps.

9   Lydia is flipping through her old journals. In a lemon cardigan, polka-dot blue shirt, and dark green tights. I'm drunk in love with her.

I ask Lydia if she's ever lied to me. Yes. But only small things.

I confess kissing Alex and Lydia admits she kissed Craig Regular at about the same time. It's as if our confessions balance; we're stunned at the reciprocity, and we both seem renewed. Or a blurring factor, like glaucoma, has been peeled away. We drive out to Goat Cove, where a crowd has convened. A boil-up in a sheltered, stony beach on the Atlantic. I find a purple starfish for Una. She puts him back in a rock pool. It's cold but sunny. We play frisbee and climb the waterfall and eat roasted bananas. Max boils the kettle. The adults loafing about the fire, keeping warm. Max hasnt said anything about our night. He has brought his rusty Christmas tree to burn in the fire. We listen to the pull and suck of the water's ebb, remembering our mother's bellies. The tree sizzles then ignites like a lantern mantle. We are all remembering gentler times as the tide claws at stones. We all want, for a moment, to return to some simpler existence, when we were all together. Or perhaps before we were together.

10 I'm at Lydia's sketching when Daphne drops in. Lydia's not home. Daphne asks if Lydia will ever have a baby. I say, If we get married, that'll be a sign. Daphne: I can't imagine being with a man and not having children with him.

I say, Congratulations.

I draw Daphne, but I've made her mouth haggard. She says, What if I put my hand over my mouth?

I draw the hand, but you still see the mouth, so I colour it like a red glove.

Looks like I'm just about to give head, Daphne says.

She says a client down at emergency declined her service. Said it'd be too hard to work around a woman who's pregnant.

Daphne: I've been pregnant all of one month and people know.

11 Lydia spent the afternoon with Craig Regular. He asked her if she's in love. Craig's been in Seattle designing software and attending Shambhala conferences. I knew she was with him because there are two Buddhist books on the table.

He asked: Are you more in love than youve ever been in your life?

I think: What an asshole. What a shit disturber.

Lydia: I thought I'd been in love with Earl, but Craig says no one can love Earl. He says he loves the guy, but Earl's not into growth. Earl has his ego and his research and that's it. Who can grow with him? He's not interested.

Lydia thought this very interesting. But Craig likes you, she says, the feel he gets off you.

I'm sure the fucker does.

I ask what she thinks of Buddhism and what he's doing.

I wonder about the meditation, of avoiding thoughts that come to you. Perhaps, she says, it's important to look at those thoughts. Craig believes meditation allows him to understand his own processes, how he does things.

Me: I need less of that. I'm in the moment so often that I need to become more oblivious of the self. I dont need the meditative encouragement.

What I do meditate on is their kiss. When I think of their kiss, how it happened by the washrooms at the Grapevine, that Daphne probably saw it, it drives me away from Lydia. It makes me think of leaving this claustrophobic city.

12 A fresh dump of winter. Moose are caught in snow up to their necks in Bird Cove. Men on snow machines try beating a path out for them, but they have nowhere to go. The moose are bawling.

Iris and Helmut have gone to look at them. Helmut has never seen a moose. While they are gone Max calls to say there's a bull moose standing in Bannerman Park. I drive over. The moose is gobbling the pussy willows and frozen ruffage.

Helmut returns disappointed. Iris: The moose got free before we arrived.

I tell them about the moose they missed in the park.

Stories. As soon as I try to write one down, it floats away from me. Trying to get a bit of eggshell out of the mixing bowl. It scoots off and wants to be something else.

13 We wake up to the sound of rain driving back the snow.

For lunch I make cheese-and-asparagus sandwiches. Lydia has made a cake. I ask what kind of cake it is. She says, It was a cake I had on the plane from Halifax. I've had it in my mind now for a week.

Youre trying to make an airplane cake?

It was good.

14 I love my binoculars. Watching a rollerblader tack down Signal Hill Road. Then I see that it's Craig Regular. Cars brake, weave around him, using up a lot of gas on the brake and accelerate. Craig wears an orange traffic vest. He's zipping, dipsy-doodling, turning down Battery Road. He has no idea I am watching him. I am two miles from him. I would love to see a car smack into him. But he is too swift. He zooms by the last saltbox in St John's, down past the yellow guardrail, and straight to his door. I hadnt realized I can see his house.

I turn to a coast guard vessel, to read its name on the bow, but can't steady the binoculars — my excited heartbeat is moving them a fraction.

15 I confess to Maisie that I have no imagination, that I have a methodical nature. It's easier to write down the present than to be present in the past.

She says, If Oliver had told me he'd slept with another woman, it might be different. But the fact is, he hid it.

Even if he'd slept with someone his own age, a peer, with the same interests, she could understand it.

Maisie: I mean, I'm not going to be the only person he could fall in love with.

Maisie says she and Oliver had friends who agreed to have affairs, as long as they didnt last and they didnt have to tell each other, but the husband got involved, long term, and eventually they divorced.

Maisie: It's the deceit that's killing me. What ever happens with Lydia, dont pull an Oliver Squires.

And what precisely is an Oliver Squires?

Lining up someone before you leave.

You might be better off telling that to Lydia.

16 Iris's cactus is blooming pink. Laundry today. Read the *National Enquirer.* The tabloids are good because often the actors dont look their best; theyre caught in unflattering poses coming out of limos or washrooms where theyve sneezed or done a line. They look tired, startled, worn.

17 Lydia says Maisie is beautiful. She has light coming out of her face. She agrees with Maisie's stand.

Lydia: If you ever have an affair and dont tell me, then it's your burden. I dont want to hear about it two years later.

Maisie is considerate. We dropped in just after she'd eaten, and she wiped down the dinner table. She was alone, Una with

Oliver. She offered us apple pie and took the smallest piece. Articulate and well-mannered, she points out your habits in a way that doesn't cause offence (she made fun of my hand gestures by mimicking them). She takes her cigarette outdoors, in her own rented house.

18 The sun is a barrel down the Crosstown Arterial, lighting the southside hills, Shea Heights, the tank farm, all the way to the mini-marina. And the top floor of the Royal Trust.

I pick up my cheque from the arts council, cash it at the Royal Bank, and buy a bottle of eleven-dollar wine at the liquor store next door. I walk into Blue Peter Steamships.

I am taken by the idea of leaving St John's by sea. I am taken by the idea of vanishing. A small vengeful part of me, or an intolerant part of me, wants to leave Lydia, and this means leaving St John's. And so I delight in the fantasy of preparing a departure.

Blue Peter has an open-air-concept office, a half-acre of carpet, and three oak desks. There's a woman, a sixty-year-old man, and a young man in a ninety-dollar shirt. I finger the young man's desk. I cradle the bottle of wine along my forearm.

I was just wondering if you still take passengers.

Young man: You want to cross the Atlantic by boat?

A twenty-foot skylight beaming in a prism above. A bank of windows to my left. You can watch ships come and go through the Narrows.

The ninety-dollar shirt says, Those days are long gone.

I walk home with the eleven-dollar wine. I am the kind of man who finds it hard to spend more than that on a bottle of wine. Lydia will often pour a glass of seventeen-dollar wine.

19 The last minutes of last call in the Ship Inn, encore of the evening. Lydia swirls her brandy in victory. Max says, As soon as you write about a culture, then you know it's gone.

The lights come up and we stand surprised and accept the applause of our own drunkenness, the embarrassments of the night, when our actions are hidden in smoke and darkness, the fictions we flirt with. Illicit lovers caught by the wrong husband.

It was opening night of the play at the LSPU Hall, and Lydia, in her small part, was terrific. She became someone else, something I can't do. I dont have the proper brain to pretend and be convincing.

We manage the stairs to Duckworth Street and speak quietly under the ear that hears all of downtown St John's. Quiet with the stories you tell, or the wrong person will hear you. Whispers from actors, from producers, from songwriters and one drummer. There are people who believe in God and people seeking God and people who are convinced there is no God. All walking up the stairs into cars on Duckworth Street.

We walk up past the LSPU Hall, the amethyst of St John's theatre. A green clapboard building that holds up a hill of attached eighty-year-old houses that cling together in the hope of money and love and insight. Not optimism, but hope. The pink, white, and green national flag of Newfoundland emblazoned on the Hall's forehead, a wild palomino, stalwart in a domesticated land, where Lydia delivered her stellar performance.

Lydia and I walk up Long's Hill and then up the stairs to my room and I sit here at the windows while she sleeps. I am so proud of her. I look at the harbour with my thoughts varnished by this supreme feeling. All spring, only the *Astron* has left port. It's a dead port. A purse seiner shelters behind a rusting trawler. Tourists will soon be pointing their video cameras at things that dont move: the basilica and Cabot Tower.

While beneath them the sewage outfall is gobbled up by seagulls. Boyd Coady says the water has changed in the thirty years since the Portuguese white fleet docked here. It was pollution from boats back then. Now it's the city's waste that colours the water as it blooms brown into the crystal green depths of the Atlantic.

I turn from this desolation to the fullness of my bed. I curl into the side of Lydia Murphy.

20 Alex tells me that most men are mediocre: I want a man I find interesting.

She was once almost married.

I ask for moments.

This very date seven years ago.

When you were nineteen, I say.

Yes, she says.

She met a man in a staircase. They went out for two years. He's a philosopher now. Earl Quigley knows him. He asked her to marry him. He had met her parents. But she said no.

Alex: I dont know why now, and I regret it. But at the same time I wonder.

I drive her back to her place on Duckworth. On the way I stop at Lydia's and point out her house. All the windows are dark. It's about midnight.

She's working late, I say.

I shift from first to second and accidentally touch her knee. Alex's knee doesnt flinch.

21 I tell Lydia of Alex's idea. Of taking pictures of men, concentrating, as they play pool. As part of the passion exhibit.

I'm speaking into the pillow. I've decided I have to tell her this.

You crop the photo so you dont know theyre shooting pool. Youre left with the concentration.

Lydia: Concentration brings a peculiar look to the face.

Me: A lot of my memories of my father are in acts of concentration.

It's like lovemaking.

Well. That's not what I think of when I think of my father.

I think Alex telling you this is a bit like lovemaking.

It's intimate. But it's art.

22 I rent *Raging Bull*. I'm walking along Gower Street at 10 p.m. Three kids, fifteen years old, start yelling.

Beat the fucking shit out of ya!

A dirty snowball hits a light pole ahead of me. I cross the

street, pass them. Another snowball whizzes by my head. I stop and stick the video in my jeans. Turn. I point to one of them.

He says, Are you giving me the finger?

They wonder if I speak English, because I havent spoken. One walks close, yelling like a mongrel, and I grab him at the collar, take him down and feel like smacking him. I have a knee to his chest. I'm surprised I've managed to catch him, like swatting a fly with one hand. The other two scream. Four more boys run up, bigger shapes. Some as tall as me. I back off and I see they have hockey sticks. But theyre in silhouette. I decide to boot it out of there. And they, of course, run after me. Running is a bad idea, I realize. Running obliges them to catch me. I turn to see about three eighteen-year-old boys with the younger pack behind them. They doggedly run after me along Gower. I run past Lydia's (they'll just beat out the windows) and jog up Garrison Hill. They are shouting for me to hold up. I continue west along Harvey Road. And make a stand under a streetlight by the Big R. If I'm going to be beaten up it will be in the light, the police station just across the road. They surround me, catching their breath, bent over, hands on knees.

We just want to know, the biggest boy says, what happened.

I tell them, my throat burning for air: Throwing snowballs, verbal threats, I live in the neighbourhood. I took one down.

Big boy: That's okay. We'll take care of things.

I say, Youre a good feller.

They walk back. My throat raw from the run, exhausted. I

can barely laugh at my own panic. The adrenaline still hot in my skin. I walk down Long's Hill, past Gower Street United, and wait in the shadows. The boys are slow returning, as if changing their minds. They pick at potholes with the hockey sticks. I walk briskly to Lydia's, but her door's locked. I dont have a goddamn key. She's on the phone. She stretches the phone cord into the porch to open the door, and I rush past her. I drink water in the bathroom and try to tell her what happened. She says, You should have pounded them.

But they were fifteen years old.

So what?

They'd have me up on charges.

What would a judge say if they did?

Lydia.

What?

23 When she says, Goodnight, Gabe, I say, Goodnight, babe. I say, You hardly ever call me Gabriel. She says you hardly ever call me Lydia.

That's not true.

It is true. Youre always calling me babe.

On the phone I call you Lydia.

Once. I remember hearing it on the answering machine when I got home. My name and it struck me how you hardly ever say it.

I think about this argument. That I dont like to sway opinion. When something sounds untrue but Lydia believes it, I find it hard to convince her otherwise. I would be a bad lawyer. I regret that she feels it, and I will usually try only once to describe my side of things. If she still holds to her opinion, I'm loathe to object.

24 I nose the green lobster into the boiling water. His tail flexes, full of bewilderment. A claw taps the side of the pot. It takes about ninety seconds for him to resign himself, for his shell to turn orange.

A dip made of melted butter, lemon, garlic, and parsley. I spread the leaves of a newspaper over Lydia's dinner table. Lydia wonders which of her boyfriends hammered the claws. Was it Earl? He'd go to the tool chest and get a hammer.

At this very table.

Corn, I say, is the lobster of the vegetable family.

Lydia: Now that sort of statement. That's where you lose me.

I think about this. Why did I make that pronouncement, which feels true to me. Theyre both large, I say. A solid colour. You boil them alive and theyre seasonal. You eat only a select part of the whole body. And pepper's important.

Lydia accepts this. She reads me a quote from Salinger, about images and how God will understand if there's confusion or misuse of images. Youre better off not getting wrapped up in the small stuff of right and wrong.

25 In the morning I tell Lydia it's time to get up. No, not yet, she says. Then the doorbell. She has forgotten that Maisie and Daphne are coming for yoga. Stay in bed, she says.

I wake again and there's no sound. And I get up. Downstairs this note. Gabe, dont leave.

It's nearly 10 a.m. when Lydia returns. And sits with me. Sometimes when she's alone she thinks of her past lives and starts to feel sad. She tells me how Earl never cried. Nothing in life is tender, Earl would tell Lydia when she was crying. He didnt see the point in crying.

We lie down for a few minutes. She's made me a little sad, but I've cheered her up by consoling her. Then the phone. And Lydia has to go. She'll call me when she's through. I'm glad you cry, she says.

As I walk home I spot a wry cat leaping to my fence. He's after a grosbeak. He's as orange as a kipper.

26 Max says he was driving in from Arnold's Cove, where his father lives. Just past Whitbourne something hard landed on his truck hood. Then a leg smashed through his windshield.

You hit a moose?

Max: No. It fell out of the sky.

He found the head by the side of the road. There was a full quarter torn from the hip that landed in the back of the truck. He drove back to Monty's Restaurant and called the cops. The cops told him what happened. A transport truck heading west hit the moose. The moose flew off its spoiler, twirled in the air, torn to bits, and landed on Max's truck heading east.

Max is dressing the quarter of moose that landed in the truck bed. Nothing wrong with a bit of tenderized spring moose.

27 Upstairs reading a fashion magazine. Lydia licking her finger to turn the pages, commenting on the looks of the stars.

Me: You often pick out women who look like you and say theyre gorgeous.

Lydia is silent. She's taken offence to that because it's egotistical. She starts listing women in town whom she has said are beautiful but who look nothing like her. She wants me, I think, to retract. And all I want is to move on — why can't I have an unsupported opinion? Why can't she just see it as funny? She thinks that I look upon it critically, that I won't go out on a limb, ever, and won't admit or see that I am acting critically.

She gets up for yoga and I rise when I hear her playing Mozart and Beethoven on the piano. I say, That's beautiful. She says, That's because my parents paid for music lessons.

28 Craig Regular, Lydia says, has spent three years in retreat. Now he's in Seattle. He rents his house in the Battery. His tenant moved out, so he decided to come home for a visit.

Lydia says my handwriting reminds her of Earl's. Earl Quigley and Craig Regular were best friends. Lydia is good at particular explanations. Reasoning why. She says that our vowels and consonants take up the same amount of space, that they remind her of rows of teeth. That it's not confined, but a loose script.

29 Ten p.m. at Max's, playing poker. Lydia and Wilf Jardine have left the table to sing and have a laugh and I feel tight. They are

singing a song I thought was my song with Lydia, but now I see it's a song she has with Wilf. I am unable to loosen up. It's about Lydia's passion. I can see a novel of a man whose movements are contemplative and their effect is not immediate.

The novel starts with them contemplating marriage. Gabriel's tension and Lydia's freedom with others. She longs, but she stops herself unconsciously and she loves Gabe's quiet goodness and he loves that she loves this in him and he loves her bigness in the world. But still we wonder about him; we dont see Gabe's worth (because it is an invisible thing), only Lydia's (external, sensuous, obvious, full of acts of will), and Gabriel hampering her and holding her back. She's not free. Then comes Alex Fleming, who sees Gabriel, understands his inner working, and suddenly the reader recognizes why he's great and talented, because Alex brings his treasure to light. Alex complements his thought and his creativity is ignited. They connect and Lydia sees it, Lydia knows again why he's great, the reason she's in love with him. But Lydia understands she can't bring it out in him. She needs Alex to encourage it and by this time he is engulfed by Alex.

All of this arises out of Lydia singing a song with Wilf. Meanwhile the cards are dealt and the best hand I have all night is two pair.

30 I can hear Maisie Pye, Daphne Yarn, and Lydia stretching downstairs on Lydia's area rug. The sun is just up. They must be pressing their faces into a wool rug that smells of Tinker Bumbo. That must be a pleasant yogic experience.

May

1 Daphne Yarn grasps a green bottle of Italian wine from Lydia's fridge. From the grasp I can see the tone in her arms, the flex in her hands. I love athletic arms. Daphne says, It's my favourite rosé. I drink it all summer long. It's not like that Portuguese stuff you drink at wiener roasts and picnics.

Then we'll bring it to Max's birthday.

I walk them down to the Y. Daphne and Lydia have begun training for the regatta. They practise on rowing machines. Daphne says she'll be six months pregnant by the time the regatta rolls around.

I notice the buildings that have gone to fire and bankruptcy. Coffee shops have choked out drugstores and bookstores. Whenever they renovate an old building, you can be sure it will succumb to a mysterious midnight fire.

2   If you rise early enough, you'll see a clear sun lift off the ocean, a bright band of hot light. The land warms faster than the ocean, which creates fog, and the fog consumes the sun.

My chili peppers are sprouting in their flats. Like a rooster's comb.

I see Max, impatient in a bank lineup. He says, You'll be able to take the wait behind this guy off your income tax.

I pay my mortgage and watch Boyd Coady lying flat on the pavement. A grating off a drain. He's bent at the hips into the drain. A boy holds his ankles. Traffic passes. Boyd stretches up with a white bucket. He dumps the slurry along the curb. A woman leans on the bank railing and cautions them about the traffic. She's wearing a windbreaker.

Woman: He lost his big gold ring, five hundred dollars.

I look in the drain. The water is not moving.

Boyd: You couldnt see that rock ten minutes ago.

You'll get it, I say.

Boyd looks at me with unquestioning faith in his ability. He doesnt need my encouragement. In fact, my words only bring doubt.

3   Maisie and I spoke of money. How Oliver wanted someone to fix the porch. Maisie said they can't afford it. Oliver looked at the bank balance and said there's a thousand dollars in it. Maisie: Several bills havent been paid. Oliver buys services, Maisie fixes things herself. Oliver's argument was that if you spend your time doing what you do best, let specialists mend the rest.

My father never hired anyone, I say. He bought raw materials, not services. Even when pouring the foundation for the kitchen. We mixed the cement by hand. We found the gravel and sand. I envied the cement truck rotating its heavy belly, a load coming down the chute. But now I may do it by hand. I know the proper consistency of cement.

4 Last night I had Lydia listen to the Rosemunde by Schubert. Lydia says she never listens to music without doing something else. Music is always an accompaniment. But we lay on the bed in the dark with only the blue light of the stereo power button on and listened to it. It's about thirty minutes long. And she saw that it is beautiful. Then she read me an article on how we are living further in the past as we learn more about it. I told her Bartlett listened to Schubert as his ship sank in the ice. He sat in his study, keeping the fire going with wax records, until the deck rail was flush with the ice. The last piece he played was Chopin's Funeral March.

5 I help Max move a rolltop dresser from Duckworth Street, next door to the War Memorial. When we have the dresser roped into the back of his truck, we inspect the memorial. The front bronze by Gilbert Bayes, 1923. Thinking of the past makes Max tell me of fishing with his father in Placentia Bay for mackerel. How mackerel get stiff soon after they're caught. He likes mackerel just as much as salmon. I say they are a handsome fish, a blue-grey skin with net pattern. Like herring. Max wants to go diving for sea urchins. The Japanese eat their

roe. I said I didnt know sea urchins had roe.

Oh, yes, he says, and studies the harbour. I can dive down to twenty feet using scuba gear.

We drive to Max's workshop and unload the dresser. Want a coffee? He has a little coffee maker in a corner. You have to weave around table saws, lathes, and drill presses to get there.

He sprinkles a pinch of salt and dry mustard powder in with the grounds. He says salt always makes bad coffee taste better.

And I have seen Max add salt to a pint of beer. And Lydia has shown me the ingredients of one brand of salt, which includes sugar.

6   There is a phone cord stretched across the bed, across my chest, as Lydia talks to Daphne Yarn. It's Max's birthday and we're late.

Lydia: Have you seen the wine? Daphne's wine? It was in the fridge.

Me: I havent.

Well, we'll have to pick up beer.

Daphne lays out ten pounds of smoked salmon.

That's a pound each, Daphne.

We dont have to eat it all tonight, Gabe.

Yes, Max says, displaying the work ahead of us. Tonight we eat all the salmon.

He is forty and someone tells him forty is the new thirty. He corrects them: Forty is the new nineteen. I can see now that Daphne is pregnant. And I feel convinced that they are happy. Something has turned in Max. Some physical change has occurred since he met Daphne. Some might say he's settling down. But he's just as active. A restlessness has been lifted from him.

I pass the bathroom door. Poofy woofy, I say.

That was one small crap for Max, Max says.

A shadow falls on his head and I can see what Max looked like with a full head of hair.

Maisie in a lemon white sockhop dress. She has baked bread, she's slicing the salmon then notices it's pre-sliced. She is set to slice it when the salmon falls into segments, as if she willed it sliced by lifting a carving knife.

Perf de derf, Daphne says. Testing the salmon.

Daphne, quiet and beautiful; there is a light on her face that shows a deep structure in her eyes and nose and those pigtails as if she has the brakes on because she's going full tilt.

7 Maisie: I wish I had done something radical with money when I was younger. Now I have no money.

Me: You have one of the most chaotic lives, and youre a fine writer. You sway rooms full of people.

What do you mean?

You attempt to persuade people on a course of action youve convinced yourself would be good for them.

I like to offer my opinion.

And yet youre insecure. Youre always buying brand-new hardcover fiction to offset some geographic and cultural isolation.

Gabe. That's professional. My one weakness.

I admire it. And your writing is sensual and particular. It's in the active, present tense. Youre funny and strong and surprisingly unsure of your talent.

Are you trying to cheer me up?

Maisie's money is tied up in a mortgage and car payments, the house in Heart's Desire, feeding Una, and for once, she's fearful of finances now that she has left Oliver.

Me: What is radical?

Brazil is radical. What Iris is doing. Anything lavish that is consumed.

Well, why not go to Heart's for a weekend? It's the next best thing.

Okay then, she says.

8 Today was a list of donts and shoulds. Lydia said, Dont use foot-bath powder in a full bath, you should change clothes after badminton, dont sneak up on me ever, dont barge into the bathroom when I'm in there, dont make coffee without measuring the grounds, dont peel carrots in the sink, dont put tomatoes in a salad, you should take my direction when driving otherwise youre being defiant, dont try to do accents youre no good at them, dont put extra oil in anything, dont serve a bowl without a plate under it, dont floss your teeth that way, this is how you make rice, dont use vinegar in a salad dressing, dont leave your coat on a kitchen chair, dont talk to me when I'm falling asleep or speak to me when I'm remembering my dreams or tell me not to swear, dont compare me, dont make

the bed that way, dont turn on the overhead light use lamps, dont use the bathroom fan switch it's too noisy, close the bathroom door if I'm in bed.

9   I find a pair of men's underwear in Lydia's dryer and theyre not mine. I lay them on top of the machine. But Lydia does not pick them up. So I ask her and she says theyre not hers.

Lydia: I've never seen them before. Maybe theyre Earl's.

From five years ago? They look recent.

Lydia: I dont know anything about them.

She's convinced they must be mine. I hang them on the box of detergent.

10   In the post office I see Max's father. A few months ago he fell — fainted — and Max found him. He was in hospital for eight weeks and had prostate surgery.

I had outdoor plumbing for a while, he says.

Mr Wareham's pupils pinpricks in the blue. He's wearing a pair of white cotton gloves and a tea-coloured coat. This man was born on an island off an island. He says he grows wheat in his backyard in Arnold's Cove. Max takes him on trips to Witless Bay Line to boil the kettle and paint trees leaning over a rough shore. He has a white shag of hair. It's funny that he has a head of hair and Max doesnt. Takes after his mother, Max does. Mr Wareham enjoys the company of women in their thirties. He has a small stainless-steel spring of joy in his ankle and a green shoot in his eye and an idea lightbulb burning in his temple.

11 I ride my bike to Motor Vehicle in Mount Pearl to reli-
cense Jethro. First time on my bike this year. It had a flat. I flip
the bicycle upside down in the backyard, wrench off the rim,
tug out the tube, dunk it in the sink. I realize I'm thinking of
that pair of underwear. Who the hell owns them?

The hole makes a flute of bubbles. I sandpaper the hole and
dab on rubber cement and let it go tacky, apply a patch
and wait for the tube to dry, and then, with the heels of three
teaspoons hanging off the lip of the rim, it's my childhood
days. Been fifteen years since I changed a bicycle tire with teaspoons.

It's a busy road. But a lull in between the two cities. With
flat properties and a little farming. Rows of plastic cones over
some tender crops. A gentle ascent into Mount Pearl. A
girl digging in the soil, her glasses glinting gold. Or the glint
tells me she's wearing gold glasses. Her father in a row of trees.
Cow manure trampled into the edge of pavement. A protest
sign against the land freeze. Ballroom dancing at the Old Mill.
Brookfield Drive-In. The word Brookfield has theatrical masks
for the two o's, reminds me of one of the entries I'd adjudi-
cated — a handwritten story and for the word *look* a
fourteen-year-old had dots and eyelashes on the o's.

At Motor Vehicle it is sunny and the skylights reflect all the
hills and land around Mount Pearl. One queue is for the photo
driver's licences and men are stroking their hair back and one
woman walks up to her boyfriend, pats his ear. You sign your
name on an electronic pad that collects the signature directly
onto the computer screen and to every province, territory,

state, and free-trade zone in North America, you can be sure. It was forty-five minutes in the lineup and then two minutes at the wicket.

I say, Do I have to sign on this electronic pad? Couldnt I sign a piece of paper instead?

I wouldnt care, but the licence left off my last letter (I wrote over the edge of the pad) and reduced my signature by 50 percent. My signature looks tiny and mean.

12 Lydia and I drive to Heart's Desire with Daphne and Max in the back seat. Jethro doesnt mind the weight. Maisie has knocked out a kitchen wall. She has discovered old linoleum. Maisie hands us a bucket of sudsy water to wash down the wallpaper. The walls have fat pink roses from the fifties.

Una asks me to rub down the butter chunks on her toast.

She has a purse, and in it a picture of Oliver when he was little.

I never knew your dad at that age, I say.

That's Daddy, Una says, when he was me.

I walk to the beach with Daphne, Maisie, and Lydia. We pass Josh and Toby, who are building a fence. Leaves are bursting out of a birch. Toby looks like he doesnt get fed much. Josh nods. They are getting older. Next year they won't even nod to me. They'll be too cool.

Maisie: We bought this house on a whim seven years ago for six thousand. I bought it out of the money I made teaching.

Me: I'm reminded of what you said, Maisie — that teaching made you realize what you believe.

Maisie: People used to give up. They would try to be a pianist or a painter, they would get to Paris and be told they werent good enough. They would become electricians. Not now.

Daphne: That's what happened to Max. Except he told himself.

13 We are driving home from Heart's. A northerly has driven ice close to shore. It pushes Jethro towards the shoulder. Daphne says her grandfather was killed at the seal hunt and brought back in a pickle barrel. They laid him out on his mother's kitchen table and the pickle came running out of him and ruined the cloth.

Daphne can't wait to get back to her greenhouse. She says Craig Regular wrote a letter to the paper. He was complaining that she uses waste of eviscerated animals from the university labs as fertilizer. It's not enough for some, she says, that I'm selling organic produce.

14 On Lydia's desk there is a photo of Lydia dancing with Earl Quigley. They are in Lydia's kitchen on Gower. The same table, same fridge, same brass chimes hanging in the doorway, same grey-and-red wool placemats, even the fridge magnets, the bulletin board behind the door — all the same except Lydia is dancing with Earl Quigley, he's bending her and they smile for a camera and this is five years ago when it would have been his underwear in the dryer and I'm certainly not anywhere near the dance.

I have walked down to Lydia's to make Boston bluefish chowder with clams and shrimp. I have to ring to have her open the door. I notice a block of cheese I bought is gone. Did Lydia eat a whole block of cheese?

Youre the cheese pig, she says.

The photo and the cheese, the underwear still hanging there, and the fact I have no key make me irritable. But I say nothing about it. I am a cheese pig.

Lydia tests the chowder and wonders if something is off. It tastes zingy, she says. Like putting your tongue on a battery.

I decide not to stay, and I can see she's relieved. You can take the chowder, she says. And I walk back up the hill. I pour out the chowder under a tree, where a dog like Tinker Bumbo will find it.

15 Lydia: You sure are spending a lot of time with Maisie.

We're writers. We're conferring.

I realize I havent been discussing the novel with Lydia. The reason is she's so busy with scripts, with the play, with funding proposals for the film in the summer.

Lydia thinks the novel could make a good film. Scenes of Bob Bartlett in the north, walking over polar ice that is floating south. Of the *Karluk* sinking, the phonograph playing. Of Rockwell Kent being accused of spying for the Germans. When I describe these images she gets excited, more excited than me. And I realize she's good for egging me on. She's much better at story than I am.

16 Just showered after a run with Lydia. Shaved a minute off Quidi Vidi, and much easier even though I ran feeling a little sore in the shins. A calm night, the lights of Pleasantville in bright focus. The oil tanks hidden behind a point of land, only the glow of lights on the bank behind them. The whole hill a dull apple-cider glow to protect the tanks from vandals.

Not a soul anywhere.

We stop at Lydia's. When she peels off her running shoes I see she has a pair of Chinese slippers inside. The shoes are too big, she says. I love how her elbows move close to her hips when she jogs. There's something oriental in all that.

We kiss and I continue on up Long's Hill. The greys and blacks. No colour except in blurred pools around streetlights in the distance, showing shingles on the edges of houses.

I run past Theatre Pharmacy, where we hugged that first Christmas and I had the rolling pin down my pants. Feel that, I'd said.

Oh, my.

I had her, for a moment. When she didnt know my body.

Starlings are walking through a grassy hill, eating insects. Green is the garbage of gardens. They are sloughing off green.

17 At Coleman's grocery store. The distorted women, freak-show faces, warped eyebrows, blotchy complexions — about four of them, their tiny husbands pushing carts. A pregnant woman with groceries. She comes out with the bags and there's a man in the passenger seat, waiting, staring at the glovebox, defeated, with a nine-year-old in the back, and

the pregnant woman, struggling into the door, forces her belly behind the wheel, pained, drives.

Thin legs on the women, big torsos, and their pushed-in, beaten faces, receding chins, thin hair crimped artificially. Then calling taxis, paying with Government of Newfoundland blue cheques that require MCP and SIN and theyre worth $301.50 and theyre buying cases of Pepsi, Spaghettios, tins of vienna sausages, cold pre-fried barbecue wings, I can barely write this as it's all so cliché.

18 It's 3 a.m. and Wilf Jardine will not leave Lydia's party. We have to con him. Trouble is, he is used to this game and is wily, wary of deception. He cranks up the music another decibel. I tell him that he has to go now. That I'll go with him. We can go down to the Spur, I say.

Wilf faces me, drunk and wincing. He is drinking shine, panty remover, he calls it. There is a yellow stain on his lapel. It makes the tweed in his coat look like sandwich spread. I'll go to the Spur, he says. But not with you.

He turns to Lydia.

Lydia: I'll go with you, Wilf.

That's better, he says. No offence, Gabe.

I call a cab and we wait in the porch. Silent.

We get in the cab and head to the Spur. Halfway down he changes his mind.

Wilf: I want to go home.

He rolls down his window and yells at some Filipino sailors.

Naw, let's keep her rolling.

We end up at the Spur and Alex is there and I sit with Alex while Lydia takes care of Wilf at the bar. I have my hand around Alex. Craig Regular comes over to talk to Wilf and Lydia, and he makes Lydia's head bend back in laughter.

Alex says, Wilf Jardine has written one good song. When you hear that song, you know Wilf is worth it.

Alex believes if you pray for someone and that person doesnt know youre praying for them, the prayer can still work. She reads fantasy novels set in utopian times. All this I find unattractive.

Wilf, she says, wants only visitors who need his help. You ever been in his house? He owns no plants.

Craig Regular is buying Wilf and Lydia a drink.

You want a drink, Alex?

19 Something in me makes me run at night.

I was exhausted, back from a dinner party at Maisie's new place. I walked through the mist and the darkness and the quiet of Sunday night. I like returning home slowly, to end the night with a known destination.

Lydia's right: Maisie looks good since leaving Oliver. She hitchhiked across the island to see her sister. One man who picked her up asked math questions like: Say you have one brick . . . Another kept stopping into museums and said, Oh, I've got a better one of those at home in the garage. There was a tire leak and the first guy tried to figure out an equation that would predict the rate of deflation.

20 I call Mom as it's her birthday. She said, Your dad came in to the kitchen, bent his knees a little, put his hands on my shoulders, and sang Happy Birthday.

I say, Youre now twice my age.

She hadnt realized I was this old.

Whenever I call her she offers me advice. And today she says she's decided never to pretend to a motive that's false. Someone once accused her of stealing money. She denied it. Then she decided to make a joke of it. She said, How else am I supposed to get by on what I make? She says, When you do that, it leaves an impression on the person. That youre capable of stealing. Before the utterance she was beyond reproach.

I think about the underwear. When I mentioned to Lydia they could belong to a lover, she accepted it. This made the idea ridiculous. But now I'm thinking of it again.

21 I asked Max what he thought of being a father. He's excited. I know he hadnt wanted children, but now he's eager. He has all the books.

We dine at the old Victoria Station. Every year it's a new restaurant, but we still call it the Victoria Station, or 290 Duckworth. Tonight it's serving Caribbean and Mediterranean food. I order stifado, a Greek beef in cinnamon broth. Max the Moroccan lamb. But the tapas are best, scallops in the half shell basted in basil, cold marinated halibut in shredded red cabbage, shrimp in red sauce. A litre of red wine.

Max drives to his place and we play chess. And then I walk home. It takes twelve minutes to walk home from Max's, through the basilica grounds. The cold, silent night. I am tired. I wake up with the shock of a cat sniffing my face. Then I remember Iris is taking care of one.

22 On Lydia's deck I can hear a delicate cheep from the neighbour's soffit. I make coffee but decide to abstain. I lean over the rail. I can distinguish three distinct bird voices. A family has begun. A little family of three. I had told Max again how I want to get married, how Lydia is hesitant. Max said the same thing happened with Daphne: She said it was too early. And so I got her pregnant.

What?

A little hole in the condom. Works great.

Are you suggesting —

I'm suggesting you force her hand. You want to get married, you want to have a kid, that's obvious.

What's so obvious about it?

The way you are with Una.

Two deep cheeps and a little high cheep.

23 Lydia and I walk along the river with Tinker Bumbo and Una. We have Una for the afternoon. And Una wants to be with Lydia. Una looks at Lydia with the eye of wonder. Lydia is a woman, a woman not her mother. Mothers dont count. It's sunny but chilly and we look at the houses along Circular Road. We stop in one driveway and speak to a Mrs Chafe. We admire the daphne and the sherbet yellow forsythia, both of which flower before growing leaves.

I wonder, I say, if that means anything about Daphne. Does she bloom before her leaves come out?

Una asks if these are oak trees. The branches are bare, so it's hard to tell. I am studying the bark on the trunks. Mrs Chafe picks up last year's fallen leaf and says no. An oak leaf has a coastline rivulet.

I would never have thought, in spring, to pick up last year's leaf.

24 Alex Fleming's studio overlooks Water Street. I can see the first three letters in the Esso tank farm. She has turned from her computer and drafting table. The screen is sophisticated. She is a woman with a lot of software.

I show her the poems I've written on the seven deadly sins. Her gaze turns professional. For the first time she is looking, in my presence, at something coldly.

Theyre very good, she says. I can work with these.

Her apartment is devoted to small art objects. Bits of rusted metal on the fireplace mantel. The hearth filled with wooden dolls. Images from magazines have been cut out and spliced. I can see a corner of her high bed behind an open door in the hall.

Alex will build seven objects to accompany my text. She says, You and Maisie are the first writers I've mentioned it to. I want to get Max in on it as well. I think it'll be you and me, and Max and Maisie.

Alex wears dark clothes, even at badminton. She smokes. There is a sinister note within her goodness. How she bends over to a serve, and looks me in the eye.

25 We pick up Max and Daphne and drive up the shore to hunt down icebergs. It's twenty-one degrees. I can feel the colour come to my face. The profiles of icebergs. A pair are linked in a green seawater gleam under the surface and I think of Lydia and me standing like that, at a distance but joined surreptitiously. One looks like a Spanish galleon, another the head of a rooster, complete with comb. A third is a lilting ocean liner. We turn shapes into objects. We do it to clouds, to rock formations.

We picnic on the grey sun-baked cliffs of Bay Bulls out on Bread and Cheese Point. Thick sandwiches and expensive leaf lettuce and a bottle of French red and crunchy pickles and ice creams and the orange guitar.

The hard wine bottle clunking against the rock.

26 There is a lawn on Waterford Bridge Road shot through with blue crocuses. I watch Lydia admire them. She has a soft spot for oddities in nature.

But then a hardness appears. We're in her kitchen. I had finished washing the dishes and she turned on the faucet with a dishcloth, getting in my way, and the cloth wiped my sleeve leaving a grease mark and I backed away, got my stuff from upstairs — the tap still on in the kitchen. I ask, Do you want the tap on? Lydia: No. In a tone that says, You left it on.

I ask if anything's bothering her.

I wish you'd taken a loaf from the freezer when you finished the bread. Is that too much to ask?

I havent had any bread.

And she gives me a look that says I dont admit to anything.

27 I decide to walk down to Lydia's without phoning first. The door is locked and I have to ring. She is there with Earl Quigley and Craig Regular, having a toke. Craig tried to get back into the States, but they found marijuana on him at the border. She'd made them supper.

Lydia: I was just about to call you.

This is her second most favourite phrase. Her first favourite is, So what's your point?

I realize I am taking the annoying side of every issue.

I size up the waist size of both Earl and Craig. I notice the underwear is gone now from the detergent box.

I recall that Lydia admitted she felt a little alone. That Earl and Craig allow her to laugh, to be connected. And here I am standing in the kitchen looking at these two men eating supper with Lydia, sharing a spliff, and I must be talking but my concentration is on remembering Earl's professional accents that Lydia falls into, of Lydia laughing when Craig holds her arms so she can't answer the phone.

If I were holding Lydia, she would be pissed off.

All night I'm quiet until Lydia inquires. I say, You dont find what I have to say interesting. When I tell how my father couldve been an excellent burglar —

Gabriel, youve said that a number of times.

Did I ever tell you? Because I'd felt like I'd told you, but you were silent.

Gabe, youve told me dozens of times that your father would say this is what a burglar would do. Do you want me to be entranced with everything you keep repeating?

Just tell me if I'm boring you. But saying nothing.

Lydia, on an elbow, says how unfair that is, thirty times I must have told her that, what do I expect from her. What I expect is for her to say, You'd be driving along like this? Would your brother be with you? Where would you be driving? Out of town? And he'd just scan the houses, or would he point one out in particular? Did your mother know he thought this way? Did you ever think he'd do it? Do you think it affected Junior? Etc. When Lydia talks about her family I'm interested, I ask these kinds of questions, I draw the stories out of her, I make her embellish. I ask for things. Whereas Lydia nods, or changes the subject, or says, So what's your point? Lydia will never be on the phone long with me, and never laugh as hard as she does with Wilf or Craig or Oliver.

How mean and small of me.

She curls around me. But my lower legs are aching. So I sleep on the couch. So I can massage my legs and move freely without waking her. At seven-thirty I go back to her bed. Get up at 9:20. I make bagels and coffee. Lydia says, Dont be sad. I say, It's a physical thing. She says, Yeah, I'm gonna take care of that physical thing.

28 I havent had a cup of coffee in a week. The last four days a headache. I hate picturing Lydia toking then passing the toke on. It's an intimate act.

Lydia was clearing up garbage behind the house and came across the dead baby starling. I pick it up. It's about two inches long, a big bum, featherless except for a tuft ball on its back, soft, little pink arm, no wings but claws, its yellow beak is not hard, ringed around its mouth like a duck's. All the promise of summer has left the nest in the soffit above.

29 It's six in the morning and I'm walking around Quidi Vidi Lake with Maisie Pye. She does this on every morning she doesnt have Una. It's part of her training, she says, for the regatta. The lake is lined with fishermen.

Why all these fishermen?

Maisie: Someone has released a tagged trout worth ten thousand dollars.

On the water there are teams of rowers practising.

Maisie says the fishermen make her wish to be sixteen and to fish in a pond at Flatrock, where her father fished — he couldnt bring her to the best spots because the place he went was too treacherous. She got tired of fishing, though. Getting caught in the trees and her father patiently untying the knotted, tangled line. Parents, dont ever think your acts go unappreciated.

The fishermen are patiently spinning and the rowers are methodically rowing.

30 There are white flowers on the raspberry bushes.

31 I went swimming with Daphne at the university pool,

which is much more utilitarian and small and low-ceilinged and choked with industrious swimmers churning out the lengths.

We shared a lane by the tiled cement and I banged my foot several times.

Daphne says, You sure speed along.

She loans me her goggles for a few laps. And I watch her underwater as she passes. Her belly full of baby. She's four months pregnant. Beautiful to see a pregnant woman swimming. It seems the perfect exercise.

Alex Fleming arrives and she has a tattoo outline of a cannalily on her shoulder. The one painted by Georgia O'Keefe, she says, except in reverse colours.

June

1 Max and I eat pea soup and rolls.

Pea soup is easy to make, Max says.

He wants us to go down the Exploits River. A four-day trip in July. Three couples in three canoes. He can lend us a canoe.

They are on the couch, Daphne's legs on Max's lap. Holes in her tights at the big toe. It's easy to see theyre in love. They are cocksure. I touch Daphne's big toe after I bring the soup bowls back to the kitchen. They have a delicate, crenellated hibiscus flowering by the fridge. Max nursing his finger of metaxa. I have a snifter of Jack Daniels. He says we have to get out of town more and explore Newfoundland.

His father has taken a bad turn, is in hospital. Max has realized most of his life has been spent in the city, whereas his father is a rural man.

My feet are sore from dancing in flat boots. Max can dance. Leading, gently pushing Daphne to the end of her arms. They are used to each other and the pregnancy makes their dance more delicate and caring. And on that couch, comfortable. Daphne flexes her bare toe.

Lydia did not want to join us for a nightcap. So I kissed her goodnight at Hallidays meat market.

Lydia will definitely want to go, I say.

2 Iris: How would you feel if your roommate kept something from you?

Depends, I say. Did the roommate get married?

Yep.

In Madeira. Helmut was wearing shorts. A man named Junko was the sole witness. Under a full moon, on the beach. A Moravian minister performed the ceremony, for the money. They had thought about getting married here, but Iris wanted it to happen outside and it was cold in Newfoundland.

Lydia can understand Iris doing this, to avoid the palaver of a big wedding. It's one of the main reasons she doesnt want to get married.

3 Distance isnt a consideration for who I love or spend time with. Lydia gets absorbed with what's around her and neglects the rest. She hardly ever makes plans but follows suggestions. She is the kind to put down the phone and go, whereas plans tend to inject the event with obligation. Such as attending weddings.

I have been to twelve weddings in my life.

And this weekend there's another Murphy cousin getting married.

A wedding, or the promise to commit, is a good place to begin a novel. It starts with our protagonists deciding if they should marry. And they dont. In the ensuing months, friends around them break up and marry other people. While they stay constant.

Lydia hates clutter. She hates it when the ice trays are empty. She says she can't find her copy of *Sculpting in Time*.

No no no, I say. I did not touch it. I've never even seen it.

Youre not very supportive, she says.

If I said I had it, would that be supportive?

4 We are on a boat trip out of Bay Bulls, to see whales and puffins. I watch Craig Regular look down at Lydia in the back of the boat, and Lydia returns his look. How can I live with that look? She jogs on the spot on the flydeck in full view of him. Lydia dances for him in her new runners. She climbed down the aluminum stairs and went over to him and danced on the spot. Seeking some acceptance, some approval. As if to say I am attractive, and you can have me.

Lydia says to me, I can't understand why you look at it that way.

Duration has little to do with whether an act is remembered. It is the passion that is evinced from the moment. And something passed between Craig and Lydia in that moment of idle jogging. Something as strong as if she'd taken him into a corner and sucked him off, or spent three weeks with him. My life will be a constant reckoning with this kind of emotional argument. In the boat I heard Daphne ask where is Lydia. And Craig Regular said, She's lying down.

Craig Regular should not know that she is lying down. He should not be the one to answer that question. Already the external world is preparing for a change.

All this is jealousy. All this I must absorb or slough off. I cannot allow it to stay on my skin. It makes me too melancholic.

5   Lydia called last night and asked, Are you mad because I've phoned so late?

Yes.

Am I forgiven?

Yes.

You sure I'm forgiven?

Do you think you should be?

Your tone conveys a certain unforgiveness.

It's that you forget about me. You have to be reminded I'm in your life.

Dont you think it's a good thing?

I say nothing.

Who's there?

Iris and Helmut.

So you want to watch that movie?

Me: If youre up for it.

Unless you want to hang on there.

No.

Okay.

Well, I'll see you over at your place.

I can pick you up.

No need.

Oh, yes, let me pick you up.

Youre not home?

I'm at Craig's.

Are you ready now?

How about in ten minutes?

I'll walk down.

I dont drive down because there is no parking without a permit on Gower. It's good I found out that she wasnt home. Because I would have been locked out, without a key. With no lights on. We often talk with a misunderstanding, like a boulder, that we have to lean around to see the other person. Even when we've safely navigated the obstacle, the effects of the obstacle can never be fully eradicated. Clearing something up doesnt dissipate the residual feeling. It lingers as if the misunderstanding were in fact the truth of the happening. To assume a false thing for any length of time makes it true. And I have pictured her with Craig Regular. Assuming the worst is the basis of grudges and resentment.

6   I'm in bed feeling anguish. I can't even write it down properly. So I dress and walk down to Lydia's and leave a note hanging out of her mailbox. That I'm upset that she invited

Craig to supper with her parents. I thought she would at least call to say what was up. I can't stand not knowing what she's doing.

I decide to go for a walk. Walking is the correct speed for rumination. Cars and even bicycles propel the body too fast through space.

I walk towards Quidi Vidi, to the graveyard on the hill. And down a straight paved path. The penitentiary is glowing in a rhomboid. I can see into its perimeter. There is a grave with Pinto on it, born in Vega, Italy.

As I walk back Lydia's brown Cavalier slows, red tail lights. Reverses. It is slightly misty. She's dropped off Craig at the Battery. She kisses me, with a strong tongue. I tell her all this. As we sit in the car in my driveway.

In bed, I ask her what Craig's like.

Oh, nice. He says he's a loner now. Lives in Seattle.

Pause.

Me: That's all?

What's wrong with that?

Youre starting to sound like me. You spend seven hours with a new guy and all you can say is he's nice.

He isnt new. I knew him back with Earl. My parents knew him then, too. They wanted to see him.

Well he's new to me, then.

Tell me what you want to know.

This, said in a stiff way.

What he's doing, his life, his ambitions, his humour.

He's managing this software design, which is a two-year

project. He's kind of goofy, he doesnt get a joke right away but then laughs and that's sort of cute and he's handsome and he doesnt own any possessions. He's given them up except he has a dog, which he loves, and he remembers Tinker in his youth. He wears business kinds of clothes now, but you soon realize he's someplace else.

So youve got a little crush on him.

Lydia: And what do you think of that?

What, should I be jealous of a handsome man who lives on the Pacific and has cute ways and a dog and youve spent seven hours with him?

She cuddles into me and I can feel a laugh in her body.

So did you kiss him?

Do you really want to know?

7   The story of my life with Lydia is the conflict of desire and being sated. Lydia is satisfied with me but dissatisfied with all other things. I'm the opposite. She appraises the world as a canvas to improve. I accept the canvas, am content to live within its confines. I dont think to upgrade the armchair or paint a room. I exist in a state of being, Lydia in a state of flux.

8   I've walked down to Ryan's Plumbing with Lydia's faucet. Mr Ryan is serving Boyd Coady, who has clear green cat's eyes. They are in disagreement. Boyd says to me, Do you know anything about plumbing?

I say, You can't be serious.

Mr Ryan dont know anything, Boyd says. He won't be able

to help you with that. Boyd points to my faucet spindle.

I walk back to Lydia's with the busted spindle.

The shadows of trees are more pronounced because of the new leaves.

Lydia is out weeding the back. Tinker Bumbo is barking at the backs of houses on Duckworth Street. He's just standing there, barking at the sun. Barely notices me.

Two girls sit on the steps of a house next door.

There's an electric chainsaw at work.

A gangly boy with thin wrists and sunglasses plays basketball in his paved driveway. Slow smack of the basketball. Thump of the net as the ball pushes through. Wind, warm, streaks of blue-and-white sky.

Lydia straightens. I kiss her on the cheekbone.

9 Lydia asks me what I'm thinking of. I say Wilf Jardine's tattoo.

Wilf has a tattoo?

The one on his arm.

She says, When have you seen it?

Several times.

Funny, I havent seen it.

You have seen it.

Oh, yes, that tattoo. Usually I dont like tattoos, but Wilf's is nice.

How did you forget he had a tattoo?

I dont think about Wilf.

You are, I say, much more into the here and now than I am.

Lydia: Youre caught up in introspection.

Do you think introspection and regret are connected?

Are you regretting something?

I'm just following a train of thought.

Lydia: I dont think you'll regret much. You think about the past, but youre not emotionally wrought by it. Youre pretty solid.

There was this man sunning himself today. He was sitting in his front door. His whole arm was a tattoo, down to the fingernails. In his late forties. It looked like he had a reptile sleeping on his chest.

10 We're having a drink at Noel Wareham's wake. Max said he witnessed what he calls his father's chain-stoking. Inhaling, mouth open, eyes wide, then exhaling, fourteen hours of this. His liver crashed, they had him on morphine, looking at photos of his kids, saying goodbye to Max, but living five more days. Sixty-eight years old. How Max finds himself imitating the faces his father made. We go to the washroom to urinate and when we're washing our hands, I watch Max make that chain-stoking gesture. Like a goldfish who has exhausted the water's oxygen.

11 To know what someone looks like by what he says, how it's said. Tone and diction. Dialogue can describe a character's facial features.

When you hear basketballs dribbled and thrown at hoops, then you know the rain has ceased.

12 Three houses have burned to the ground on Cook Street. I watch a tractor yank down the charred chimneys with the shovel on his crane. As I sketch this in my journal Boyd Coady peers and says, Is that like a book youre putting in everything that happens to you? I say that is exactly right. And show him some drawings. Boyd's son rides over on his banana bike.

All I can see of the southside hills are the silver pipelines that snake up to the tank farm. And now comes the ridge against the sky. The contour pulsating in and out of greyness.

13 Max Wareham is wearing a denim cowboy hat on his back deck. There is a lilac tree. Daphne Yarn clutches a bunch of flowering sage. She keeps admonishing me with it.

We've agreed on the canoe trip: down the Exploits, mid-July. Lydia will do it. And Max and Daphne are in. Craig is up for it and Alex would like to do it, and Maisie, staring at Oliver, who is oblivious to the conversation, says she'll go if Oliver's not along and she doesnt have Una. Max: Who here invests in the stock market?

About half the hands go up.

Alex and Craig Regular dance to country music. Oliver bids goodnight and pockets his half bottle of Grouse Scotch. We all know he's going to meet his pregnant paralegal student. I hear Maisie's voice rise and say she disdains a limp penis because it immediately becomes a urine thing instead of a sperm thing.

Max: It has not been admitted yet on our media that power

rests not in Parliament, but in big business and multinationals.

Craig takes Lydia aside and I look at her face. In that moment of nervous knowing, of climbing into bed with Craig, I see her face and it is the same face, the face I know, and that comforts me.

She says, Max, can I have a refill?

Max: Lydia is some bossy.

Lydia turns to confront Max. You want to get into it, Max?

Max: No.

Silence.

Maisie: You may as well get into it.

14 Failure is a comfortable place, it locates you within a familiar frame. Success thrusts you into new territory. It's more work to succeed. The best-laid plans are vulnerable to sabotage from the self. Self likes to lay out old maps, because it is easier to live within old maps.

Sunny. The windowsills full of cilantro and bell peppers. The basil just up in flats. The dogberries are sheltering us, an arbour. Lydia is over for lunch. She says, Tell me about yourself.

She says it in a challenging tone. As if she knows it's difficult for me to funnel actions into principles. She is judging me again, even as she tries to open up and be honest. Her question is in fact a statement. And so I dont answer.

15 I run for twenty-six minutes, my shank aching. I run around Quidi Vidi while Lydia and the sculling crew row up the lake. I watch them practise the turn. Then I run over to

Lydia's — she'll have arrived before me. How quiet it is at the back of her house. I hear her on the phone. Last night a distance between us before I left: I was peeling apples while Lydia rolled out pastry for rhubarb pies. She was at the counter, standing on her toes to press out the dough. She was jealous of the book borrowed from Alex. She thinks I want to be with Alex, which I dont care to argue. Yes, we all fantasize about being with others, the what-ifs.

Lydia is sitting with palms up and outstretched, Tinker Bumbo at her feet, the phone crooked to her shoulder. She is flapping a man-made shoe in the air. She is talking to Craig Regular.

16 Boyd Coady is standing inside his pickup truck's open door, adjusting the knot in his tie. As if he's releasing energy, a clenched muscle.

I'm giving Max a hand with a job. I love seeing weight displaced. A lintel over a door. The lines of energy being diverted over the weak spots, such as windows. The crush of weight detoured. Dams on gravity. The turn of bricks into a bridge over a window. A bridge is a prayer.

Max has a photo of a fly's enlarged head glued to his tool chest. This photo tells him a lot about the twentieth century. The beauty of science and the power of life. His father once scraped the inside of his lip with a spoon. Not telling him why. Then showed him the cells under a microscope. That vitality taught him insignificance.

17 Iris lends me her flashing rear light and a small triangle of reflecting banner. I bicycle out to Cape Spear in the dark. The name Shea Heights painted on a water tower like some military post. Strickland's Salvage hidden behind a tall wooden fence. As though if you saw the beautiful wrecks behind it, you'd feel compelled to steal them. The beautification committee has bulldozed and paved an area for an open market. You could land a small plane on it.

It takes an hour to ride to Cape Spear. I claim a spot on the grass above the World War II cannon in front of the bunker. The cannon faces a bonfire licking the cement wall below the stage. The singers look nervous about the cannon facing them. Or are they cold. I huddle into the grass as the wind picks up. An anonymous thermos of good Scotch is passed around. Then I see it's Max's. They wave and I join them.

Clear night, dark sky, streak of milky way, Daphne calls it a fried egg on its side. The city to the north is two pots of jewels separated by Signal Hill.

Max offers a ride home, throw the bike in the truck, but I want to whoosh back in the dark. There are no streetlights and I have no light. I pull up hills and then descend, plunge into the valleys of the road. I can make out the centre line and the side line and keep in the middle. But the condition of the road is a mystery. All I can sense is the whirring of my wheels and I can tell their distance from the sound they make. There is no motion except wind. It could be that I'm standing still. I look back and notice the frenetic blinking of Iris's red light.

18 Woke at six-thirty, the mist anchored in the harbour. Propped on an elbow I can see this bed of sneaky fog. And then coffee with Iris and Helmut. Hot sun. Everything lit.

On the table is our box of co-op vegetables from Daphne's organic farm: deep green bok choy, rhubarb, a green onion, parsley, tatsoi (a small bouquet of greens with a slender peach-coloured flower in the centre), spinach. Everything special and select.

I wait for Lydia to call, and she does. She invites me down and I go.

19 The rain wakes me at six, and I get up and make coffee. I wrap Lydia's Bodum in a cup towel. I notice her faucet is fixed. I watch the rain, tons of it, slash down. Lydia smells the coffee and comes down for some.

Me: You fixed your faucet.

I didnt fix the faucet.

Well, someone fixed the faucet.

It wasnt me.

She's got an admirer who fixes faucets. Craig Regular fixed that faucet.

20 At the Ship with Maisie and Lydia. Theyre having brandies and Earl Quigley says he's alone at the bar — could he sit with us and listen.

It's rare to see Lydia and Earl together. I like to see it. To see the one youre with talking to her ex provides a window onto a previous life in action.

We had been to Alex Fleming's photograph exhibit. And there was a picture of Maisie and Oliver wearing cowboy boots. It was seeing them again in their life together. Maisie said, Even though Oliver's affair was the catalyst for my departure, I had already begun to drift from him. She hated how, when they married, his sink became their sink. His mess was their mess.

Maisie: I dont ever want to clean up our dishes. Una's I dont mind. But not the man I'm sleeping with. There's no fun in that.

Me: What about a guy who fixes your faucet? Just on the side?

Maisie: That's what I want. I want a weekend man.

And yet there is something in possession, marriage. In becoming an object. Something erotic in that. We all agree with this admission, even Earl.

21 Wilf walks into the Ship looking uncomfortable. Then he sees us and relaxes. He is in a suit he wants to wear in Lydia's film. He looks like a Beatle in it. Wilf, at the age of fifty-two, has become a promising actor. That word, promising. Wilf buys a pint and sits with us and sighs with relief. Wilf: When you open up the Ship Inn door all by yourself. Youve walked downtown alone. You dont want to be alone. You feel like a dog and you want a bit of company. Well, you open up that door and you steel yourself. It's got to be all one motion, no hesitation. Open the door and stride in, but a slow stride, maximum exposure. And you make your way to the bar. And

all the way there you keep your eyes on the bottles and the mirrors and youre hoping, youre hoping there's someone in there who knows you. You hope you dont make it to the bar before someone waves you over, grasps your arm, says, Hey Wilf, how's it going? Yes, sir, that walk to the bar is the loneliest walk in the world.

22 I lurch for the birdie. I lurch and a hockey player strikes a two-handed blow across my calf. I fall, twist, turn to face my attacker. No one. The floor hockey crowd is on their half of the gym, separated by a net curtain. Badminton players look down at me. I roll, seize my leg, grimace. I see Lydia looking down. Oliver: Would you mind rolling over into your own court? And Lydia: Okay, let's keep playing.

But there must be an image of agony that transcends their lust to play, for they form a huddle again, over me. Lydia kneels. Oliver offers a tensor bandage and a shoulder.

I'm wheeled into emerge. Dr Singh feels the calf. He recommends ice. Lydia wheels me over to get crutches. I swing on the crutches back to the car.

Want to get fish and chips from Scampers?

Lydia loves getting the fish and chips, she skips in, as if she knows I really want it and getting me what I want pleases her. I realize I'm a hard man to get something for.

I watch her from the passenger side. She stands under fluorescent lighting and orders, both elbows on the counter. She turns and mouths to me, through the take-out window: A drink? I write NO backwards in my breath on the car window. I try to write it in a soft way. To incorporate the thanks.

23 In bed with my leg up. Lydia brings me juice, toast, poached eggs, and coffee. I try the bathroom. When the foot is below my hips, that's when the pain rushes down. A bucket of liquid needles sloshing heavy into my foot. It's as if blood can't return to the heart.

I have eaten a bowl of grapes and a clementine. I watch Lydia fill a grocery bag with wet lettuce. She slashes holes in the bottom of the bag, knots it, and, outside, whirls the bag over her head, like a pail of water at the beach. She is drying lettuce. She turns quickly and I watch her hair twist to meet her head. She is so determined.

Max delivers frozen pea soup and a bag of cherries and a loaf of bread and a salad with a cookie. It hurts to even stand up straight. The blood burning in the back of my leg.

24 The laburnum is floating, yellow cobs of dots. A woman, who has forgotten the name of palliative care, calls it that place where you goes and that's it. Daphne's on duty and she props my leg over folded hot blankets.

They tilt the X-ray bed. Tie two rubber tourniquets around my ankle to find a vein. Daphne tries twice, sticking me with a small needle attached to a thin glass tube. It's called contrast dye.

They wheel me in for an ultrasound. The specialist is wet from the rain. He hasnt operated the computer in three weeks. He coats my leg in cold gel. He sticks the scanner up to my groin. I see, on the screen, the vein and artery in cross-view. He pushes and my vein flattens. My artery doesnt budge.

25 Lydia's father fries me a splendid mackerel after my venogram. We have the mackerel with cauliflower and lettuce.

On crutches, I swing back home. I can't push the clutch down, so I have to walk. I remember the man in Corner Brook who had one leg. Lived in the Bean and wore denim. He was active, tough, and got around on wooden crutches. He had strong hands. Amputees no longer do this. They have prosthetics or wheelchairs. It was a time when missing limbs were visible, the drains open, the sewers flooded over Valley Road when it was just dirt.

At the fire station four firemen in blue shirts sit in portable chairs on the wall looking over the road. They watch my progress.

Maisie and Una visit with a loaf of bread, an apple, a grapefruit, and a sesame-seed snack. Maisie's given up smoking and resumed running, to supplement her rowing. Yesterday, twenty-eight minutes. There's so much to do, she says, and here's another thing.

What thing.

The not smoking, she says.

26 At about two Helmut calls. He is leaving port at four oclock.

There is a defined half moon accompanying the sun. Lydia and I drive down to say bon voyage to the crew and their company boat. Helmut invites us on. All the men are tanned, with thick forearms and tall. Most are American. I leave the crutches and hop aboard. A famous marine artist has painted a school of tuna across the bow. The navigation is tied to satellite imagery. Helmut shows us St John's harbour on a screen as it looks from the sky. We let him have a minute with Iris.

Boyd Coady says, loudly, I'd rather fly to Boston. Saw one of those tupperware boats caught in ice last year. Sunk before you could blink.

Helmut asks Lydia to take the video camera, to catch them heading for the Narrows. He starts up the auxiliary outboard and spews forward, ducking under the boom. He describes a wide curve and returns to the dock, cutting power. Helmut leans to collect the camera, waves, then slips on the wet gunwale. He falls into the boat, hitting his head, and two of the crew come to assist him. But he's up quickly and laughing and opens the outboard throttle, embarrassed.

Iris jogging to Cabot Tower, to wave them off. Gulls sit with their chests against the pavement.

They will sail to Boston on a dry run before heading to Brazil, where Iris will meet them.

Boyd: You wouldnt catch me in one of those contraptions.

He's German, I say, as if that explains something.

27 As I walk up Cabot Street a ten-year-old girl asks me to stop the ball. I stop it with my crutch. I look tough with the crutches swung over my shoulder. The neighbourhood so shoddy. A dog in a second-storey window, silently clawing at

the inside glass. A man with an apron opens the door to a house adjacent to Leo's Fish and Chips. He's smoking. He goes back inside.

Often I am afraid of new life. Of pushing into the new. Maisie says when you have a kid there's an eight-hundred-dollar-a-month grocery bill. I watch Boyd Coady feeding a baby in the back seat of a Chevette, his seven-year-old standing beside him — Boyd looks fiercely down Long's Hill to the Narrows. Helmut in that storm last night. Lydia saying to Iris, He must be some loner to do that. And Iris: Helmut is looking for love. He's mad at me.

28 The caplin are sighted in Flatrock and Torbay. I have two five-gallon buckets in Jethro's trunk. I pick up Lydia and Tinker Bumbo and we head north.

There are men on the stone beach preparing cast nets and as evening falls they light three bonfires on the landwash and this will guide the fish in. There are wheelbarrows and buckets and families making it a picnic.

The caplin will look like a force of bad weather. And they will strike fast and roll.

The men wade in a little with their cast nets.

The water is green and darker green and there are white boulders and kelp fanning in slow motion and I can see a flounder sitting passively in the green.

The green pitches to black. It swarms black and darts like a vision behind the eyelid. About ten square feet of soft grey-black curve and then a slick of silver pins as the curve darts and separates around our feet like a beaded curtain.

There's no way to get them in a bucket.

But in a few minutes a wave launches in full of their silver bellies. The bonfires light up their silver and they wriggle in the smooth wet sand and stone.

The caplin crest and tumble on a high tide and we fill the two buckets in a minute. We watch children scooping up these frantic deaths into carts and dumping them into buckets. The rims of these buckets flicking and dying.

29 We are in a Chinese restaurant ordering won ton soup, spring rolls. Lydia puts her hand on the belly of the teapot. It's hot, she says. The restaurant is full, bathed in yellow spotlights. Lydia admits she assumed she'd be with a social animal. Her idea of a partner.

This makes me wonder if Lydia is good for me. How her work requires her to be in the centre, where possibilities can grab her. The world notices her waiting and snaps her up to direct and act. Whereas I need the small, ignored corners of the earth, to write about them so that people won't forget. Or even know for the first time.

There's a woman two tables down who looks like Lydia at forty-two. I could love that look.

30 I am making lamb as the Moroccans might cook it. Lydia: Youre a good cook for a guy. But then, I've always gone out with good cooks. Usually, men dont waste time on salads.

She says she's been keeping tabs on her food and noticed a

bunch of bananas and a jar of caviar went missing.

Lydia, I dont know what to say. You think I'm sneaking stuff out of the house?

She looks at my heel and says it's full of blood. The bruise in my calf has sunk to my foot. I can't forget that she has said she's keeping tabs.

You dont rave, do you, Gabe? Earl used to rave. But you know what? He'd shut up if you told him to.

I want to say something about the tab, but this shuts me up. Lydia convinces me to drive her to Cape Spear to see the humpbacks. Warm and sunny. The whales are heading north. They loop up their dorsal fins five times, then arc and slink up their tails and dive deep. It's as if their size grants them a different speed dimension to work in. All the movements appear in slow motion.

One humpback heads straight for us in smooth torpedo form. The white of his flukes crimped over to the top black like a pie crust. A blast of spray from his spout. The spray drifts up and along the horizon, like an exhausted fireworks.

July

1 I grab another beer from Oliver's fridge. Craig Regular is telling Alex that all new computers have a clipper chip installed so the CIA can backtrack into any computer and scan information stored there. His colleagues in Seattle have told him this. Also, if Quebec separates, the U.S. will invade.

Alex is wearing plastic bracelets the colour of apple juice.

People won't go for bar codes on the wrist, she says. They'll rebel at the objectifying of the body.

Craig: But that's not the same as a chip encoded with information. It'll start with criminals. Then we'll all be given a telephone number for life.

Craig is working on a science-fiction television drama on the side. He doesnt care about story or character. He's interested in creating moments of suspense. Learning how to do that. If you can do that, he says, there's room for you in TV. It's important, he says, for writers to watch TV. Craig says this with utter conviction, as a point of fact. There is something women like in an opinionated Buddhist. It doesnt matter the opinion. It's the decisiveness. Men are not as attracted to it, especially in women.

2   I'm at the Ship to join Max. Max is at the bar with Oliver. There are strong words and Oliver raises his glass of gin and tonic and pushes it into Max's eye. Max recoils and swings. You can hear his knuckles on Oliver's temple. He grabs Oliver in a headlock and hits him twice again with his left hand and Oliver slumps over his stool — for a flash his dull face is towards me, his cheek on the stool, a string of saliva an exten- sion of the chrome rod of the stool. Then he regains his feet and staggers past me to the door.

Max: That's one fucked-up man.

Me: What did you say to him?

Max: Nothing. It's a musk I give off.

Me: If Oliver wasn't drinking he could level you.

Yeah, but he's always drinking. I was sticking up for Maisie and he went aboard me.

Were you obnoxious?

Max: I said to him, Oliver, you can't say you didnt try.

I order a pint. What you have to realize about Oliver, I say, is that he's sensitive. If you challenge him on what he knows he gets defensive.

Sensitive people, Max says, are the most insensitive of peo- ple. They are sensitive only to what hurts them.

3   The phone rings, and I get out of bed to answer. It's Alex Fleming.

Gabe? I thought I was calling Max. But you'll do. What do you know of Craig Regular?

He's thirty-eight, I say. He went to school with Earl Quigley. He's a software analyst. He owns a house in the Battery —

I mean, what do you think of him?

I think of a mean thing. Lydia says he's not that funny.

Alex: Yeah, he lacks a sense of humour. But he wants to see me.

I really can't advise you, Alex.

Would you miss me if I started seeing him?

That would just make it all more interesting.

Craig has invited Alex to take a ferry along the south coast. White beaches and cliffs. And he thinks they should go as a team on the Exploits canoe trip.

Good for you, Alex.

In bed, Lydia sleepily: You were on that phone too long.

But later she curls into me, wanting me close. She will have no recollection of saying this.

4   Why the interest in Craig Regular? Lydia: He's new. In this town, everybody knows everyone else even if you havent met them. That explains Craig Regular.

It's true. I've never said more than five words to Craig, but I know all about him. He drinks Guinness. He doesnt smoke. Max said he has donated sperm to a lesbian friend who wanted a child, and Lydia says Earl told her there was some rumour Craig may have had a terminal illness and that's why he went West and has been gone for six years and came back and dropped ten pounds and bought a place in the Battery.

Lydia: People suspect he's inherited some money. He likes to go on bird counts and is a vegetarian as well as Buddhist and I saw him once at a string quartet concert and I've also seen him at a film festival in Toronto and once, at Christmas, we passed on Gower Street late at night and we stopped and kissed without saying a word. That was after I broke up with Earl. Craig has a little cabin on the Salmonier Line and he used to design the student newspaper and Earl says in school he was a good goalie.

Fact: I know everyone in this town even if I havent met them and they know everything about me, which is frustrating. So when someone new comes to town, or someone returns, like Craig Regular, everyone lurches towards him, especially the women, because it's such a relief to meet someone you dont already know.

5   How does a fight begin? It begins because of our contrary natures. It begins when Lydia arrives and says how things could be improved at the house I share with Iris. That the kitchen is poorly laid out, that we should move the shoes and jackets, that the red carpet collects dust, rip it up, that I should do something with the basement stairs.

All these things are valid, but I'd prefer her to say, Look at the forsythia. Or, I saw something interesting today. Instead, she says, Talk to me. She demands to be told something. And so I'm mechanical. The phone rings and it's for her, so I go upstairs. Then she starts in. That I left a communal atmosphere, that it's up to me to return rather than for her to go upstairs. She leaves and does not tell me she's leaving, so I hit the sack.

She asks so many questions until I say, Yes, yes, and yes to your next five questions too.

She has this gesture of pursing thumb and forefinger together, as though dabbing a watercolour and pointing out my flaws.

She wants to be able to shout from different rooms. Whereas I dont find that civilized.

Then she gets into the fact that I'm ungrateful, and that I'm a prick, and that I never apologize.

She says she wants to break up.

6   She has left me alone. Power always rests in the one who decides. So I feel our argument is incomplete. I'm restless. I decide to fish for urban trout. I bicycle down to Virginia River, fly rod tied to the crossbar. I choose a small wet fly. A branch of a pin cherry leans over the water, and I know there must be fish in a pool below it. I land two mad trout on two flicks. Both are the length of this book opened out. Seeing their white bellies and tanned sides wriggle on the hook, heavy, straining in the grass for water.

I bike down to Maisie's with the fish in a bag knotted to my belt. Maisie is looking thin. Lydia is there. And she smiles. I try to read the smile. The smile is considerate but weak. It's not a polite smile, not a forced smile. It's a loving smile, but a smile that says she's fine with a separation. I sit with Wilf Jardine. He's going to work on Hibernia in two weeks. His brother, who worked on the land rigs in Alberta, got them a package deal. Land rigs, Wilf says, are a cross between the military and slavery. Got to give good head to the foreman.

I give this some thought.

That's just a figure of speech, he says.

Wilf thinks my thought was a literal consideration. There's a way to hold your face that will convey a not-serious consideration. I may have to learn this.

Wilf says, If you want, I can get you work out there. The pay is outrageous.

I tell him that I'm out of commission for a year. I make a wriggling motion with my fingers to indicate a keyboard.

I show him my trout.

Oh, they're nice. Brook trout. How are you going to eat them?

In rosemary and lemon, baked.

Have you ever cured any? You take equal amounts of sugar and salt and mix it with dill. Press the fish for three days. Delicious.

7   I was to meet Lydia at the Grapevine at nine. And she is sitting next to Craig with a Bloody Caesar.

Lydia: I had to get someone else to buy it.

Who?

Craig.

Youre going to make me jealous.

Well, you werent here at nine.

At one point, Craig's hand reaches over her arm to make a point. Craig introduces me to his friends, This is Lydia Murphy's lover.

This pisses me off.

I am worried. That Lydia will fall for him. The trip with Alex is off, Craig says. Alex is crazy. He is oblivious to my relationship with Alex. He is not circumspect. Near the pay phone I ask Lydia if I should be jealous. A little bit jealous, she says. I realize I had been relieved when I thought Craig was with Alex.

Lydia wants to drive me home, but I decide to walk. Two days without Lydia make me want to take a third. She is getting up early to shoot a time-lapse of the sunrise and needs her rest. Craig has offered to be her trigger-puller for two hours. It is so ripe for her to sleep with Craig Regular tonight. He's shirked off Alex and Lydia is tired of me. But all this will be said tomorrow. If anything happens — if Lydia is shit-faced and they lunge and she doesnt even remember much but that she was drunk — I will not remain with her. In fact, that's the reason I decline her offer. I want to open the floor to her negotiation with Craig. To see if it will happen. Masochism is jealousy's backside. How can I become unjealous?

Cold fact: Lydia's utter joy of Craig makes me realize how little she enjoys of me. She laps up Craig — and isnt this what we want? To fully enjoy the other person's being.

I have left her to the wolves and her own lone-wolf desires. I walk up Long's Hill feeling like a boring man. That I can't entertain. I have this feeling badly.

8 Craig uses the word ebullient. It isnt used with full confidence. But I can see Lydia with a man like that. She is massaging her breasts as she talks to him by the fridge. They are both concentrating on the conversation while I'm focused on their body language. Lydia is not aware that her hand is cupping each breast. Everyone catches an uncertain word and inappropriate gesture. Everyone has evolved to the point where nuance is a primitive knowledge. We all understand and are not blind to slippery characters.

We are still planning the canoe trip. To go together. But of course Craig will be there. And so will Alex. I must decide to lighten up.

9 Lydia is such a summer extrovert. And I am a cold and lonely. I left Lydia a delicate saffron poppy and a bowl of curried chicken thighs. She is having a smoke with Wilf and Craig on the lawn. I watch her slap Wilf Jardine's knee and clasp Craig Regular's arm.

Wilf says he's almost tempted to take a kayak down the Exploits. Just to witness what might happen with the six of ye.

I call Max about planning the canoe trip. I tell him about feeling down. He puts Daphne on. Daphne laughs hard at my jealousy. She says she hears Lydia's feelings for me. And that Lydia says good things. But theyre not as fun to repeat.

Daphne tells a fine story and is quick with voicing her feelings. She is sensitive to slights, but she forgives easily. She loves a good dinner party, but also enjoys quiet time with a man. She, like Max, is at a point in her life where she prefers the rural over the urban. They will be spending time in Brigus.

10 I buy eight empty salt-beef buckets at Murphy's at the Cross. Lydia and I are in charge of breakfast and supper on the second day. We have curried chicken marinating. We pack our tent, food, and clothes in the salt-beef buckets and thread a rope through the handles. We split the rims of the lids so theyre easy to pry off. We pick up Max's red fibreglass canoe and two maple paddles. We are ready for the river.

11 We drive six hours to the Millertown Junction. There are six of us in three canoes slipping into the river. Craig and Alex, Max and Daphne, Lydia and me.

Craig and Alex capsize on the first rapids. Their canoe, submerged in water, is wrapped under a ledge of rock. We pry with two logs as levers. The canoe pops out of the current, bouncing back into shape.

One moment: it's night and we're away from the three tents, at the shore where a tributary feeds into the river. A perfect Beothuk camping ground. I wouldnt have thought this if Max hadnt reminded me of the Beothuk. I had forgotten this was the heart of their land, where they built fences to force caribou through narrow gates to the water. The canoes are hauled up and earlier you could see the light of the sun through their hulls. We watched a beaver hard at work. Now it's dark. And Lydia clenches a penlight in her mouth as she bends her knees in the water to rinse her new toothbrush. The penlight arcing a jittery circle of yellow light, illuminating stones in the water, her bare legs, her cheeks, and her hands. Earlier we are washing our hands in a bowl of soapy water and Lydia forgets, takes her Swiss Army knife and rinses it in the water. She cuts my finger across the knuckle with the blade. I'm sorry I'm sorry I'm so stupid please forgive me. It is the knife I gave her.

12 Lydia's father has warned us there's a falls along the river, but it's not marked on the map. Lydia and Daphne offer caution. Craig says we'll do the next rapids and then set camp. Craig: If anyone gets wet, it's better that it happens now than tomorrow morning.

We shoot the rapids.

Lydia and I in the lead canoe. Instructions: if any heavy rapids, pull to the side and inspect the river.

We see high whitewater ahead and pull in.

But Max and Daphne keep going.

The third canoe follows — Craig and Alex shrugging. So we join them.

But ahead I can tell Max is in trouble.

I stand up in the back of the canoe. I can see Max and Daphne lean and capsize. We pull into shore.

All I can think is, Daphne is pregnant.

They have gone down several steep shelves of rock. They

are hanging onto the sunken canoe in the last pool before the falls. The current is fast. You can tell from how theyre balanced that their purchase is tender, up to their necks. They are leaning into the river.

Max is nimbly leaning back into the current, holding the nose of the canoe. The falls are twelve feet and very rough, massive rocks. Max calm in the face of a ridiculous situation.

I throw a rope and Max secures the canoe. Craig hauls the canoe over and I steer it in. I throw a rope to Daphne. It's not clean around her. She loses her footing and swings, she swings towards the edge of froth, gripping the rope in her armpit. I see Craig lean to dive in. The rope snaps taut and we pull her in. Then it's Max.

It's six-thirty, the sky grazing the tops of heavy spruce. The food tubs were not roped in. So their gear is floating downriver. It begins to rain. Daphne a little in shock. We set up tents on the only clear spot, rocky and steep. A dreary scene. Build a fire, a fire is good, you hear about fires, everything you read about a fire is true. A fire never offers despair. A fire is pure hope, a true raw heart.

Make some tea. Tea is the drinkable equivalent of fire.

We portage the canoes. We spot a tiny cabin behind the bluff of a hill in the rain. We decide to break in. Max assures us the cabin owner wouldnt mind, considering our predicament. The rain plummeting.

We scuttle our miserable camp, our last stand, and make for the cabin. We ruin a screen on the window breaking in. There are six bunks. Six of us. A fine woodstove. Drying out the gear.

We leave money on the table to replace the screen.

We all try our best to lose our stiffness. We're too serious. Or perhaps it would be best if someone admitted how close to death Max and Daphne were. And Daphne pregnant. But it's too early, or too severe, to admit to anything, and we play cards and drink Scotch and light candles and kerosene lamps.

13 Lydia: Take a gander at the map.

Me: You mean, take an exploits at the map.

What?

Gander River. Exploits River.

I knew you were gonna say that.

We take a vote and decide to continue down the Exploits. We're sick of the cabin. We feel better in a canoe, even in the rain. We make it to Badger by nightfall and camp at the edge of a farmer's field. Max walks into town — the highway runs very close to the river, so even when youre out on the water youre never that far from civilization. Craig strings up a tarp and a line to hang clothes.

The farmer and his wife come by. They are politely leery of the fire and their grass, which could transport a line of flame straight over to the sheep barn. They tell us that the Badger Chute is around the bend and that we must portage it. Search and Rescue, the farmer says, are hauling people out of that every year.

Max returns with a bottle of dark rum. And Daphne mixes drinks. It is clear Daphne has scolded Max and Max has apologized.

Craig repairs everything. A missing tent pole. He leans over to apply duct tape to the heels of Lydia's sandals.

14 We reach the chute and size it up. We portage the gear over the knob of rock and stand studying the chute. I try to stand as if I know what I'm gauging. Craig and Alex want to do it, which convinces us. Max and Daphne have already begun to portage. We flip a coin and Lydia and I win the toss. We tow our canoe upriver a little. We have to cross the current and then swivel midstream and hit the chute at a little off-centre to avoid a massive rock. It's difficult to see what is under the boiling froth below the chute. I throw in a carrot and it bobs safely enough. Lydia says, But we're not a carrot. The wind picks up and Daphne clambers along the shore to us.

It feels ominous, Daphne says. You guys are the only ones not to have capsized.

The others have gone over on tricky rapids, shelves, and ledges. It does seem a little foreboding.

I say, How often will we get to shoot the Badger Chute? The worst that can happen, it seems, is we'll put a hole in Max's canoe.

Max: Dont worry about the canoe.

Daphne: Put pressure on them, why dont you?

Max: I'm just saying.

We are close to the road, so there's no problem with hitch-hiking back to the cars and getting out our gear.

Lydia: Let's do it.

We sit by the canoe and I quietly go over the path with

Lydia. Hit the lip of the chute about two feet to the left of that first bit of whitewater, okay?

Okay.

This is the first time I have seen Lydia take blind-faith instruction from me.

We kneel on the floor of the canoe for a lower centre of gravity.

As I push off I see Craig hoisting their canoe over the rock. They've decided to portage too.

Everyone watching at the rocks. We hit the lip perfectly, which slows us and then, gathering determination, sucks us down from the peak. Heavy water plunges over the sides. We are swamped. We avoid the big rock and strike the whitewater and float over yellow boulders and push through, the stern fishtailing but then brought back straight. We're through. We turn and paddle hard to shore against a strong current. To hearty cheers.

Later, a moose and her calf cross the river. A horned owl blends into bark. A rabbit hunched in the undergrowth. And finally, Max's car shining by the embankment.

We lift the canoe from the water. I hand Lydia my knife to cut open a mango. I watch her slice the fruit in half, remove the pit, and score the fruit into cubes. She pops each half up like city blocks and hands one to me.

15 Back working on the novel. Outside my window I can see Boyd Coady on an aluminum ladder. He's scrutinizing the work of the roofer. The roofer is carefully rolling a glistening

licorice mop over the aluminum edges. This mop has magic in it. They say there's a halo around the sun today. But I can see it in the treacle of the mop. Boyd yells down, Okay, boys, two more hot!

Below, the boys fill a black bucket with steaming tar and hook the handle to a thick rope. They hoist it on a pulley lever. The liquid tar jiggles but never drips on the clapboard. The pulley is like the ones on clotheslines, except it's made of cast iron, not white metal. I am comforted to know that pulleys are still used. Every civilization has discovered them.

The boys take a break and sit in the shade on the tailgate of their red pickup. Boyd and the roofer sit on the pressure-treated wood of his wife's flower boxes. All over, city roofs are being tarred and shingled. Repairs have been decided on. Is this seasonal or a sign of money? The fixing of what has already been built. Maintenance.

I borrow a scalpel from Iris's dissection kit and slit the seed pods of poppies. I make a tea slurry from the pods and drink it. It's bitter. Nothing happens.

16 I get together with Maisie to tell her the canoe trip. She's astonished at the falls, and sorry she couldnt go. She hates to miss anything. It makes me want to write down what I know of Maisie. I should write it now. How she ended up with Oliver. And now she's on her own. I first knew her when she was seeing Max. Max thought Maisie loved him. I can believe it. So when they broke up, Maisie dated a lot of men (including me) and then she found Oliver. A month later Maisie was

pregnant. Maisie was still in love with Max, but she knew she was pregnant with Oliver's baby. She could feel it. It was just a weekend fling with Oliver, but enough to make her pregnant. And Max admits he still slept with Maisie occasionally. Almost for old time's sake.

So Max was convinced the baby was his. And Maisie wanted Max to think it. Maisie said to Max that he wouldnt see the baby if he didnt come back to her. So he went back.

But when the baby was born, Una, you could see Oliver's looks all over her. There was not a drop of Max in her. When Max saw the baby, and saw that Maisie knew, he closed up. He left her. So for a year it was just Maisie Pye and Una.

Then Oliver's sister would offer to babysit, and she'd bring Oliver over on the sly. Bring Una up to see Oliver's parents too. And then Oliver made it understood that he wanted to try things with Maisie. They started going out. They had never gone out.

Were you in love with Oliver?

Maisie: I loved him. But there was always something lacking. It's very complicated and hard to talk about, but I can see myself falling for a sensuous man. And Oliver is none of this.

17 Out on the grass of Long's Hill. The arugula large enough for salads. Lydia picks a handful. She's by for a half-hour lunch break. She has begun pre-production. I make a green salad, and lay out slices of avocado, tomato, and feta. Lydia likes her greens separate. And this preference has grown on me. Before, I did not have an opinion on salads, but now I prefer them green.

She says, The least you can do is offer me a coffee.

I'm all out of coffee.

Sure, you took the whole bag from my cupboard.

Lydia. I did not take an ounce of coffee from your house. I add, Perhaps you should ask someone else that question.

She says she feels unimaginative and everyone is down on her. Surrounded by cube vans, thick cables of electricity, thousands of watts of light, thirty-seven crew members waiting for her call to roll camera. The amount of money riding on a shot. The pressure.

18 Max and Daphne invite us to Brigus, but Lydia can't go. As I drive I think that things should only ever be half lit and half known. It is false to know everything. The earth, the moon are only ever half spheres. We believe the rest. To portray the whole story is false and grotesque. Even the edges of what we see are blurred. There is only a circle the size of your eye you can be sure of.

As I gas up at Canadian Tire I spot Oliver. He is on his twenty-year-old green Raleigh. He bought it new from Pike's. It has a dynamo in the front-wheel axle. He's wearing clips on his cream slacks.

That bike, I say, is so you.

I tell him I'm off to Brigus. Put your bike in the trunk.

Okay, he says.

I've brought baked chicken and a quart of Ontario strawberries. And now Oliver and his bike. I dont care about allegiances. Oliver may be an asshole, but I still like him.

There's a new crop of mosquitoes and people are polite to Oliver. They are welcoming him. Everyone asks me how Lydia's doing on her shoot. I say I've barely seen her.

19 This morning, the first real emotive moments of love, and this because Lydia's marrying Wilf onscreen.

Do you mind if I marry Wilf? she asks.

Before this, she says she's going to loan Wilf the money for his mortgage.

Lydia: I can see you dont like it.

No. It's just I'm concerned about lending money to friends — remember how you felt about it last time?

But she comes over to me and asks if it's okay to be Wilf's wife.

I'm fine with it.

You are?

You dont have a crush on him. Why should I mind you marrying onscreen an old fart who wants to jump your bones.

20 Oliver Squires is sitting on the red carpet. He has warm hands. Strong hands from the all the bicycling. Since Maisie left he is a bicycle fiend.

He says, There must be a word to describe how you carry on normally, or habitually, even when you want to scream or be raw or be away from an energy that isnt satisfied by you.

I can only shrug and Oliver, very proudly (and why not?), pedals off through a red light on Long's Hill.

You have to be motivated by love, guided by reason.

21 I'm the best man on-set. I watch Wilf Jardine take Lydia's hand before a justice of the peace. We are outdoors in a copse of pine near the fluvarium. Earlier I'd seen fat trout swim past the underwater windows as Lydia's cameraman took shots of the couple passing by the salmon. The trout were happier than me. One looked at me sympathetically, and if he could, he'd put a fin on my shoulder.

Six white cube vans feed juice to the shoot, electric cables begin certainly and then vanish in the grass, only to reappear around the perimeter of the set. An army fording a river.

The extras blow on bubble wands and a man toots Stand by Me on a saxophone.

I hear Wilf and Lydia say I do. And we all believe, for a moment, that they are married. Perhaps the only person who does not is Lydia.

22 I started going out with Lydia a full six months before she started going out with me, and I celebrate a kind of kinky-perverse-celibate-monotheistic-kind-of-solipsistic-devoted-like-a-dog thing near the end of July to commemorate my pathetic attraction and initial infatuation with this woman but this is a private matter that I keep to myself and write here and never include Lydia in the picture.

23 Lydia drops in. She just got back from the lake with the girls. They've shaved a minute off their time. Lydia has them feathering their oars. She said, If you add up the square footage of all those blade surfaces, it's like holding up a sheet of plywood

to the wind. Tonight she's meeting Wilf Jardine to go over a few scenes.

She kisses me and is off now for a quick pint. Do you mind me going off? Good.

I remind her that Max says the weekend is good for the Flat Islands. She says, Can you pack for me?

I work on the novel until I hear her return. She recounts this conversation she heard Craig Regular having with Oliver Squires at the bar:

Craig: So how are you and Maisie?

I dont give a sweet-smelling shit about me and Maisie.

Pardon?

A flying carnivorous fuck.

Oliver.

I dont give — and I pause for emphasis, boys — one snot-haired jism about that loud-mouthed trout.

Jesus, Oliver. What's up with you?

I'll tell you what's up there Mr Craig Regular my friend. The jig is up. Up shit creek and as far as I'm concerned it can stay up her hairy-arsed self-important self-centred woe-is-me crease for all time. You can string her up by the jeezly tits.

Me: This is getting ridiculous.

Lydia: He's got to get over her.

It's hard to get over someone leaving you.

Perhaps he should have thought of that before waving his dick around.

That's what he's wishing.

And now he's having a baby with her.

24 Lydia needs a scene on an abandoned island, and Max takes us over to the Flat Islands, out of Burnside. Tremendous swell. Daphne, pregnant and wary. We take in the lee of an island and wait. I have a boiled dinner ready, though no pease pudding. The best salt beef is the kind with two circles of bone.

We hunt up gravestones. Lydia says raspberries and wild roses grow where people used to live. Lilac bushes are a dead giveaway, Daphne says.

Graves from 1838. Samsons. Methodists. We meet a man and his three kids. He's clearing up crab pots. Coiling rope.

Making a film, he says.

When he speaks he looks at his feet, but when he's listening he stares you in the eye. Kids throwing themselves in the tall grass. Lydia points out a rusty bedspring. I figure the kids know of it, but the eldest bangs his head on it. It's as if Lydia created the bedspring and then drew the boy to it. He rubs his head, says to his dad, I bashed me head in! but forgets it as he sees a white sail at the horizon. The man tells Lydia she can film anything she wants. His wife inside the house the whole time.

25 Life is the battle between attaining comfort and rebelling against it.

26 It's Friday and I am feeling a little sorry for myself. I wonder if everybody suffers this in their loneliness.

Lydia worked late and then we went to the Ship. I had wanted to spend just ten minutes alone with her, but she wanted to go have a drink with the film crew. She said, Theyre all going down.

I didnt tell her I wanted the ten minutes.

When we got out of the car, she raised her face to mine to be kissed. And said: Youre a good boyfriend, you dont ignore me.

27 I overhear Maisie Pye and Daphne Yarn talk at the bar. Maisie says, Drinking does nothing for your relationship. It may be great for getting fucked, but not to meet men.

Alex arrives and I ask how things are with Craig.

A disaster. I ended up in behind his house in the dark curled up in a ball, crying. My emotions are all over the place.

I've got photographs. Of the canoe trip.

Oh, let's see.

There's one of Alex in her canoe navigating the rapids. Craig is lying down in the back with the paddle gently steering.

Alex: Now that tells you so much, doesnt it?

What.

Well, look at my arm, so stiff. Like I'm twelve and I'm try-ing to be cool.

I dont see it that way, Alex.

Wilf Jardine comes in and we watch him as he leans over to Lydia.

Excuse me, he says. While I kiss my wife.

Lydia, in bed. What did you think of Wilf saying Excuse me while I kiss my wife.

It was funny. But I wish he didnt feel like he was doing something wrong.

Good.

He didnt see me.

It's just for the past five days we've been married on-set. And he lives the part.

28 Lydia is at Craig Regular's now, playing crib. She has called. I say, You two alone?

Yes.

That's cozy.

She says she will be by soon. But she waits an hour. She waits on purpose until it's too late. I say this. She says, I dont want to be made uncomfortable on the phone. She doesnt have any friends. Any time she spends with friends I resent. And Craig's been a major help to her on-set. Any time we spend with other people she instigates. We fight for fifty minutes. And now she has gone home because she has a long day ahead.

I've got to lighten up. Cut her some slack, as she says. Saying cozy was out of line.

Iris in the house the entire time.

Lydia would prefer if I just asked if Craig was interested in her, was she interested in him, okay? Instead of this stuff. She said, If you were man enough.

She'd thought that Craig and I could be friends. She used to have a lot of male friends whom she didnt sleep with.

29 These days have been cold, the hills wearing hats of fog.

The whitecaps pushing out the Narrows yesterday morning. The sea starts here. Unleashing waves that will rush to
Portugal.

The first strawberries ripened this morning. I gave one to
Iris on a small white plate.

Feeling still so exhausted, beaten down. Max said, It's good
to see you up in spirits. Last seven times I've seen you youve
been in misery. I thought you'd forgotten how to be happy.

I feel worn out and unworthy. Not being strong enough. I
had wanted so much to be big.

30 I ask Maisie if she sometimes found herself in an uncomfortable silence with Oliver. Often, she says, we'd be doing
different things in the same room, but it was understood we
were together.

But what if you were eating a meal together.

Maisie: I can remember that happening, but it's normal for
a couple — especially if they live together — to run out of
things to say. Eventually you know all about them. I asked
Oliver once if he felt uncomfortable with anything, and he
mentioned the mealtimes. At first he'd tried to fill in the lapses
of conversation, but then he realized our main reason for eating was to have food. And then he was okay with it. The way I
see it, a dinner party is when you converse, and dialogue is the
prime reason for being together — but regular meals are just
to eat.

I tell her Oliver's having a hard time of it.

Maisie: I've heard.

I confess my despair. That my journal is full of it, and Maisie says, Well, Gabe. You have to write the low points as well.

31 It's the weekend of the food fishery, and Max invites me out.

Max: A pound a foot will hold a boat.

Meaning a forty-foot boat needs a forty-pound anchor.

He says that when he was young, he'd ask his father how he knew when to turn in to port in the fog. You couldnt see anything and they didnt have sonar. His father said, Well, son, I'm on my second chew now. When that's gone, we turn in.

He was given his father's boat. Max has put in sonar. All the fishing boats have a metal diamond on a mast that acts as a radar reflector.

We can see the cod sitting on the sonar screen, a white mass in the blue water above the orange seabed. The caplin are just below the surface. Out on the water, the puffins are feeding on the caplin.

We throw over our jiggers. We let the line down to the bottom, and then haul in about four feet. Then we jig.

I get one quick and haul it up. It's just a dead weight. It takes thirty seconds of hauling to bring it to the surface. I see the cod's white belly and the arc of its black, freckled side. I've hooked it through the gut and it flops over the boat rail. About four pounds. It wrenches its tail up in agony.

Max jigs a sculpin. It's yellow and green and spiny. He beats it against the side of the boat until it falls off the hook.

Those are the only fish we catch.

The cod are full of caplin, Max says. They are little purses full of silver coins.

August

1 On our way to Gallow's Cove. Max and Lydia and me. We
stop at a Mary Brown's to eat fajitas. We sit in the parking lot
to eat them. We look over the lot and across the road and over
another paved lot to a Sobeys. There are about three acres of
bare property that caters to automobiles. Fajitas perched on our
high, bent knees. Then we wipe our fingers in the new grass
and drive on.

The Cove is slanted green into the sea. There are cows, a
weathered fence to duck under. We scan the field for a bull. It's
the most easterly farm in North America. We descend towards
the ocean, you can hear a cluster of gannets in the cliffshore.
We check the dung of cows. Under trees we find chanterelles,
small but we pick them. We look for psilocybes. Max finds a
lone one.

Another month, he says.

I say, I've never done mushrooms.

This begins something for Max and Lydia. They swap psychedelic experiences. It happened in the fall with Lydia and at New Year's for Max. The full moon ascends and blurs behind a jacket of cloud. It smudges the moon into Saturn. The ocean is surging white against the blue, upraised slate. Max was with Maisie Pye then, and that's why Oliver has never liked him. This, under the influence of the mushroom. Lydia was with Earl.

Max has forearms from manual labour, from laying pipe in the Northwest Territories, from living a summer in a canvas tent while building a hunting lodge. Each time I'm with him he has a previous life to reveal. He can always illustrate a point with a personal story. It's as if, left to think long enough, Max could summon an entire personal universe.

2   We're at the Ship and Craig Regular buys me a beer. I hate how he pretends to like me. He says his house in the Battery has had plumbing for only twenty years. In the seventies there was a honey bucket.

Alex says she photographed a sentinel fishery crew throwing a thousand grapefruits into the sea. To mirror cod egg dispersion. They got back a hundred. She didnt think they'd get any back.

And then we see Oliver in the corner. He's watching Maisie laugh at the bar.

I go over to say hello. Oliver says, Dont you hate it, Gabe. When the one you love has a laugh with someone else, a laugh you never hear from something youve said?

On the way home Lydia says, I like Oliver. Even if he is an asshole when drunk.

It's true that Lydia prefers the company of men. That Maisie has always aggravated her a little. Because I get along with her so well.

3   I pick up Lydia in Jethro and drive west to Brigus. We stop to investigate a bog for bakeapples. I have a bottle of red wine, a clear bag of green arugula.

We walk through Daphne's garden. Mini tree farms. Ginko. Across the water I can see Kent's cottage. Bartlett's house is hidden in hawthorn bushes. What I should do is come out here and write.

Daphne says this age will be lost because our records are so fragile they are prone to any catastrophe. She says our handling of the past — concentrating it in libraries and museums — makes our records vulnerable to disintegration. We may be the first generation to accumulate a vast knowledge of the past, but this knowledge will be lost for the first and only time, along with the evidence.

4   We walk the length of Water Street with Tinker Bumbo. To the War Memorial, where the kids smile, facing the water. They like Tinker. They line up to pet him. At Fred's we check out the folk concert lineup.

Lydia says, I'm gonna take you home now.

We look at the fabrics in that Nepalese clothier. And back

to the car. I do not protest. We hold hands. I try to recall where the Napoli pizzeria used to be. I'm surprised at how old photographs show the same structure, merely a difference in detail.

At my driveway we kiss, the headlights on the red gate.

Lydia: Can I visit if I'm feeling tired — tomorrow morning?

Yes.

I won't be able to talk to you, just sleep. You won't be offended?

We kiss in three stints during this conversation. Three pauses in the goodbye. I'm gonna miss you, I say.

5   We stop into Max's on our way to the folk festival. The thing about Max's house is that it's so big and beautiful that he has to take every job that comes to him. He's a slave to the house.

They are eating blue burgers — blue cheese in the ground moose meat.

Daphne tells us how important it is to stay open and be friends with new people. That it's true that when you get to be thirty this effort diminishes, but without the effort you may as well end it. You have ended it. Max, in his undervest and smallpox vaccine scar, confesses he prefers the company of women.

Lydia: Gabe does too.

Max: Or is it the feminine side of people?

Funny, I say. It's the male side of women I like.

6   In the novel I have the boy grow up and come to St John's. To this city. Composed of roofs and walls and chimneys, windows, stout maple and dogberry, and the bank of hills on the other side of the harbour are streaked with pipelines to a tank farm. This is all I see, but I have to imagine it as it must have been eighty years ago. Telegraph poles. A patch of harbour with not a wave on it. I hear the long rub of tires on pavement, the motors echoing off hills and buildings. Every morning I pick a plateful of raspberries and eat them with a cup of coffee. I can smell the raspberries on my fingertips. It is very early in the morning, the hills would not photograph well, washed out by the sun. The fog always sleeps in the harbour and then the sun, when it lifts off the water, chases the white fog into the hills. As if the hills soak up the fog. The sun a bright orange cod after caplin.

You can hear the rivet shot of a hydraulic punch as workers dismantle the last stretch of wooden wharves in St John's. These wharves were here in the twenties. Making room for Hibernia facilities and the light blue Maersk support vessels.

7   Regatta day on Quidi Vidi pond. One ticket holding up the wheel. Sometimes the water is too bright to look at.

A family of ducks in the shade under a wooden walkbridge.

I bet a quarter on the crown and anchor and win a dollar.

Four boats race at once. The coxswain holds a cord to a buoy. She also controls the rudder, on cords. Lydia's film crew is next.

A girl in a booth displays a stuffed black fox. Samosas and puri and overboiled hot dogs in stale buns. There's a brisk westerly. Close to thirty degrees.

I see Una with her friends. The kids have twenty dollars each: ten for gambling with, ten for eating.

Max last night, mimicking his father. I'm all right, he says, except I got the hole droppin out of me.

Lydia's team is second in its heat.

8   I serve Lydia pasta outside at the picnic table, with home-brew. She's wearing three shades of brown. And pink eye in both eyes. We lie in the grass. I've picked raspberries and I feed them to her. Lydia pretends to be a baby. A baby, she says, would not like raspberries.

No. A baby'd push the raspberries out with his tongue.

No, he'd do this.

And Lydia pushes out with her lips and tongue.

And he'd straighten his legs.

Get away from me.

There are no movies playing, and badminton is over for the summer. It seems like we can't go out tonight, I say. And later. So, darlin, do you want to hang out together or do you want to get on?

Lydia: I want to hang out here and be your baby, baby.

In the park kids wag glowing haloes of rainbows. I ask Lydia and she says theyve been around a couple of years. How do they light? It's fluorescent goop, she says.

9   Eight of us aboard Max's boat in Placentia Bay. I love getting out of town. Sunny, steaming southwest of Long Island. Trying to remember how Lydia's foot looked in a white nylon: the red polish on her toenails showing through. As if her foot were dusted with sugar.

We see eagles in the distance. Some sea stacks that look like ancient pillars of rubble. I've had about five beer with absolutely no effect.

The horseflies are bad.

Discarded scallop shells shine along the bottom near the wharf in Harbour Buffett. Their reflected glare allows you to see more of what's on the bottom. Connors dart and coast around the legs of the wharf.

The wharf is the deck of an old oak schooner. All the houses are gone now, resettled to Arnold's Cove in the sixties. This was where Max was born. He has shown us photos of when his father moved the house to Arnold's Cove. They jacked the house and rolled it down to the water on logs. Then a barge shipped it down the length of Placentia Bay. They didnt break one pane of glass until they got to Arnold's Cove. Max says his father didnt mind the idea of resettlement. It was the speed. In the summer of 1967 there were two hundred people in Buffett. By September there were none.

And then what was left was pirated.

Even five years ago you'd see the shells of houses, still standing but their spines broken, about to collapse. You could see the size of the communities. But now all that's here are cabins. People are starting to return. The cabins are mushrooms growing on a dead log.

Max, looking at the topo maps, says we can go across to Merasheen, but if the wind is from the south, you just dont know.

Max has fibreglassed the boat — eight sheets on the hull, sixteen overlap on the keel. And six sheets cover the house. Fibreglassing saves on maintenance.

We pass the whaling station on Merasheen. Across from Rose au Rue Island. Abandoned in the forties. A pasture to the south where the whaler's quarters were, now caribou graze there. Rusting boilers, a vat, and the sticks of a wharf. On the ocean floor we see the outline of a sunken whaler, its hull arcing through the green depths.

10 This morning we ate blue mussels a friend of Max's raked from the bottom around the island in Buffett Harbour.

The friend says, Max and I we're the one age.

Big mussels that Lydia boiled in wine and garlic.

We watch two old women tend their drying fish. They stroll over to the chicken wire mesh, where the fish lie split and salted, to turn them over. The coastline is like a polygraph to see if the island's lying.

Off the wharf I catch a few connors with Una. I'm using raisins for bait.

If you can imagine a tarnished beer bottle capable of wriggling, that would describe a connor.

Daphne: We like being near running water. Because we're 90 percent water.

Driving back, in the dark, I almost hit a moose. I have Lydia, Maisie, and Una in the car. The moose is all legs, and then the legs join a torso. I never see its head. But I brake and swerve around him, I see fur against my right headlight. And Lydia says, holding my arm, You did well there.

11 How did I know Craig Regular was going to address me? He asked, Is this just olive oil? He was speaking to Lydia and something lifted in his chin that made me look, something that stopped us gently in our expected progress while he asked in a tone slightly lower to indicate an aside. Yes, it's just oil, I say, and he resumes the soft talk on editing film on computers, dipping his torn baguette in the green pool. I am intimidated by taller men. I'm not used to it.

12 Lydia is supposed to have her period today. I ask in the morning and there's no sign. It's the only thing she's never late for. On our bicycles we see Oliver Squires on his back step, soaked in heat, elbow propped on bare knee, eating a thick wedge of watermelon. Hottest day in thirteen years, he says.

I ask him, What were you doing back then.

He pauses. Thirteen years ago. Walking around the hill. I met Maisie. Yep, that's when it all started.

Oliver says, If you die 366 days after an assault, the assault is not considered a homicide.

He says, A woman in Labrador shot out the appliances in her home today, then lightly stabbed her husband.

Lightly?

Oliver believes that in a dream, parts of a house represent parts of your self. He is eating this wedge of watermelon at his back door. On the stoop. Hidden from public view, but still outside. And we catch him wolfing into it, a secret act, an act of private joy that Oliver could not appreciate indoors. His eyes find ours while his teeth are sunk into the meat of the watermelon. Such a hot day.

13 We wake up and I ask, and Lydia says no. I say a gentle prayer. For Lydia's period. I have never had a prayer unanswered, though I'm careful what I pray for. Lydia is calm about it all. She says her breasts feel sensitive, and bigger.

Lydia believes the world can be split into dreamers and writers. For the dreamer, words are strung together easily, you can fill libraries with their answers. But only a writer can tell you what life has meant. A writer cringes at how easily the dreamer pours out words. Politicians and bad writers are dreamers. Art is made in the kitchen. Whereas dreamers speak in front of the king.

14 Lydia says, I'm pregnant. She says this declaratively. We are going to have a child.

Let's get married, she says.

Okay then, I say.

I love you, she says. And she means it.

I have a rippling ecstasy coursing through my shoulders. I have never permitted myself to plan the future. And now large chunks of clear landscape have risen up.

I have thought so long to make Lydia pregnant. Her belly swollen, cupping a hand to her stomach. I wanted her changed like that. Carrying a baby. Cradling her. What an incredible nine months this will be.

I confess that I'd prayed.

Lydia: That I wouldnt be pregnant?

Me: I was careful. Because of the monkey's paw curse.

You prayed I wouldnt have a monkey's paw?

I prayed that you werent pregnant, yet. I wanted to make sure I wasnt praying that we could never get pregnant.

You wanted our baby to come later.

Yes.

Lydia: Maybe I should pray.

Okay. Something positive. That whatever happens will be a good thing.

Yes, that we'll have lots of good times no matter what. That whatever happens it'll have your looks and my brains.

15 We bicycle to Quidi Vidi gut. Boyd Coady is fishing for sea trout. He nods to Lydia. I ask if they will take a fly — he is using a spinner. Boyd says he's seen people flyfish, but theyve never caught anything. The fish are too nervous, scared by the line.

A couple of skinhead bikers search for bait under boulders. Now three short-haired boys and a girl, about fifteen years old, are fishing. She's got a waterproof radio. Sporty waterproof electronics are always yellow.

A tourist couple have walked behind us on the concrete breakwater.

One of the boys catches a sculpin. A friend has joined them: Have you brought me a smoke?

The boy is bashing the sculpin against the rocks.

Boyd says he had on a German brown that was sixteen inches.

Sitting on the concrete breakwater, poured in 1961. The Atlantic bearing down between the Narrows. My tall ginger bike glinting in the trees, leaning against Lydia's.

16 We sleep in the tent in Daphne's backyard at Brigus. I am making notes about how the rock is tilted into the sea, the grain of rock on an angle, like a giant's handwriting. Daphne in her maternity dress frying blood pudding and pancakes with Max's partridgeberries. Out the window I can see the gentle curve of Brigus. I can see where the sealing ships would lie at anchor to dry their sails. A second pot of coffee on. Sun and wind. The night wind was strong, slapping the tent fly like a sail. A few dangerous moments of wet windshield, headlights from other cars refracting on the wet, making it hard to see the road, the median. Reaching for my wipers.

A note from Lydia. I read it as soon as I got the fire going. She had jogged through Brigus with my baby inside of her. She was definitely pregnant. Running and pregnant with my baby. And then she felt her period start.

I feel my own blood sink, a depression that a ritual had begun. I realize that I had wanted her to be pregnant. There was only remorse, no relief, at the news.

17 Lydia sad and sick from her period, doesnt want to play soccer. Oliver Squires, after a bad kick: It's like a Heisenbergian particle, you concentrate on its placement and the velocity is shot to hell.

Oliver challenges Max in the Tely Ten road race. Oliver ends up passing out from dehydration. Oliver back from a week in Mexico, his face seems to be slowly crumpling, his good looks turning sour. Abundant nostril hair, pushed in eyes.

I watch Max lift to head a ball, but instead he sneaks his fist up to his neck and punches it upfield.

18 I water Iris's flower boxes using the shower nozzle through the bathroom window. I watch a plane descend and, for a blink, the sun goes out. Beyond the fence Boyd Coady is growing snow peas.

Lydia calls and says, Thanks, Gabe.

Youre welcome.

It's beautiful. It's so cute and excellent quality.

What are we talking about?

Your little television.

Lydia.

I found it this afternoon. You know, I thought I didnt want to live with a TV, but —

Lydia. I didnt get you a TV.

Lydia: There's a television in the living room.

Well, perhaps someone else left you the television.

What?

I drive down and there it is. A very good, portable TV.

I think we should call the police, she says.

Just think, first, I say.

19 I am fishing with Max. At one point the outboard motor stalls. I try to remember my childhood knowledge of choke and gas and ignition. I get it going. Like remembering youve memorized a poem and can recite it years later.

We fish for salmon on the last day of the season. Max lands a black fighter, about four pounds. We store him in the cooler and climb to Mount Misery. We scan over two hundred square miles of land. The distant ponds agreeing to the topographical map. I tell Max about Lydia almost pregnant, and he sees I'm sad. He says, But you were both happy about it. That's a terrific sign. And perhaps that's the lesson offered, not failure but a signal that youre ready.

20 Lydia calls from Wilf Jardine's at 1:15. She's too stoned to walk so I suggest getting her.

I stand in the porch but she doesnt see me. She has her hand on Wilf's knee. She's drawing his attention. Someone tells Lydia, Gabe's here.

Sitting on the bathroom sink at home brushing her teeth she says, I'm really attracted to Wilf. Can you see why?

I describe his rough energy. But that's not it, she says. It's more his armpit.

His armpit?

Lydia: His spirit.

In bed, we're honest. She says I've only ever lied to you once. She says, I wanted you to come over to me and kiss my cheek and say, I'm here for my baby, in my ear.

I thought if I'd done that you'd have been embarrassed at such a public display.

But that's discreet, she says. She says, Why did you walk away from me and Wilf?

I didnt feel a part of it. I dont like seeing you stoned, you laughing at not-very-funny things.

At 5:15 I'm still awake, walk around the house, I massage Lydia's feet.

21 In the morning she asks if we made love last night. This too angers me. She could have slept with someone and not known. I ask about the lie. Lydia said it was with a guy who had a girlfriend.

It struck me that I knew who it was.

She says, Youre not upset, are you? It was nearly two years ago, before we were going out.

I say, You have to understand that I had decided on you. You might not have been going out with me, but I was going out with you.

But you knew I wasnt going out with you.

Lydia lingering on Wilf's knee.

She wants me to relax, be comfortable. Get to know her friends more.

22 In the porch doorway we argue. It begins with me following Lydia down, wanting a kiss before she leaves. She says she can't because of the towels: all the towels in her bathroom were gone. And I felt like I couldnt say anything to you because you'd take it the wrong way and write it down in that journal.

You read it.

Yes.

Lydia.

Everything you write about me is rotten.

I write down things that vex me. I dont write down the good things.

Well, why dont you?

Happiness is too hard to write and boring to read.

She won't kiss me before her run. Only as a begrudging against-her-will kiss. I say, Not even a neutral kiss?

You mean like kissing a statue?

No, youre right. It's all or nothing when it comes to a kiss.

23 I roll my trunks inside a towel and drive down to Lydia's. There's a strong wind in the tops of trees. Leaves add so much sound. The tomato plants have sprouted.

Lydia is sitting on a cooler, clipping her toenails.

We drive out to Horse Cove. I spot Max's truck stopped in at Jardine's. They are buying fudgesicles. A man, bare-chested, is slicing bologna. He is singing.

Max says, The Jardines are full of music.

We take the route to St Thomas and then Laurie Road after the guardrail.

The shale cliffs tossed vertical.

I put together a salad at Horse Cove.

We swim and play Scrabble. Daphne gets two seven-letter words in a row. Drinking rum and orange juice. The kids throwing rocks at the boulders, to have them bounce back.

When did you first think of Max?

Daphne: First time I clapped eyes on him. I said, That man I'm gonna marry.

Are you getting married?

Max: After the baby.

24 In nature you see only half of a thing at a glance. But in writing you patch together bits and sides. More than is natural. It's a full map of the world, but in two dimensions. A flat map is not the globe. Something is lost in seeing it whole. Or too much seen gives the wrong impression. Nothing is as grand or foul.

Lydia and I make a list of all the things we've lost. The bread, the good cheese, the green bottle of wine, a Sydney Lumet book, a cutting board, a small rug from the bathroom.

We hunt through her house and notice a plate missing above the pelmet. The curtains from a window in Lydia's study. A pair of shoes.

We add the two items found: underwear and the television. The police suggest installing a monitoring system, and Lydia has agreed.

25 I help Max set a course of cinder blocks under a house. The basement excavated and the dirt thrown to the side for a vegetable garden. Max says, On the job, when the foreman yells for mortar, the labourer throws in a handful of stones. That slows up the bricklayer — he has to pick out the stones. The stones are called the hearts of the labourer.

He shows me the plumb. The line is the line, he says. You go just inside it with the bricks, you never touch the line. If you move the line, then you have no line.

Max knows a bricklayer who doesnt know eighths. If the measurement is seven-eighths, he will say a strong three-quarters. Five-eighths is a weak three-quarters.

He says how many bricks it takes depends on the job. If youre paid by the brick, then if you have to break a brick in two — for instance, around a window — you throw away the other half of brick. If youre being paid a wage, then you save the half-brick and use it on the next course of bricks. Those half-bricks add up.

26 We're invited to a barbecue at Alex's, but Lydia is shooting an underwater scene at the fluvarium. Craig has become a volunteer, helping the cameraman.

At the barbecue, Wilf sings a song whose only line is: Please come back to me.

There are murmurs of a swim. Alex wants me to stay behind, but it's safer to swim. So she comes along. We follow Max to Long Pond, which is rimmed in distant orbs of street-lamps. A wharf that sinks a little when we step on it. There's a wind here, cooler. Max strips off and is in first, his cry. As Alex undresses I see her small breasts. We all jump in. Except Oliver. We lose the moon and a short, swift rain falls. I can't feel the rain, only see it puncturing the surface of the pond, and the punctures look like nipples, a pond of nipples. Then the moon returns. A quarter moon.

Look at the moon.

Look at the ass on that moon.

Oliver: I can't believe you havent thrown me in.

He looks big, with a gut, and old.

I tell all this to Lydia and she says, At about the time you were skinny-dipping I had parked the car with Craig by the fluvarium. We caught that rain. We were probably looking right over at you.

27 Una skipping in the baseball diamond. We are following our noses. This is what skipping would be like, Una says, if it was an Olympic event. She whirls fast.

I ask, Why isnt it?

Because it's a kid's game.

She says, In India they dont skip rope.

Why not?

Pause. Culture, she says.

She knows this because in both movie versions of the *Secret Garden* they discuss India and skipping.

Maisie and I have decided to enter the CBC short-story contest. I'm culling a story from the journals. I havent written a story in months.

28 We take sea kayaks out into Bay Bulls. I watch Lydia lean back and paddle along the coast, across from Bread and Cheese Point. A cave with a baby gull bobbing in low tide. Lost and fluffy. Panels of rock slanting into the sea. A ledge to keep off or you'll be capsized.

Farther out puffins with caplin draped in their mouths. Puffins find kayakers unusual and dont move. Until youre right up on them and then they hop and flap, push off the water with their stubby wings, and plunge-dive.

On the way back in the baby gull has reached a purchase. But he's alone and bewildered.

29 Oliver says, Everything of importance has resonance. It all has immediate links. Maisie, he says, goes for the throat in her fiction. And that's what it should do. It matters how you leave someone. If you want to feel good, then choose to love and leave when you dont like her. Leave when youve done no wrong and leave when youre not feeling jealous. Have a good footing.

I have seen Oliver too often at the Ship. And who has seen him with his prize, pregnant paralegal student? Only me.

30 Craig Regular steps out of Lydia's bathroom and we chat for fifteen minutes. About his six-week gig on a local software program. Oliver got him discharged from drug charges, so he can get back into the U.S. He's leaving in ten days.

All this time Lydia is drawn to him, and Craig speaks to her. Then he wants to make a coffee. Lydia shows him how her stove works. There's something coquettish about how she leans on her hip as she twists the knobs. There is something brazen in how his head tilts over a collarbone to admire the propane flame.

I call her when I get back home and she says, I'm going to call you back. And I can tell that Craig is by her ear.

I am nervous. I dont want Craig so close to her ear.

31 The police are rigging a video-camera system through Lydia's house. They are very polite, ashamed if they have to do a little damage to the mouldings. The cameras are tiny, with high resolution. Apparently there are three, though as soon as they are installed I cannot see them.

I wash a cast-iron pan in the sink. I have my weight on one leg. I often rest on one leg to give an ankle some relief. The body does things the mind is oblivious to. Lydia is firmly planted on two legs. She's slightly back on her heels, feet apart, ready to go. I am more floaty, balanced, ready to bend with whatever comes. Lydia anchored, resists any oncoming.

September

1 My story is about the impossibility of holding onto water. Of the moments of love sifting through your hands. Trying to hold them and yet they push through and pass. Maisie's story ends with a man's fluorescent shirt, so blue it's like someone poured a drink down his neck.

I want to hold the majority of Lydia. I want this established. She offers me this much, a quarter. And when I ask for more she is defeated. She says, with resignation, that what she offers does not seem to satisfy me.

And then I'm down to a tenth.

This morning as I press her close to me and there is resistance. A moment at the top of the stairs when I lean in for a kiss and she steps away. All this makes me ache. I have holes of aching.

2 I am taking a few days on my own. I have forgotten about the city. About the small images that fill in a day. There is a man in an apron smoking in a doorway beside Leo's Fish and Chips. He is talking to Boyd Coady, who sits wedged around the radiator under the hood of his pickup. You could drop the hood on Boyd and click it shut, he's that far in.

3 I'm running around Quidi Vidi. As I run I'm talking out loud about Lydia. How she trivializes my love, implying that my love means an appreciation of her body and social graces, but not her talent. As if I could love someone whose talent I didnt respect. And yet I'm constantly in jeopardy, feeling that I'm not getting enough love, which must drive her nuts.

I am grumbling out loud. I swear as well. It feels good to swear at her.

Soccer-pitch lights shedding white on the path. I have to shut up as I pass people. I watch fifteen minutes of a soccer game, excellent players. High-school girls in the bleachers and I understand there are boys playing. The girls chatter about bad shots, hitting the scoreboard, that shot's got steroids in it. A corner. Both posts are held by defence, standing almost inside the posts. I run on. Up King's Bridge Road and then Gower, past Lydia's car. On Long's Hill I see Boyd Coady in the cab of his pickup. He is playing accordion. His truck windows screwed up.

4 I turn on the radio and a listener asks, When's it a good time to move a bleeding heart? The gardening expert calls her

my dear and it's patronizing.

Lydia has on a small, checked jacket with big mother-of-pearl buttons. She speaks of the salty beets you get in Toronto. She misses the beets. I tell her how I instantly fell for her and havent changed over two years of loving. That it's a rare beauty that Lydia doesnt seem aware of. She's not clear about what I mean, this unconscious beauty. That's just it, I say. Youre unaware. But still she has drifted from me.

I walk to the store for a newspaper. Wilf is there and asks if I see Twix bars. He is bending and pointing into the glass cabinet. I have never noticed this cabinet for chocolate bars. Wilf has big hands and I see that he is very big. He's wearing tinted blue glasses. He is holding, by the neck, a guitar in a peculiar black case, like half a guitar.

That's an odd case.

You play, Gabe?

I play a little.

He's unzipping the case because I have remarked on it.

Play us a tune.

I appreciate his novelty. I remember there is a music school two doors up. As Marion passes me the paper I catch her quiet face.

Me: No, I dont play in public.

Just a little song.

I couldnt, Wilf. It's good you play.

Marion says to Wilf, Do I know you? I feel like I know you. What's your name?

He tells her.

Have I seen you on television?

Wilf: I've been on television.

That's where it was then.

As I leave Wilf encourages me to play in public.

5 Lydia says her film is accepted in Vancouver. That's great, I say. That is so great. And she gets a bottle of wine and we drive out to Flatrock to watch the water surge against the breakwater. She leaves in ten days. Gone for five. She says that after that we should take a trip to Corner Brook. To see my parents. To visit the cabin at Howley.

Craig will be in Seattle. Just down the road.

6 I'm sitting next to Boyd Coady in the bleachers. Boyd worked in a restaurant in Ontario, near Woodstock. Been working on rodeos since he was sixteen.

Boyd: I saw Alice Cooper at the TSC. I used to hang around the university.

Me: Oh, what did you study?

Boyd: I never went there. I only hung around.

His hair rich brown and parted in the centre. Well-taken-care-of hair. His face scarred. Beady big brown eyes. A tattoo of a snake on his ring finger. He comes from a big family.

There's eighteen Coadys, he says. Same as the Roaches up on Freshwater.

He points with his arm. I've got to make phone calls to Santo Domingo and Los Angeles tonight, he says. Family.

The arc lamps glow on the backs of outfielders. I sit in the bleachers with the university team, which is arriving for the night game. It is September, they have begun a new term. Earl Quigley wants to take a group portrait. He has massive thighs.

The home team behind ten to one.

Boyd says, in an effort to lift them: It's a tie game, let's knock in a few runs.

A woman sits on a legless folding chair. Down by the dugout Earl stares up at Boyd. There's no need to be like that, Earl says to Boyd. And Boyd rises to meet him. There is history here.

7 I am cleaning a pound of squid. Stripping the flesh of ink-freckled skin, cutting the abdomen rim to push out the cartilage spear. Removing this spear is like slipping a belt off your waist.

I melt a chunk of butter in the black pan. I slice the tubes into rings. I flick on flour and scatter them in the pan. Just seconds. Until the edges shrink and contort in agony. Slip them onto a plate and squeeze half a lemon on them. Spray them with salt.

We eat with our fingers. Lydia says we can shut off the video system while we're in the house. But even so I feel monitored. There is one camera on the front door, one in the living room, and one in the kitchen.

8 This morning I woke up to a honking. It looked like flags had been strung across the harbour. But it's the world's eighth-largest cruise ship. The radio says be nice to the tourists,

let's not charge for the water. It makes me want to go down and knock heads.

Last night I bumped into Iris and we walked home. She was waiting for an e-mail from Helmut. She said the team is holed up in a small port near Sydney, waiting for the leg across the Pacific.

Iris stopped suddenly at Garrison Hill. I'm taking you out of your way, she said. No, youre not. Oh good, I just assumed you were going down to Lydia's.

It's obvious to Iris then that we're not getting along.

We walk around the basilica. We investigate a doorway and a concrete alcove to the rectory. There is a cemetery full of priests. She says, Everything we did in Brazil was fun. Even brushing our teeth. You know what I mean?

9 Oliver Squires is putting on weight and he's letting his ginger hair grow. Oliver Squires and Maisie Pye have officially separated. They have joint custody.

Oliver told me of the day when he knew. A boiled potato had fallen on the floor and he was damned if he was going to pick it up.

Oliver: I was working and Maisie wasnt. She was writing but I was at legal aid from eight till six. I'd ask her to iron a shirt for me. I thought that would be nice, to have a clean shirt. And when I came home something cooked. I know this sounds ridiculous or old-fashioned, but I figure if I'm working this is a little return. But Maisie wants to write, she was writing and one time she did cook this thing but spilled some and we ate with a potato on the floor and we walked around it for three days and I knew then that was it.

When Oliver tells this to me he has a solemnness I rarely see in men. He is deeply sorrowful.

Max too lost Maisie. Once, about eight years ago, I asked Max why he went with Maisie. We were at the Ship Inn and Max was on his way to the washroom. Above the men's is a pistol. He said, How old are you, Gabe? I said twenty-six. He said, When youre twenty-nine you'll see. It all changes when you round thirty. You'll want children. You'll want a house. And you'll need money.

And now Oliver is cut adrift, and Max is marrying Daphne. And I am dispirited at thirty-four.

10   Alex calls. Can you come down? I drive down. She says she asked Craig to marry her. And those words hovered over their weekend. He left for Seattle today and she thought it was time to be rash.

Alex: We were planting bulbs and Max came over and made fun of our domesticity. And by Sunday we were more and more married. And I felt diminished. For the first time I was looking for a way to get away from him. Craig said to me: What's getting in to you? And I told him: The energy we have comes from not being married. Being married would kill it.

Craig: Youve just figured that out? Then he added, Let's leave it. Alex: Craig doesnt like conversations that look like theyre headed for arguments and ground he isnt sure of. And I knew then it was the end.

Me: When youve been alone for a long time, as Craig has been, you become rigid. It's hard to consider someone else.

Alex: Men become selfish.

11 I see Boyd Coady talking to a little guy. Boyd has the guy pressed up against Jethro. A van line, he says, kindly moved me from Mount Pearl to Long's Hill.

As I walk past Boyd yells out: And as the saying goes, I'll take you down to Casey Street and beat the face off ya.

I stop. Boyd walks up to me. He recognizes me. He says, Just twenty minutes ago, Gabe, the U.S. military flew over the city leaving a line of smoke this long in the sky.

If I closed one eye I could make a flaming maple come out of Boyd's head. And the man by the car could have a deep green oak. How an orange tree is so much more festive, and summery. Yet the green tree is summer and it stands to the left of the flaming maple. How time shifts to the right, like writing.

Now let me finish, Boyd says. Left a streak in the sky, the U.S. military, over the city. I'll say no more on this.

He pushes his hands into his jeans pockets and walks back to the little guy, who is still leaning backwards over the hood of my car, as if he enjoys it.

12 Max Wareham's father collected stamps. In 1944 a surcharge of two cents was printed over the old stamps. A group of them on Merasheen set out to buy up sheets. You were allowed two sheets at a time. Mothers, kids, everyone had to buy sheets. The cartel lasted a couple of weeks and then they sold them to

mainland collectors. Max's father, Noel, made $1,500. He bought a cabin and land, a clothes washer for the wife, a phonograph — mahogany, plastic buttons. Macpherson, a rich man, bought one. Macpherson heard a second had been sold. To whom? Oh, to Noel Wareham, the fisherman.

The house Max grew up in was moved to Arnold's Cove. He visited it and could smell the same smell.

His parents' bedroom had seemed huge (it was two rooms knocked together) but now it was average, although it had two chandeliers.

Max left Newfoundland to work in a Christian camp in Manitoba. He lived in the basement of a church and worked in factories. He got to know the working class.

As he tells me this he loses a contact lens in the car. I find it perched like a dish on his knee.

13 Lydia calls to see if I'll drive her to the airport.

Sometimes, I say, I feel like a humourless curmudgeon.

Something very ill at ease about all of this.

Then Lydia kisses me at the automatic doors. And I can tell that it's okay that I'm unhappy. She gives me a key to her house. To check on it. And I'm to take care of Tinker Bumbo. The first time I have a key.

14 I drive out to Brigus to meet the man who lives in Rockwell Kent's cottage. He's an odd American. He owns the house but lives there only in the summer. He says the big difference between cities and the wild is you have to make your

own happenings in the wild. You have to act if you want one moment to stand out from another.

I tell him I'm writing about this house, about Kent and his time in Brigus. He says the carpenter's name is on all the studs. And it isnt the man noted in the books, but a man named Percy.

There is one weed beside us, and I guess it. Plantain. I had found it in my wildflower book: seaside plantain. And here I am, beside the sea. This is how the world is ordered. The categories were working.

I take a tour of Kent cottage. Named after Kent, England, not Rockwell Kent. The ceilings are low and the hill so steep and close behind the house, I feel tense, that a rock slide could do me in. Things seemed to be 20 percent smaller than they are now.

15 I am sitting in the kitchen while Iris is compiling data on olfactory responses in seals. Tinker Bumbo is snoring beside her. She notices my drawn look. She says, confidently, that Lydia will never leave me. And I won't leave her. And you'll have a baby. Trust me, I know these things. My first five senses arent that hot, but my sixth and seventh are superb.

16 I call up Max because it's Friday and no one has called and Lydia is in Seattle with Craig and I'm going mad.

Max: Do you know she's in Seattle?

I say, She's gone to Vancouver, and how far's Seattle?

He says it's important not to give in to conjecture. He says,

Why dont you come over and watch a movie?

Theyre in bed with a bowl of popcorn and Daphne is very pregnant. She's due in six weeks. I sit in the bed with them and we sip beers. I brought the beers. I am in their bed, under the sheets, in my clothes, with their new baby just a few inches away inside Daphne. I could not ask for a more direct allusion to a missed life. It's a good French film.

Max and Daphne have painted their bathroom. Daphne: At first, Max had returned with an onion skin and I sent him back for an eggshell.

17 I always sense a panic at the thought of change. And then, before change happens, there's a period of tranquility. It's as if I work out my fury and then accept what I dislike. There is an aversion to any kind of change, good or bad. I was so jealous of Craig, and now that Lydia's spending a weekend with him I am at ease. She'll be home tomorrow and then we'll drive to Corner Brook.

18 Lydia is back from Vancouver. Had I been to Alex's show yet? Yes, I said. You went with Maisie? Yes. You drove her there and you drove her home? Yes.

She says, I wanted to go to Alex's with you.

Well, let's go.

Forget it.

She has spent the weekend with Craig, and she's jealous of my time with Maisie.

She says she did not go down to Seattle. But as it happens, Craig was in Vancouver.

So you saw him.

Lydia: We had coffee.

And then.

And then what? Yes, a bunch of us went out for a drink. And.

Nothing happened, Gabe. He was staying at a friend's apartment and he asked me to come back so he could change. He put on a cream suit. That's all.

We go down to the Ship to celebrate her win (best short film). Wilf, of course, is all over her. It is Wilf who has made Lydia. No one understands Lydia like Wilf. And I see the look of adulation for Wilf in Lydia's eye. I can't stand it. I grip my beer bottle and Max witnesses my behaviour.

Max: You want to go to the boozecan?

That sounds like an idea.

And we stay out all night.

19 My wife has slept with Wilf Jardine and she's also slept with Craig Regular and I bet I bet it happened during those hours in that apartment when he changed into a cream suit through her encouragement, that ended in something that ended for she was too short in the telling too short in telling me everything and what am I to do now that my wife has all but told me she's had an affair and with a New Brunswicker (the only thing lower than coming from Corner Brook). And Wilf. It is early morning and I've walked up from downtown, pounded

on her door until she dropped a key from the window and I stagger upstairs to confront her with this. I am bold and say okay what about you and Wilf and she says Gabe youre drunk youre stinking drunk now get into bed no I'm not getting into bed until this is unravelled. I say, Okay this is a secret, but Max said to me Gabe I dont know if I should say this, but she's looking pretty absorbed in that guy, and I looked and there you were staring into Wilf's eyes like you adored him and it made me well it —

Look, if youre going to wake me up, accuse me, and want me to say I've slept with Wilf then youre mad and go on home out of it now and I'll call you tomorrow if youre lucky.

You want me to go.

I want to go to sleep. I was asleep. Youre stinking drunk.

I'm not drunk.

It's six in the morning and you wake me up and call me your wife when I'm barely your girlfriend and you want me to confess and it's you who should be apologizing for saying that in front of everyone saying, Are you going down to the booze-can with Wilf? when I'm having a night out with Daphne and youve made it clear youre out with Max and I've come over to you to say I'm going down to the boozecan and you ruin it by saying that in front of Daphne and Max, man youre lucky I dont just leave you and then! you go to the boozecan and come here wailing to me that I talked to another guy.

20 She's mad at Max. Why are you mad at Max?

Because he said that thing to you.

What thing.

Gabe, I dont know if I should say this, but she's looking pretty absorbed in that guy. That is so rotten.

Oh, Lydia.

Do you see why I'm mad?

He didnt say that.

You said he said it.

I was . . . He might have made a joke about it.

What did he say?

He might have said Lydia's got that fella's attention.

Pause.

So it was joke.

Yes. I took it badly. It was my jealousy.

So you were an arsehole.

I was upset.

Why can't you admit you were an arsehole? How I wish you could just say, Lydia, I'm such an arsehole.

Can I say asshole?

What?

Can I say asshole. Arsehole is so hard.

Say whatever you want.

Lydia, I'm such an asshole.

21 We've been invited for supper over at Max's, but I decide to wait. I am standing under a maple for shelter. It's been raining all night, a cold rain. The leaves are outlined in light and they overlap, like hands rubbing. There is Max's house. Windows in red trim. Rain dripping. How I'd prefer to stand here and wait

rather than be early and talk. A car pulls up and I recognize the sound of the exhaust. A car door slams, and it's Lydia. But I want to hang on. I havent seen Lydia since yesterday morning and I was sooky on the phone. That I'd have to walk down to see her. I was home and I called her place but there was no message. It seemed like she hadnt tried to get me. So I was feeling sorry for myself. I so hate getting this way. Standing under a tree — she would never do this. She is so unlike me. I urinate by the fence, it's dark in this corner.

She'd said, I'm at the Ship with Wilf. I'm not sure what I want to do tonight. I may just go home. She'd said, You can come down if you want.

There is something so uninviting in that. If you want. I wanted her to want me to come down. I didnt want her to shift the want to me. I was home and I'd gone to the early movie so that we could be together later. But here she was calling me and saying this is what she's doing. It's raining and I dont want to walk or drive down there.

I know when I walk in it's going to be uncomfortable. That she caught my sookiness on the phone. Last night, when she phoned to ask me over. But I was, for once, content to stay. But she wanted me. And I liked telling her no. But she gave in so quickly. Okay, she said. And I wanted her to beg more. Like I do. But she resigned herself, didnt yearn. She ends by saying, Sure you dont want to come over? I pause, Should I? She says, No, dont come over, I'll talk to you tomorrow, goodbye.

I keep the receiver to my ear, waiting for her click. But she has paused, waiting too. But I can say nothing and those silences so often between us, our language not folding into conversation but solidifying into isolated fragments. And she hangs up.

All of Max's windows lit up, burning around the edges of curtains and shutters. I bet there is no one else out in this weather by choice, waiting under a tree, obviously in a mood.

22 We pack Jethro for the trip west. It's an eight-hour drive to Corner Brook.

I drive as Lydia sleeps. She is peaceful in sleep. I reach behind for a blanket and as I do this I turn the wheel. Jethro is hurtling quietly down a rough steel grey shoulder full of spruce and ditch, and now a terrific new sound occurs, which wakes up Lydia and startles Tinker, and my arm shoots over to brace her.

The sun dead ahead the light of gods or inquisitors the gold of speculators.

We plunge sideways down the embankment. A hundred kilometres an hour over a boulder. Just stop now Jethro pleasy please and Lydia wide-eyed as if I have dropped a snowball down her neck. We lurch forward in our seat belts and stare at each other.

A rap on my window. A young couple who have climbed down to us. I have to push hard to open the door.

Is everyone all right?

He ducks a look in and seems shocked that I've gone off the road in good weather. Embarrassment that I've been reckless. If only there were four more cars in the ditch.

That was some dive you took.

He calls up to a woman, Theyre fine. Then smiles. That's my wife, he says.

They offer us a lift. As we're getting in their car I notice the sign in the rear window: Just Married.

Congratulations. We've been thinking about getting married. Woman: Dont do it.

Then she looks at her husband and laughs.

We'll take you up to Glovertown Irving. You'll get a wrecker from there. Nice dog.

A wrecker. The next step. A ride to the Irving and get a wrecker.

23 We spend the day in Glovertown. We camp out at Kozy Kabins. The wrecker brings Jethro to a buddy of his who fixes Hondas. All he needs is an arm or a rod or something I can't remember but it's steering-related. It involves torque. In the morning we're on the road again.

I had stroked the word LOVE in the Glovertown roadsign. But Lydia might have thought I stroked OVERT.

I tell Mom and Dad about the accident. How Jethro was off the road in a second. Mom interrupts: Did you say death row?

We sleep in the room of my childhood. Feet hanging over the bunkbeds Junior and I grew up in. You grow at night. Best to write in the morning, when youve grown.

24 Lydia watches my father work. He has a mahogany table leg

clamped in a vice, its claw foot sticking up, clenching a ball. He cradles a carving tool. If you keep both hands on the handle, he says, you'll never cut yourself.

We watch him carve around the filigree in the knee. I realize that my father is a handsome man. That I probably won't be as handsome when I'm his age. For some reason I'd thought the human race was evolving into better looks, but it's not the case.

He understands the physical world: electricity, plumbing, capillary action. He has built all the furniture in the house, and the copper ornaments contain his planishing. He has opinion and decisive comment whereas I am hampered by the acceptance of multiple views. I have learned no trail through the world. If I could show him batts of insulation.

25 Dad asks where Long's Hill is and Lydia says, It's the very bitter end of the Trans-Canada, Mr English. You never put on your indicator. The Trans-Canada turns into Kenmount Road and Kenmount turns into Freshwater and Freshwater turns into Long's Hill and Long's Hill is where Gabriel lives.

We visit Junior at his shed in the woods. He's studying stories of Labrador. He wants to move there. He wants to be the Member for the region. He asks me how difficult that might be. He says it's only an idea.

The shed is a garage on the first floor and a living quarters above it. Two snowmobiles lie under tarps flanking six cord of wood. He has a sky-blue Ford Fairlane standing on a sheet of plastic. When I ask, he says, You ever hear of the wick effect? Moisture coming out of the ground, it will attach to the metal of your car and rot it. A sheet of plastic acts as a vapour barrier.

He keeps one window open a crack to avoid condensation.

Inside he has a hole cut in the floor and a plastic bag full of milk, eggs, and bacon. It's cooler down in the garage, he says. I got no electricity yet. I've got no running water either. I'm living on potatoes and moose.

26 We drive to the cabin. We paddle up to Boot Brook at sunset. It takes twenty-five minutes to get to the point. Windy. It's almost ten oclock before we start fishing. I tell Lydia to fish in the calm water of the brook. Past the white stump that has sat in the current and, in low-water times, been fully exposed. I used to believe that Boot Brook produced calm water. That calm water poured from the brook, and at dusk, this still water spread over the lake and made it smooth.

We catch a few fighters.

We paddle back in the dark. The lake is vast and quiet under the stars. First the Big Dipper and this leads us to Polaris, and from that we get Cassiopeia. About two miles down the lake we see the lights of a car on the bridge to Howley. The lights cross the water and wink out.

The caribou have pulled carrots out of the ground to munch the green fern, but a two-legged animal has been at the spuds.

Lydia puts in a fire and we drink beer and play crib. We

decide to leave the generator off and just light the oil lamps.

There's no one else on the lake. You can hear the water lap against the big rock.

In the morning Lydia cooks the trout with bacon and squeezes lemon over the fish and packs on the pepper. We eat a loaf of bread by tearing it.

27 On our way out to the highway a moose stops us on the road. I get out. I approach the moose. It's a nervous calf. He backs up. I hear Lydia, out her window: Gabe. Behind you.

I turn to see a cow moose ploughing through the ditch, her head low. She starts up the grade. I put the car between us. The moose is determined. She clambers up Lydia's door, kicks herself onto the roof. I watch her teeter up there, turn around, metal popping and kinking like a pop can. The moose stands on Jethro's roof and stares at me, some massive hood ornament. Then she scrabbles down my side, feints my way, and veers left to her calf. She pushes her calf and they trundle off into the scrub.

Lydia stares at me through my window. She gets out. The roof is covered in stretched craters, like the punches super-heroes put in metal.

We drive back to St John's and shower and head out to a party at Max's.

Max says to me, Youve got to loosen up. There's nothing going on with Lydia. She loves you. She's crazy about you. Okay, so you guys fight. Who doesnt fight? Youve got to be a big man.

Me: I know it. Thing is, I'm battling exhaustion.

Max reflects on this. Youve got to stop looking and listen with your heart. Your heart will know. Is your heart getting fed?

I go to the kitchen because Wilf is there. I lean up against the counter beside him. Alex comes in, barefoot. Wilf puts out a hand.

Dont come in here, Alex, cause I broke a glass.

This is clearly a lie.

But it forces Alex to sit at the table.

Have you tried the soup?

The soup is delicious, I say.

And Wilf turns and sees me for the first time.

Alex says, Would you mind getting me a bowl?

I ladle her up a bowl. I can't find a spoon so I give her the ladle.

Wilf turns to the chicken wings. I join him. I say, How did the show go?

What?

The show at the Hall. You were the special guest.

What?

I'm thinking maybe he forgot about the show. I dont want to be the one to remind him.

Youre talking about the show next week, he says.

Oh, that's it.

Yeah, that show. It went well.

And he gives me a little grin.

Went really well.

Lydia walks in and Wilf says, It's time for you to have some kids.

Alex: You dont need kids.

Wilf: Sure you do. He nods to me. And you dont have to worry about the donor.

We walk home to Lydia's, exhausted.

Lydia: What do you think of what Wilf said?

Me: I think he's pretty brazen.

Lydia: He's funny, though. Can't you see how he's funny?

28 I sit in on one of Earl Quigley's lectures. Earl is talking about the physics of decay. He describes a coffin birth. A pregnant woman dies in childbirth. She is buried, and the soft tissues degenerate. The fetus slips out of the womb into the coffin.

I look at Lydia in the mirror of her study. How I can see her face ageing, and what her face will be like. As if the mirror distorts her or she is not Lydia. So I can see her face as skin and bone and not an identity attached to it.

It's like holding a drawing up to a mirror to see if it's balanced.

Lydia picks out a green-and-yellow striped dress her mother wore, when she was younger than Lydia. She tucks it under her chin, swaying the hem. The carved edges of cheeks and chin. I realize I am holding some professional distance from her.

29 Maisie, on the phone: Did you get mail?

I havent checked. Have you?

It came. There was none.

Want me to check?

Okay.

Want to come with me?

Okay!

I'll get the portable phone.

Pause.

Me: You hear me?

Yep.

Okay, I'm going out the screen door, hear the creak? There's oregano still, I'll just rub some between my fingers, smell that? The dogberries are deep clusters of —

Gabe, I got the picture.

Okay. Oh, my God, it's in there.

What's in there?

A letter from the CBC.

What? What's it say, Gabe.

It's definitely about the contest.

How come I didnt get anything?

It's a thin envelope.

I can't believe it. Youre putting me on.

It's true. I'm gonna open it. Hang on. This is it.

Oh, man, why didnt I get one?

Shit.

What is it?

It's a rejection.

Gabe.

Yeah.

I didnt get anything, Gabe.

30 Eight city workers stand over the big pits carved by the back hoe on Tuesday. There's a broken sewer pipe and theyve watched water and toilet tissue slip through it. The pipe belongs to Number 6 Young Street. So now theyre shovelling by hand to remove the length of pipe.

A wasp crawls over my bare foot as I'm on the phone. It's a yellowjacket. They are licking up the aphids off my chilli-pepper plants. I watch one bite chunks out of the flesh on a cantaloupe rind in the compost heap. Black currants are still ripe on bushes.

I'm surprised when good weather lingers into fall and bad weather remains into spring. I've never gauged correctly the true nature of the seasons.

October

1 I drive out to Conception Bay. I'm on my way to teach creative writing to high-school students. Jethro's studded tires rumble on the sunlit pavement. I feel tough. I let go of the wheel and the steering stays true for three hundred metres.

Two students have signed up, the librarian says. Youre in the basement.

Two?

I follow her downstairs. There are small plywood and metal tables. The shelves are full of Robert Ludlum.

Glenda is sixteen, wearing an off-white raglan with a poppy. Her bleached bangs cover her dark eyebrows. She speaks to me with confidence, with erect posture. When she gesticulates, she bends her arms at the elbows and sways her arms. Her elbows she plants on her hip bones.

Hedley arrives, with his mother. His mother is not much

older than me. Hedley is fifteen, smaller than Glenda. They shake hands and introduce themselves in a social and comfortable way. His mother says, So it's until four oclock? And that's all she wants to know. She's a pretty but harried woman.

I start by saying that this chair is a chair. And if you wrote your impressions of the chair, what you wrote would become the chair. The writing is not about the chair, it is the chair.

The way Hedley and Glenda exchange a look tells me we're going to have a good time.

2   I am picking up Lydia from the LSPU Hall. Wilf is smoking in the bar, clutching a beer with thick fingers. He has a perfect physique yet he lives on chocolate bars and cigarettes. Ragged white hair. He's been a songwriter and an actor for thirty years. He once moved to Toronto, to do merch, he says. Sell merchandise for a folk band.

Terrific show, Wilf.

Dostoevsky says the human being is an animal that can get used to anything. And that describes Wilf.

I've come to like Wilf. He would be surprised to hear me think that I suspected anything. He thinks highly of me. His love for Lydia he puts down as unrequited.

Lydia, he warns, is one fucking talented woman.

3   I run and circle back to Lydia's. She wants me to go for a walk. I say I am beat. She steps back to admire the curtain rod she has for her kitchen and stands on my finger, then my bare foot — she's wearing big clogs. I yell in pain. She says, Well,

you were in my way. And I say the obvious (It was you standing on my foot), to which she leaves the room. For a half-hour
she's on the phone and so I lace up my sneakers, wave goodbye, and run home. I call up Max and go to the Grapevine
for a beer. From there I call Lydia — no answer. I walk back
up the hill at nine and she's not there. At ten I call and she
answers. She's mad at me for leaving without telling her, after
she'd invited me out for a walk. So we go through it, and she
thinks I should apologize for yelling at her, and so I do. I ask if
I can come down, and she says, I want to be alone tonight. She
says she stood on my hand because I'd moved a chair to the
wrong place, and so she had to stand on my hand. And I say,
Why can't you admit you stood on my hand because you werent looking?

In the morning I walk down and she lets me in, but she's
serious. I see she's been cleaning the kitchen and living room.
She has thrown my things (a pair of socks, sneakers, three
books, a sweater) into a corner heap. It's so offensive. She com-
mences to talk on the phone. So I tell her I'm off to the
library. It maddens me. It makes me want to never return to
her place. I'm not welcome.

4   On the way down to the Ship, I spot a kingfisher on the
phone line in the rain.

I confess to Max that I'm upset. And I'm not sure what
it is. I resent the little fights Lydia and I have. She's late or she
gets angry if I peel potatoes in her sink or she says I dont insti-
gate evenings out.

He says passive-aggressive behaviour is insidious. He says, You two look so good together.

He remembers seeing me after we'd come back from Toronto. Asked what I was doing. And I said, Falling in love.

Max: It sounded beautiful.

He says, Hank put faith in Audrey.

But Hank left in the end.

Max: And then he died. On New Year's Day.

I am drinking blackberry sodas. I am eschewing alcohol. Max asks if I've ever eaten the testes of urchins.

Max: Use scissors, cut them open, wash away the stuff, get to these orange sacs, about five to a teaspoon? Urchins are hermaphrodites. Eat the testes raw. Taste of the sea. You know that taste on the shore? Or when you have cod right off the water? Something that gets lost after a couple of hours. Whelks.

He pauses.

I've eaten whelks. I've eaten periwinkles steamed. I've been eating a lot of sea crap. Milt from herring.

Alex is looking great. I tell this to Max and he raises an eye.

The truth is, Lydia loves me. When we fight, she is upset that I'm hurting her. She's angry because I'm an asshole. It's true she feels she's done nothing wrong, but her anger blooms out of love. Whereas I see I've upset her, and I'm afraid of Lydia's anger, but I never blame her for the argument. I try to see where I went wrong. What I resent is that she never does this, sees where she's wrong.

5   Vinyl siding is going up in strips. Why. Why not a vat of liquid plastic that you ooze over houses. I would like that. I'm not opposed to plastic. But if it stood for what it was and did not pretend to be wood. If you could be proud to call it genuine plastic. You start from the roof with a nozzle. You mask off the windows. Ooze the hot plastic over roof and sides. Nudge it into soffits. Encase the house in plastic. It would look like snow houses. The smooth rounded surface of Gaudi architecture. This would appeal.

6   Oliver says the fights he had with Maisie eroded the beachhead of love between them. They'd apologize, but he needed good times to restore the love. Whereas Maisie became immediately in love with him again. So she could afford to fight more often than him. She was hurt, too, when he told her about the beachhead eroding. The fights never diminished her love for him.

7   Lydia has painted her cupboards a light orange. She is mixing a bowl of vegetables. She is cutting carrots. Her rings scrape against the stainless-steel bowl. She says she'll just be a minute. She has flour on her sleeves.

Lydia is chopping the carrot very slowly. The wind gently lifts the back end of her house, just a fraction of an inch, but it lifts and cracks. I have boots on and they stamp on the linoleum. The linoleum is too soft for my boots. The phone rings and Lydia is waiting for me to grab for it. But I dont. She is supposed to be finding the books I left here. She grabs the phone with its long cord, she needs to dip under the stretched-out cord to look on top of her fridge for the books. Her hair gets caught in the cord, and for a moment, she balances on bent knees, trying to untangle herself, and she blames me for the tangle. Oh hi, she says. Yes. Sweet on the phone.

She finds the book under a chair.

Do you have the dust jacket?

Oh, she says, covering the mouthpiece. I took it off because I didnt want to tear it.

Well, at least it's not torn.

I dont know where I put it.

8   Max serves me up borscht made with Daphne's beets. There's homemade cornbread and mint ice cream. We drive Daphne to work at emerge. Then we make our racquetball appointment. We're cramming in nights out before the baby's due. My wrist is getting stronger, I'm returning his serve.

Outside by Max's truck a drunk man asks for a ride home.

I lives in the senior citizen's home on Thorburn Road. It's way before you get to Vatcher's, he says. I'm in some pain. Pain for the past three years. I dont know what I'm doing in the home, I'm only fifty-three. My wife is on a heating pad eighteen hours a day. I try to have sex but it hurts too much, but I does it for her. My God, I thought the pain would stop after what I've been drinking and I had some pills too. All kinds, but it won't go away.

Max looks over at me.

Drunk man: Everything goes right through me. Maybe you'd best take me to the hospital. That's where I'm gonna end up. Take me in to emergency. I'm real sorry about this. What's your name?

Gabriel, and this is Max.

Good to meet you, Gabe. Max, good to meet you too. I'm Alphonse Tucker. See my thumb, I can't move it. Yes, in through this way.

Max idles the truck as I take Alphonse by the elbow and help him through the In Only. He knows the way. Daphne Yarn is down the hall. I nod to Alphonse. I say, He's been drinking and he says he's taken some pills.

Daphne: You got an MCP card?

No, but I'm in your computer. Alphonse Tucker.

We take chairs beside the glass wicket. Daphne says, 4 Wigmore Court?

Whatever, he says.

He searches through his pockets, pulling out pills. The pills are small and blue or large and yellow. The yellow ones are marked Dupont. He cups them, slowly, to his mouth and I put a hand to his wrist.

Now, Mr Tucker, says Daphne. You won't try that again, will you?

He clenches his fist. He will not relinquish the pills.

Daphne stands, says, Put them in my pocket here and you can have them when you leave.

I'm surprised that he almost falls for this. He moves his hand over to her pocket but then retreats.

Do what you like then, she says.

He tries to swallow them again. Daphne rakes the pills from his hand.

I say, I think you'll be okay now, Alphonse.

It's good of you to do this Gabe, he says in my general direction.

Daphne asks his date of birth.

1944. That means I'm twenty-seven.

I'll see you, Phonse.

See you, my son.

I wave to Daphne.

Max and I play snooker and meet Oliver. There is no animosity in the men. Oliver says, Did you know Dali experimented with his diet — he took notes — to make the perfect shit?

Max says, Do you know why shit is tapered?

Max answers his own question: If it wasnt tapered your asshole would slam shut. He laughs. We used to say that all the time when we were kids.

I go to the washroom. I pee red. Oliver is at the next urinal. I'm peeing red!

He says, Did you have any beets today?

9   This is my last barbecue of the year. I've decided to invite both Maisie and Oliver. Oliver has brought salmon. It slips off the spatula onto the dirt path. Oliver looks at it. Then grinds the fish into the dirt with his heel.

Wilf, drunk, leans forward and slips off his chair. His head above the table, making his point, then keels over sideways onto his back, stretching his neck up, still talking, and making perfect sense. He's a man for whom liquor affects his body first.

10 I walk to Lydia's in the rain. Leaves stain the sidewalks almost like a spore print from mushrooms. The trees tight with clusters of dogberries. It's going to be a hard winter. The silver dollars have turned brown, and you can peel them now. Inside is rice paper. The furnace cut in this morning and I have hauled out my portable heater. I have lived ninety-five days on the heat of the sun alone.

I get a fire going using coal. A little drunk on Scotch as Lydia watches me. As if a foggy light, a heavy air, makes it hard to blink. I read aloud an interview with Gordon Lish. Lydia has made a steak in peppercorns, mustard, cream and white wine, garlic. Can you light some candles?

Me: Where will I find a match?

I dont know, you'll have to imagine where they might be.

Every interaction drains me of goodness.

11 Me: I was mailing something. And I got the paper.

Lydia: What were you mailing?

It was an application.

A what?

There was a job.

Great.

It's to write a book and you get to travel and interview seniors and I think you design the book too — I'd love to get it, and it pays twenty-five thousand.

Wow. You'll be, like, closing in on fifty thousand then.

Yeah. I'll have to find a woman who wants seventy-five thousand.

Sure.

Does that piss you off?

I think it's kind of mean.

I think it's mean to keep mentioning fifty thousand.

It was a joke.

You keep mentioning it.

I never knew it bothered you.

I told you I didnt like it.

Well, I'll never ever mention it again.

You know, you can be spiteful.

Say it.

That's all I want to say.

You should say it.

I've already said it.

You dont want to elaborate.

I think you get the picture.

Well, let's forget it.

12 I am feeling rather spiritual. That I'd like to spend more time alone. Read books I hear are good. Study and write. There is no one else I want to be with. But I could grow into being a man who can't live with a woman, no matter how accommodating the woman is. That is the worst, when you see lost men. Oliver is a little lost.

Boyd Coady tells me his parents live in Eastport. Theyre in their eighties with no electricity. They have an outhouse. His grandfather is still alive, at 109. He had twelve children, and only Boyd's father is still around.

Boyd: Grampa says if Dad dies, he'll have to go cut his own wood this winter.

13 For thanksgiving I'm invited to Lydia's parents'. While Lydia pours the gravy into a glass jar, her mother is plonking in three ice cubes, to help separate the fat. Her brother is sorting the coats and boots in the porch and saying, Let's get this place spotless. Lydia carries a bag of garbage out to the garage, and then returns with her boots still on. Her sister is laying plates in the oven to warm. Mr Murphy says, You want a drink, Gabriel? And he pours a generous glass of rum with orange juice. I'm putting on the cabbage. There's one two three, nine for supper. Tinker Bumbo is snoring on the loveseat.

Mr Murphy: It calls for salt.

Lydia: It do boy, it do.

Theyve invited me for supper but I'm brokenhearted. Too many fights with Lydia. And they love me and I love them. That's what breaks my heart. Theyre a good family and I'm losing them.

14 I look outside and focus on the twenty-two black wires strung on the telephone pole in the yard. If youre looking down Long's Hill at the burgundy and scarlet and mustard and

rust of Signal Hill, then the twenty-two wires converge and disrupt the hill in a random graph of thin crescents of colour.

This pole is leaning a little, carrying the weight of electricity and communication. A thirty-foot timber cut from the Gander region. It stands just outside the rebuilt Chinese and fish-and-chips restaurants. Where they sell laminated placemats of the Great Fire of 1993. The Old Big R engulfed in Halloween nighttime flame. Fire licked in ladders up phone poles on Harvey Road, transformers exploded. In the grocery store fire burnt turkeys in freezers. And last night, on the rough parking lot that once was the grocery store, I had a fight with Lydia. We were sitting in Jethro, discussing breaking up. At one point, a point where we've all been, where you are exhausted with your predicament, willing to take any ship, I realized Jethro was sitting in the aisle for fresh fruit and frozen products.

15 We've had our last fight. It's finished. I hate her. Let me explain why I hate Lydia Murphy. Because she says that I'm mean-spirited. That I'm a prick. That I dont admit the real motives for my actions. That I won't apologize. If only I'd apologize.

Nothing I do seems to make Lydia laugh. She will laugh at Max in a glowing love. Maisie laughs. Wilf will take my questions in wonder. But Lydia shuts me down. No, she'll say, that's not right. No one wants to eat that gravy with fat in it. But the truth is, only she doesnt. I try using the turkey baster (we're waiting on the gravy) and she tells me not to. I've asked her to take care of the gravy and she goes off with Wilf. Later, she yells at me, you didnt say it had to be done now.

We play 120s and she takes sixty points off my score when I went thirty for sixty. Instead of laughing at my bad luck in a good way, she's mean and punishes. When I ask about the sixty points she isnt sure. You just like being mean to me, I say. Then take it back, she says. Take it, take it. She is stern in front of the others. When I ask if saying hearts is strategic — the ace of hearts becomes the ace of trump, reducing trumps by one — Lydia says, automatically and impatiently, Doesnt matter. She wins, but do I care? It's not with joy.

We call a taxi to go downtown, but the cab driver says he won't take five. I'll walk, I say. And Max and Maisie and Wilf say, we'll walk too. It's only Lydia in the cab. And I see her sitting there in fury.

What's tiresome in all this is that I will explain why I was upset and it's as though I havent said a word. Lydia returns to her original argument. And, always, it's me who is wrong. I will apologize for hurting her — she expresses hurt through anger.

We look at each other, bent on fury and exhausted. And resigned. There is even a touch of love, perhaps sadness, when we agree we should part ways. It's too much anger. I'd rather be on my own.

16 Thinking that when people break up, they should have to write out a statement about their feelings of what happened, what went wrong, who was at fault, and how they feel. Purely subjective. These statements should be kept together on file

down at the archives for anyone to look up. Both for curiosity and for personal interest (you can look up the history of a man or woman youre interested in seeing).

17 The police invite Lydia and me to come by. We walk over to the station. The station is behind a doughnut shop, but the police, we hear, are not allowed to use that shop.

We watch the edited surveillance tapes. We see a man enter Lydia's porch door with a full garbage bag. We cut to the kitchen. He empties the bag into the washer and starts it up. He opens up the fridge door and helps himself to a can of apple juice. He goes to the living room with the can of juice, flicks on the television, and sits himself down in the recliner. There he sits until the wash cycle is over.

The man is Boyd Coady.

18 Lydia's called. She doesnt want to break up. But I'm broken. I'm sad and exhausted. She's not a bad person. We just dont get along. We both love the talents we have. She's funny. She's wilful in a way that is good for me. But being together is destructive. Moments build until the smallest things irritate us.

I'm taking a road trip around Conception Bay. I just dropped off a hitchhiker in Bareneed. There is a set of stairs left by the side of the road, like a huge tired accordion. The old oilcloth runner. Loads of trap skiffs. I can see the back side of Bell Island and Kelly's Island. But all the old houses are going. The new bungalows with treeless lots. Occasionally you'll see a saltbox close to the road with a bunch of fruit trees overgrown and choking the garden. A shed in back painted the same colour. But sagging on the foundations. Too late to save them. They needed to have been kept up ten years ago.

19 The trees on Long's Hill have crosses painted on them. I just called city hall.

The mayor: The arborist has been by. Said those trees are 90 percent gone, boy. Carolina pine and two elms. Ninety percent gone, like me.

Me: We all gotta go some time.

When I pass those trees behind the kirk's retaining wall I can feel the weight of the hill, the slope, the inertia pulling down the hill, the job that wall has to do. The work of a wall happens below ground. Beams of cement that creep under the road to counter the raised surface.

20 On the footbridge over Waterford River I watch the ducks. They know that to cross, they have to swim at an angle to the current. Dogs dont know this. A dog will cross a stream pointed directly at the far side, and end up downstream. But a duck calmly paddles at two oclock or ten oclock. Their beaks the green of unripe bananas.

I am a dog. I am stupid.

I pick partridgeberries and blueberries above Shanawdithit's monument and below the Irving oil-tank farm. But I end up collecting colours. Alders, berry bushes. The sun is lower and the leaves are like tiny red ears aflame. I segregate patches of colour by looking through my curled hand. How Helmut used to direct his camera lens at small areas of caribou moss and rock pools. Looking for the particular.

As I'm driving home I catch Maisie holding hands with Earl Quigley. On this day, anyone would be happy in anyone else's company.

21 Max comes by for a game of chess. He says he was driving by during the murder. He heard the shot. A brother shot another brother outside Theatre Pharmacy. It was over a woman, or drugs, or it was a hit sponsored by another brother in jail.

He crushes me in zugzwang.

We walk down and see the corner of the hill cordoned off with yellow police tape. The stain where the dead man lay. A mother is crying into a television camera. Along the hill, all the Carolina pine that had X's have been sawed down. They look like a field of butchered elephants.

22 It's midnight. I am drinking cold vodka with Max, staring down the hill where the murder took place and the trees lying on their backs like dead elephants. You can see the spire of St Andrew's Presbyterian Church now. I've never been in the kirk, Max says.

Neither have I.

Max wants a length of the pine, so we drive down in his truck. He says the arborist was wrong, the wood is solid. We balance a length on his tailgate. It must weigh five hundred pounds. There's a fine veil of rain hovering in the air. The billowing police tape still circling the murder scene at Theatre Pharmacy. Their slogan, beneath a turquoise woodcut of a bedridden patient, on prescription bags: When illness comes, next to your doctor you depend on your druggist.

Max says, I'll put the pine in hay. For two years. This will prevent the wood from checking. Then I'll carve it.

He has blocks of wood at the shop in various stages of drying.

Max says the murder may have to do with territory. The pharmacist sells to dealers in the early morning.

The police tape, the crime, the chunks of trees, I can empathize with this carnage. A part of me has been murdered.

23 The sun, low in the sky, hits the walls flat on and the floors are dark. Light through a piece of stained glass can travel through two rooms and pin itself on the panel above the phone.

I walk by Lydia's house. I see her planting a hundred and one bulbs. She has kept the bulbs in the front porch. I have seen Lydia store beer, cooked ham, turkeys, undeveloped film, thawing fish, bicycles, cases of soft drinks, dormant plants in this porch.

Hi, I say.

Oh, hi. Want to help?

We find a trowel, a planter, a pick in the basement. Work gloves. We look at the key and discuss the height of allium, grape hyacinth, dutch iris. We dig among tree roots, we exhume previous bulbs. Harvesting potatoes with my father, spiking one with the pitchfork. Bright flesh in the dirt.

There are the black skins of chestnuts, split to reveal the smooth, varnished knot. The grass still green. There is new grass, even when snow approaches.

We spend the afternoon gardening and it is easy and sad. We are kind to each other, but our hearts are heavy with rain.

24 Tonight my house is full of industry. Dark windows and desk lamps. Radios on low. Iris is polishing up her thesis on sperm physiology in yellow-tail flounder. But I ask about the floating eye, the change in colour. She says most flounder are left-eyed, meaning the left eye floats over to the right side. But some are right-eyed, for no apparent reason.

Iris should be scanning Internet sites for new articles on the role of olfaction in the social behaviour of harbour seals. But she is sending an e-mail to Helmut. They are in Hawaii. In six days they set sail for San Francisco, then south through the Panama Canal. They are replacing the mast. She describes the design, injecting the material with plastics.

But it's still wood?

She pauses. Gabe, there's nothing from nature in these boats.

Her door ajar. I see her glowing blue from the light of her laptop. The soothing clack of a keyboard. There's a moon breaking through the top of the sky, but fog has settled over the hills. Shipyard lights, clustered like ballpark lights, burn through in a haze of urine. The fog a beard. Sky a bald, shining pate.

25 Today I picked up my father's jacket. The cuffs were frayed, so I brought it to Tony's Tailor.

Tony: You have your ticket? It'd be easier.

It's that coat hanging there.

Tony: Youre the one with the cuffs.

Yes.

It came out well.

Did you notice the back?

No.

It's all one piece of cloth.

Tony snatches the jacket from my hands and holds it to the light.

I've seen that before.

It was my father's jacket, I say. He wore it when he was my age. Before he had me. I used to think he got married in it, but my mother said no.

That's the difference, Tony says, between men and women.

26 I walk down to the Fat Cat with Max. Earl Quigley makes his way to me. So how are you, he says. Never mind, dont answer — can of worms, I know. Look, call me and I'll buy the coffee.

Yes, I said. A confessor would be nice.

Earl went out with Lydia for four years. And now I've seen him with Maisie.

Then Max. Max is such an affable man. He is the word affable. But then I am just another man and we have no obliga-tion. So the freedom to be easy and drink and tell all.

Wilf asks Lydia to get up and they whisper and they sing the song I thought was our song, Wilf on guitar. Lydia sings with her thumbs hooked through her belt loops.

Earl Quigley wins the door prize. I never know where I've put my ticket. The pints are cheap until eleven. And I want to get plastered. I point to my empty glass.

27 For the first time, the black roof below is covered in white. I wake up to the branches, sparrows hurrying for seeds, their claws wrapped tight against bare trees mostly white. Bunches of dogberries slivers of red under caps of white. And I think of the first time I held Lydia, bowled her over in the snow when she came back for Christmas. Our first Christmas after a fall of courting, of letters, of plane flights. And now she is not here. Our first snowfall apart.

It's not that I return to the past; rather, the snow makes the past hurtle forward.

There is not much new to say about snow, or broken love. Lorca: I am thirsty for odours and laughs, I am thirsty for new poems, poems with no lilies or moons, and no love affairs about to fail.

28 At the Ship with Max. It's 2 a.m. When Max lived in Merasheen they had no electricity. He salted fish, he caught fish, he killed cattle and chickens, the whole thing. And now, in a few days, he'll be a father.

240

29 The ground covered in torn leaves, mainly green, the violence of rain and wind. Dogberry leaves are stuck to the wet door frames. Already people are wearing their poppies. This bugs me.

The city has been ploughing in the public swimming pools.

I hear from Daphne that the police have found lots of evidence. Boyd Coady used seven houses in the neighbourhood. He'd break in, find a spare key, make a copy, and then study the patterns of the people who lived there. When he knew they were gone, he'd go in.

He left the television at Lydia's because she didnt have one, and he liked to watch TV while his laundry was on.

The underwear fit him.

He admitted he took small things. He liked the things.

Sentencing is next month.

30 Walking Alex home from badminton. As always the night has grown calmer and a little warmer, as if heat is coming off the earth.

I'm having a conversation about everyone knowing everything. This is my belief, that instinct over body language is a sophisticated, primitive knowledge, as old as sharks. Our new found intellect thinks it can hide true feeling through omissions in language, but it forgets the body is talking the entire time. Anything we hide we are hiding only from ourselves. As long as someone is not practising obliviousness, he will know how you feel and what you feel about him.

31 Halloween and I'm dressed as Question Man. I have a pair of cardboard glasses shaped into question marks. I wear a belt buckle with a question mark. Alex is dressed as a sheep and she asks me for a light. She says, Question Man, do you have a light? I'd thought Alex was a rabbit, but she's Sheep.

I dont have a light, I say.

There is a freshly dug grave and a straw man with a pick through his head. The head is made of newspaper stuffed in a yellow sock. There is a thick-lipped sardonic smile. I see Lydia speaking to the pope, who wears a tablecloth and a tea cosy on his head. The pope is Craig Regular. When the hell did he get back in town? There is no defining element in the men Lydia finds attractive. All shapes and character types. Always a surprise: Wilf breaks into big American musical numbers. Craig is goofy but smart. Earl has an academic intensity. Some are sweet, others are sexy. Wilf has a charisma, that's undeniable. But he's an alcoholic.

I take a burning plank from the fire and hold it to Sheep. The plank has cinders and blistered edges. She bends towards it. The plank is hot on the fingers, but I still hold it. I know Sheep thinks this is dramatic.

The harbour is shiny. The planks we are burning are the same kind the house is made of. The updraft is making a ghost float.

Inside, Sheep takes me by the waist and says, Dance with me, Question Man.

Lydia comes up to me, and offers the final question of the night: What is the function of regret. And I say, it allows you to understand that there are other possible lives to lead.

No one, thankfully, asks me Leibniz's question: Why is there not nothing?

November

1 I wake up. I wake up in the dark and there is someone leaning in to my room. It's a woman. Come on, she says. She must be tugging my shoulder.

Gabe, come on.

It's Lydia.

We're going to Max's, she says.

It's the middle of the small hours. Max is propped by the gatepost, giggling in the dark. The giggle tells me he's loaded. Maisie is sitting on the rock wall.

A boy, Max says. I've got a boy.

I'm afraid to take his arm from the gate. I am too sober to enjoy them. But we walk arm in arm up the road.

Max says there was a seam of black, the blood vessels breaking on Daphne's face. He cut the umbilical cord. The cord deep blue and red.

Shhh, Max says. He misses the keyhole with his key. He tries again. I try taking the key from him, but he resists.

Are they in hospital?

Max: Theyre upstairs. Let's go around the back.

And we sit on his deck and whisper loudly.

Daphne, he says. With a finger to his lips.

Have you got a name yet?

Havent got a name. Maybe Eli.

They are all about five beers ahead of me. Max and Lydia had called but my phone was unplugged.

Max finds us a round of beer. I realize they are in conversation. It's a conversation I can't follow, but there's a raw nerve of excitement, of the new boy in the world.

I drink my beer and let them gush on. At one point, Max says, Some people never become themselves because theyre afraid to be fools.

2   Sometimes, at night, late, I will see Boyd's pickup idling, parklights on, in behind the Big R on Long's Hill. Boyd Coady stands across the street, hands in jeans pockets, looking in a gallery window at a print on an easel. He was on his way home and had to have a look. Longing for something in the print. The print is nostalgic, an outport at dusk, yellow squares of light indicating windows, woodsmoke, a reflection in a still sea. Boyd is longing for this. He lived there once.

3   I'm at Maisie's house. From the porch I can see Maisie leaning into the sink to pour herself a glass of water. In the

porch Oliver Squires says, I have two sisters. One's dead. There's one I'd love to drown, and she's not the one who's dead. Yes sir, I know exactly where I'm going to drown her.

And then Oliver leaves.

He leaves because he can't stand seeing Maisie. Maisie says Oliver gets into moods. He can't enjoy himself at a thing like this. He thinks he has no friends.

We all think, in the end, that we have no friends.

Maisie: He'll be worried for me.

Why.

Oh, that I'll drink too much and lose control and someone might take advantage of me, I mean it's ridiculous.

You left him. It's all about power.

Maisie: Yet he's glad to be with his prize student. He's delighted about her being pregnant. He just can't get used to me being with other men.

Me: That's common. I have that. It's having to let go.

Maisie: Yeah, men are great. But sometimes they try to be controlling and it just doesnt work.

4   I arrive late for badminton and Lydia is there and I have to play on her court. It's hard to watch her have fun. I'm glad to be free of her, but I dont want her happy.

I leave early because I dont want to be ignored any longer in front of others. Lydia took offence because I suggested that when she's passing the birdie to us, she lob it with an under-hand shot instead of her inaccurate overhand. I know that the overhand tends to smash the birdie and, coupled with its inaccuracy, is jarring. But Lydia found this irritating and chose to ignore it.

Lydia has to run an errand, so I go to the Ship. I buy a round. Maisie confesses things have been bad with Oliver. He's not good about their daughter. Essentially, he wants to have the baby, have his student, and get back together with Maisie, and he resents that she's not interested.

In the past, she says, Oliver has often thought of breaking up with me. But then wanted me again. I spelled out his wish list and he very soberly agreed with me. Girlfriend on the side. I had to explain to him that I'm better off without him.

Me: I think we're all better off alone.

Maisie: I think women are better off than men.

I think men are starting to catch up.

Maisie: It's as if everyone has had enough of the one they're with.

Lydia enters the Ship and walks to the bar to use the phone. She is calling someone. She is the kind who guesses at a number. She often gets a wrong number but this is part of her push into the world. I miss it. She doesnt mind saying, Oh, sorry. She is lavish with apologies. I try to limit mine. It's true I'm mean with my apologies.

I have to stop watching Lydia.

5   There's a bonfire in the field below me. A gang of boys feeds branches of the dead pine into a bed of molten rubber tires. Some steel-belted radials are burnt so that a mesh skeleton of tires remains, standing amid the inferno like some

macabre effigy. At ten they run out of fuel and begin hauling pickets off the fences. Off my fence. A fire truck wobbles into a lane, and fat hoses are dragged up to the fire. The kids are swearing at the firemen. Cinders are landing on shingled roofs.

6 Now that it's definitely November you can see through veils of dying shrubs. The world is going bald. Hedges you can see through. You can stare into a house. There are no secrets. With the trees bare you see the whole city sitting on the hill in its underwear. The striptease of the city is complete. Honesty reigns and the honest picture is barren and mean.

The grass melting through snow. Grass still green. Sedum still erect and burgundy.

7 Maisie says there are five things she needs in a man: sense of humour, emotionally stable, treats me like a queen, a good listener, intelligent.

I tell Maisie I think she is beautiful and can't understand why there are no men. She says she knows of men, but theyre all taken. St John's has a dearth of good men. Daphne found one.

Me: What about Earl Quigley?

Maisie: He's set in his ways. As you get older your standards get higher.

I said there were things I needed from Lydia that I never got, so I ended it.

Maisie: Dont settle for less than you want. Better to die alone searching than settling.

Max is not so sure.

Maisie: Dont ever compromise for the sake of a man. That's my motto.

8 Max has come into money. His father's will has been settled and there's a massive windfall. At first I'm a little stiff. Then Max says, I'm egocentric because I was the only son — Mom gave me love I thought Dad should receive. And Dad, it would have been embarrassing for both of us if we'd verbally expressed our love. But I know he loved me.

We are in the Ship guzzling our pints, raising one for old Noel Wareham. And what to do with the money.

He says he'd like to give Maisie some and Lydia. And put away a pile for Eli and Daphne.

It has to be anonymous, I say.

Otherwise it'll change how they are to me?

Just dump a bundle in their mailboxes.

Would you be jealous if I gave Lydia some?

I think it would be a beautiful gesture. Let her make a movie on it. Offer a proviso.

Yeah, I'll be executive producer. The interest, he says, on a half million is twenty thousand a year.

Max is drinking pints of Smithwicks. I'm on black and tan. He feels the money is a weight. And having to settle his father's affairs. The house in Arnold's Cove. He had antiques. There was a key to a safety deposit box. There was nothing Max wanted except the boat.

Max: I didnt even want to go to the funeral.

9   Maisie stops in her car and I get in. Just to drive around. I
open her glovebox and it's full of fall leaves.

Maisie: I filled that a few weeks ago. I want to have it there
this winter. So whenever I get sick of the sleet, I'll just open up
the glovebox and stare.

She says Oliver left a message on her machine last night. He
was disappointed she wasnt in.

Maisie: It wasnt obvious that he was being polite.

I have an ache of sadness in my ribs, where they cleave. As
if an axe has split me partially in two.

10 Walking up Carter's Hill: two girls and a boy singing,
London Bridge is falling down, my fair lady-o . . .

And then, Take the keys and lock her up . . .

And I remember I've never had a key to Lydia's place.

Even when it's the boy's turn to get caught in the collaps-
ing steeple of the girls' arms, they sing: Lock her up.

A man opens a door for a woman and calls her darling and
she calls him dearie. She says the word weathervane and the
door closes. Tenderness.

11 I meet Wilf Jardine down on Water Street. He is on his
way to the welfare office. The fridge is looking empty. No
shame in him at all, it's a joke to Wilf. I know he uses jet fuel
in his kerosene heater. His buddy at the airport gets him the
fuel. He makes ninety-proof alcohol from a still, the charcoal
takes away the impurities. He doesn't buy booze or heat. All he
needs is food.

12 Tonight after racquetball, in the sauna, I ask Max if Alex Fleming is seeing anyone.

Isnt she seeing Craig Regular?

That's old, Max.

He says Maisie Pye has officially broken up with Oliver.

Max, you are way behind.

He says, Okay. Oliver made a pass at Daphne, can you believe it.

Now that's news.

Max: He did it because I used to see Maisie. I told Maisie, and she said, If they get together, what will that make us? I said, Wary.

Max, of Oliver: It's two things at once. It's as if he leaves it all out there, and then it's as if nothing's there at all. Of himself.

Max is cautious of what he says around Oliver. It will come back on him sometime later.

You did punch him out.

Max: That was self-defence.

My open ear is what Max needs. He doesnt need advice. Max needs to air his beefs about Oliver.

13 Oliver says eating mussels is the same texture as chewing on your lip.

We're in the Indian shop at the east end of Duckworth. In back the vat of frying. And then the woman, on her mat praying directly through the harbour. She is wearing taupe.

We walk along the path around Signal Hill. I dont really like Oliver, but we share the word bereft.

Oliver stops, turning on the path, interrupting to say, Look at that. The bone white shine of the path behind us, leading to the city. I look at Oliver and he is crying.

It's just the wind, he says.

14 Alex Fleming grew up in Quirpoon. She says, Theyre gonna shoot the big Hollywood feature in Rocky Harbour. It should be shot in St Anthony. They should get Maisie in on it, to write it — no offence, Gabe. But Maisie should write it. And Lydia should direct it. Did you read the book?

I can tell, before I say anything, that Alex has a definite opinion, and it's probably negative. In fact, she has an opinion on everything. At least, initial opinions. She seems willing to relent. I say that I didnt finish it, that I found the voice false. I heard the author speak at the Learneds and she claimed that she heightened, or torqued, the language in order to best capture the place and people. I found her persona arrogant. I dont agree that caricature is the essence of novels, that you have only three hundred pages and life is much longer. So you need to condense and heighten.

Alex has been clenching her thin fist on the table. I can't stand her, she says. She stayed in our bed and breakfast. When she came to St Anthony she was poor. She stole that book from Maisie. Maisie had it all written down and she took it. That voice belongs to Maisie. She didnt make anything up. That's very dishonest. I know these things: ethics, that's my area of study.

Alex says the author even slagged her mother at that lecture at the Learneds.

Me: I dont remember that.

Alex: Well, it was a veiled reference to her as being stupid. You were there?

I heard about it.

I think I would have remembered that. And about Maisie.

Yes! Maisie!

Maisie was in her writing class.

Well, then you know.

She's a good writer.

But to myself I know other things. That she helped Maisie with her manuscript, that she encouraged Maisie to send it to her publisher.

I say, I thought Maisie said good things about her.

Oh, I'm sure she does. All I'm giving you is my slant on things. Maisie thinks the world of her.

15 Maisie confesses she has always laughed — her family laughed a lot. She didnt realize until later that other families didnt laugh as much as hers. Oliver's family is serious.

She has always taken my demeanour as sincere. Most people think I'm not being genuine. I've watched myself on videotape and I understand how they make the mistake. I hesitate. I look like I'm lying.

I have always been drawn to kind people. I love witnessing generosity and subtlety. If I were to begin a religious order, my first article of faith would be to commit sneaky acts of generosity.

I am drawn to the Catholic demeanour. Maisie, Max, and Lydia are all Catholic. Mainly because Catholics seem to laugh more than Protestants. They seem less restrained. You have to be slightly embarrassed to come from an English background.

16 Max and I are drinking homemade red wine in the car out in Ferryland. We were going to walk out to the lighthouse, but it's too windy and wet. So we have cheese and olives on a board over the hand brake. The wine in paper cups. Max remembers his mother saying, That's it, I've had enough. I'm gonna go up in the graveyard, dig a hole, and bury myself.

Max: Mom would take the shovel and we'd start screeching. No Mom, we'd say. Dont do it. She'd say, Too late, I'm gone. And we'd watch her march up the rise to the graveyard on Merasheen with the shovel on her shoulder. We'd be bawling at the door, begging her to come back, We'll be good, Mom, promise. Our faces all crumpled up.

Well, eventually she would come back, after spending the afternoon next door, drinking tea.

Mothers, he says, go through a period of madness.

He says his arm still hurts from when Eli was born. He kept Daphne's head down when she was in labour. For five hours Max's arm crooked around her neck, bending her.

When Max tells me this he pats himself on the shoulder, on the ribs. As if to reassure his body that it's all right.

17 Oliver drops by. He's in his legal-aid suit. Smiling

uncomfortably. As if a pain is spreading across his chest. He has been returning Maisie's junk mail and he's just off to the mailbox. For one, from an environmental agency, he has scribbled on the envelope, Stop sending mail, or I'll club a seal.

I show him an untitled recipe Lydia left on my fridge: Keep it white. Peel and dice potatoes. Sauté in butter. You dont want any skin in there. Make love to your potatoes. Glazed, melt. Chopped onion. Translucent. Cover, barely, with water. Put lid on, simmer. Stop. Cool down. Lay on chunks of fish and scallops. Let the steam tickle your fish for four minutes. Break apart. Milk and cream. Never boil. Sometimes sweet corn.

That's pretty erotic, he says.

I find things like this all over.

And he understands my sentiment.

18 I walk towards the harbour, thick snow on the dogberries. Thinking back on when I asked Lydia to marry me. Part of the reason we did not marry was my own reluctance to answer yes to Lydia's every okay. The truth is, I knew about responding with okay to every hesitation a woman gives you on a commitment. As soon as Lydia hesitated I pounced on it. I was relieved. I wanted the decision not to get married to be her responsibility.

I pounced on it in a very subtle, disinterested way.

I had that sort of tone in my voice when I met Lydia's hesitation with my own brand of hesitation.

This is a maddening personal trait. To slip out of responsibility. To pretend an act is someone else's decision.

The truth is my future is always a dull extension of the

evidence around me. That's why I'm frightened to have children. The new.

19 At the cash the woman says I remind her of Prince Charles. This one's got royalty in him, doesnt he?

Oh, he's much more handsome than Charles.

No, Charles as a young man.

The other woman, keen to assure me I'm better looking, says, When he's older he'll be far more handsome than the prince.

20 There's a big wooden fence out by Mount Pearl. It's supposed to be a barrier between the houses and the highway. But as you accelerate, the fence begins to blur, the gaps between the pickets link up, and suddenly the fence vanishes. You can see, with no interruption, the houses in behind. But the houses can't see you. If you slipped off the road and hit the fence at the right speed, you'd slip right through it.

21 Max: Let's do some heavy drinking.

Yes, I need a few heavy drinks.

You need a chaser.

I need to be chased.

You will be chased. You have to stop chasing in order to be chased. Youre too exposed and everyone sees the wind blowing through you and they won't touch you while that wind is blowing. No one likes a man with his heart wounded by another.

I need sutures.

We're gonna get you some sutures.

22 I phone Lydia. She says, I'm just reading an old paper.

What time did you get up?

Oh, nine-thirty.

Me: I'm just up.

You sound like youre not up. Like youre way under a blanket. You sound horizontal.

Me: You sound half asleep.

Yeah, I'm just noticing that. It was getting up. From the table.

So how are you.

Lydia: I'm good. I'm really good. I went for a run.

I'm not feeling too good. Oh my God, my nose.

What is it?

It's all puffy on one side.

Are you okay?

I feel okay. But the side of my face.

You must have fallen.

I must have. I was with Max until the sun came up.

You got home okay?

I was pretty drunk. But I beelined home. I must have hit a lamppost. No, I hit a tree.

23 Helmut will be home for Christmas. They placed first, Iris says. She shows me their web page and the maps of their progress and Boston harbour. They were eight hours ahead of

the next boat. Five months of racing and they won by eight hours. There is an article all about the racers, and a photo of Helmut and the team in today's papers. He has long hair, he's thinner. I recognize him by his hands.

24 Alex and I sit on the cold concrete at one in the morning, down in the heart of the town. The river flashing below us. A river takes you out of the human landscape and transports you into a terrain without clocks. A bridge is a place of confession, of consolation. Confessions are anything you know to be true.

Alex: I want to write a song as good as a Wilf song.

Yes, a song.

I want to fall in love. I mean, really fall in love. Don't you, Gabe?

Yes.

Can you imagine it?

It's hard to separate it from the sexual side.

Not for me. I've got a picture of the perfect man.

And what's he like?

He separates what I say and do from who I am. He doesn't criticize me. You know, men do that all the time.

Well. It's hard to know the difference between criticism of acts and criticism of the person.

I know I'm sensitive, she says.

We hold hands. It's meant for comfort. It is like holding your own hand, or patting your own sides to offer encouragement. It is dark, the river rushing under us, the air a little chilly. I have fished this river, and fishing takes the mystery out of a river.

It's true that all rivers connect. The sound of a river belongs in the same folder as all other rivers, and nothing quite compares, and so the memories of what has happened at other rivers is easy to summon. And so rivers are nostalgic and nostalgia means returning home, plus pain.

25 They call out to me as I'm walking up Long's Hill. The night so empty, sound travelling for miles.

Maisie: Let's go for a beer.

Max: One beer.

Maisie: We'll split a beer. Three ways.

Okay, I say. Say, arent you parents?

26 I walk to the art gallery, and pass through the graveyard. The graveyard on Mayor always puts me in a mood. Boyd Coady is combing his dog there. The dog is tied to a pipe railing with a blue ribbon. There's a number spray-painted on some of the pines above the Farrell graves.

I ask him why.

He says he just needed things. He needed to do his laundry.

Did you fix the faucet?

It was not a big problem. A washer, he says.

And that's your TV?

She didnt have a TV. I like to watch TV. It was the TV that did me in.

Me: I thought it might have been the underwear.

And Boyd looks at me as though I'm nuts. It's evident he knows nothing about the underwear.

The sky darkens at 4:30.

At the gallery, the commissionaire is reading a self-image book. I ask what it's all about. It helps you improve your image. This war vet, sitting at a desk between rooms of Chinese prints and wrought-iron sculpture.

27 I drive Iris to work at the marine lab. Jethro's wipers are broken. Iris says she's cooking supper tonight. She has brown eyes that remind me of a small ceramic deer I had once when I was eight. It came from a box of tea.

I tell her that I saw Boyd, that I talked to him.

I can't believe you didnt hit him. With a stick. If I were Lydia I'd clean everything I own, she says.

28 At St Patrick's Church we watch Max Wareham and Daphne Yarn wed. Their son, Eli, in a pram with a blanket the same colour as Daphne's dress.

I flip through the book of hymns, and learn that the angel's sole purpose is to praise God.

Lydia reads a passage about the good wife. And she changes it. She adds vice versa to all the commands on the wife. She is sitting with Wilf and I hear him say, You changed the Old Testament on a whim? and she whispers, It was sexist.

Also in the hymn book, the word chrism.

Daphne's mother ties a knot at the back of her necklace, to shorten it on her clavicles.

29 Max's house is larger than it looks. One of his knuckles is carefully scarred from a chainsaw and plastic surgery. He has thick wrists. His legs are thin. When he sits he is careful. He has an old man's caution about sitting. His features are young. It's only in the sum of his actions that he becomes his age. I have seen a pained look cross his forehead. This pained look is new.

He once asked Maisie to marry him, and she started chatting to a man at another table. I have told him that he fears success. What? When something good comes by you sabotage it.

He nods slowly at this.

30 Been reading Thucydides. Where he says he's not interested in the applause of the present, but writing for future attention. Here I am, 2,500 years later, reading his words, feeling his person.

The ancients were equal to us in diplomacy and civilization. It might take them an afternoon to bone up on warfare (theatre of the air), and then they'd be a match for anyone. Technology does not outstrip diplomatic methods.

December

1 Today I polished shoes. I took my old leather coat and stitched the armpit. I soaked my feet in an enamel basin. I threaded new laces. I scoured the bathtub. I drew a sketch of the harbour. I bought the *Manchester Guardian*. I finished a novel. It takes just as long to read a novel as it did ten years ago. It still takes nine months to have a baby. If a woman walks away from you, it's with the same gait as if it happened in the eighteenth century.

I have stopped eating pasta. I will make pastry and bake a pie. I will ignore the clock. I will wash down the windowsills. I will study the town with binoculars. I will extract the precise quality of love that objects possess.

2 We are learning carols at Oliver's. Max's new baby asleep in Oliver's bedroom. Una sitting by the piano hugging a stuffed cheetah.

Me: I dont think this is what Maisie had in mind.

Oliver: I think Maisie can have her mind changed.

Think she won't mind?

Oliver: I think she'll look in and say this is something else.

Maisie arrives. She has a box of beer and the carol sheets. A studded leather belt that makes her tough. She's letting her hair grow. She had asked my opinion on this, quietly, and I'd said let it grow. Around the piano she has Daphne and Alex while she plays and they try harmony.

Me: How can you know the next note?

Maisie: It's all written down on the sheets. You dont have to guess.

I look around for Oliver's pregnant student. I've forgotten Oliver is circumspect.

Being shocked at how badly Alex sings. Knowing she has said she can't sing but never knowing it was that bad. She was reticent about singing and we were all, separately, encouraging her and finally she blurts out a random note and at least her ear understands it's outlandish or maybe she recognizes now the reaction of others to tone-deaf singers but she stops after three notes and retires to the couch.

Oliver leaves on Silent Night because he can't handle singing a song that possesses serious, sentimental conviction. He doesnt have the bone you need to shift the corniness aside, the irony and the slyness to allow the heart room to manoeuvre in the mood of a genuine song. He left to get a beer and I wonder if he is bereft of a clear bone of sincerity.

Then I see he's just gone because he can't handle Maisie back in his house and all of the above is false.

Max and Daphne are leaving with Eli, and Max admits to taking a half-carton of egg nog topped up with my Old Sam. He has it tucked in the tweed pocket of his overcoat. Sorry about this, Max says. Will make it up to you. He opens the mouth of the carton to show me the contents. This is while it's sticking out of the coat pocket. I love the fact that he thinks he can do this. I love the comfort.

3   Maisie says, After Christmas, I want to party hard. I want to go out with Max and Wilf and I want to have a good time.

What about work.

I've been working. After Christmas I'm going to devote myself to partying.

I meet Oliver in the bathroom at the Spur. He says, You just missed out. A guy was sharing a line of coke. Man, it burnt my nostrils. I couldnt tell the guy it had no effect because it was a freebie. But good coke, Gabe, doesnt burn at all. If it burns, you know it's full of Old Dutch.

Oliver, Maisie says, is a guy who plays both sides. She says this with admiration. He's a lawyer by day and a hound at night. He's up at seven every morning and out till four every night.

4   Two cats in a tree. In the taller branches a brilliant blue jay. With a seed propped in its thin black beak.

Beyond them a barge docked in the rain. A man operates welding gear. Acetylene torches under a blue tarpaulin, flashing in the fog.

The smell of brewery as I jog past Lydia's.

I watch a man operate a Taylor down at the dockyard. He is lifting a blue Ace container off the back of an eighteen-wheeler. He turns (his rear axle turns) and lays the container onto a stack three-high. I know the hoister is called a Taylor because I've called up Oceanex.

What is that loader called?

They're called hoisters or tailers, either one.

Which is better?

Depends how much you want to spend. I prefer tailers.

How much would one cost?

About $700,000 Canadian. What do you want to lift?

Oh, about the same thing youre lifting.

You get them through Materials Handling, Bernie Faloney, he's the man to talk to. He used to play for the Hamilton Ti-Cats. The hoisters are French-made and theyre good, except when they break down, theyre a you-know-what to get parts for.

And who makes tailers?

Taylor makes them.

Oh, it's Taylor.

The eighteen-wheelers wait in line, snorting exhaust, the Taylor operator does not hesitate. He spends less than five seconds at the side of the transport truck, his hydraulic front end (at least forty feet high) clamps onto the container — is it magnetic? — lifts, the rear wheels pivot, he swings towards the neat stack of blue containers awaiting an Oceanex vessel. He pivots the rear wheels, returns to the next truck. The previous truck now making a slow loop around the stacked containers.

5   I attend Boyd's trial. I sit with Lydia and we share a look. That beyond it all life is peculiar, we're healthy and blessed, and we are curious. We are not going to be mean to each other. Oliver Squires allows Boyd to confess to taking 114 items from eight houses in the neighbourhood. His neighbours are all present. Boyd says it wasnt personal. He just needed things now and again and he was tired of waiting in line to pay for things. He says he's sorry.

The judge sentences him to three years.

6   Alex says things tailored for me. The ideas seem to be performed or moulded to what she thinks I'd like to hear. It's flattering but annoying. Because I want her to be herself. Lydia never did that, unless she was talking to Craig Regular. Perhaps we do it to those we have crushes on. I hate seeing it in Lydia, because it implies the person she is talking to is out of her reach.

7   Alex says, Have you ever been to the synagogue? Come on, let's go.

It's Hanukkah. A wall of windows made from Stars of David.

Alex: You might be expected to wear a keepah — there's a box of them at the door.

Is that the same as a yarmulke?

Yes.

Does this one fit?

It's fine, Gabe.

In a cold room plaques of the Israeli Declaration of Independence, proclamations during the Yom Kippur War. In 1931 Hymen Feder donated three dollars. A Chagall print of Moses with the Torah.

Alex says all synagogues smell the same. A mixture of must and stale seeds. She says only five people attend Friday meetings. It's outport Judaism, she says.

How do you know so much about it?

I keep an interest in what goes on, Gabe.

We sit in the warm room at a table near the stage. There is to be a children's play. The play has a scientist refusing to go to the Hanukkah party. When her friends leave, she is killed during a chemical discovery. Moral: beware the works of man.

We are sitting with a doctor and his wife. They are both learning Hebrew. There are no vowels. Alex asks if shellfish can be kosher. No, the doctor says, because they are scavengers on the bottom.

He sticks out his hands and scrabbles his fingers over the tablecloth, the cloth gathers under his fingers until a glass topples. Scavengers, he says again.

8   Una and I watch Max filing pyrophyllite. He sits cross-legged and wears a surgical mask. The soapstone is from Manuels. He pulls down the mask and smiles. Newfoundland,

he says, has the best stone in the world. He's doing this piece for Daphne, it's slightly abstract. Near his knees are wedges of cast-off stone. That's a tail of a humpback, Una says.

Max says, You can have the humpback.

When I say a new word, like pyrophyllite, I have a propensity to forget it.

Una's game when we're walking home: Why does underwear start with an H?

Why?

Because they lie in a heap on the floor.

9   Maisie's favourite found poem is: thick fat back loose lean salt beef. We are walking up from the Ship. She opens a frail yellow umbrella. The poem was on a piece of shirt card in Vey's corner store for ten years. Now Vey's has been sold, renovated, and is for sale again as a house. There was a pot-bellied woodstove between the aisles.

Maisie says there's wonder in this life. I say, And bewilderment. Thank you, Gabe. That's the word.

10   Alex says, There's your Christmas present. I look behind me, Where. There, she says. In the near vision I see a tight filament of dental floss and a small box hanging from it. At eye level. You look in the box. The box has a glass front that's been sandblasted except for an eye, which you can look through. At the back of the box is another eye. It is a photograph of my eye. Then she shows me bits of furniture she's made: wooden arms for a chair. Human arms. She's adding pearls and chunks of mirror. Alex

has sculpted an ear that she carved by feeling her own ear. She carved from touch. Translating touch into vision.

Alex wants to build a corner camera. You stand at an intersection and the two barrels of the camera take a picture of both streets converging. The photographic paper is at a right angle and you mount the photo in the corner of a room to get the correct perspective. Of two streets meeting. I say, Does such a camera exist? Alex: No. I'm going to invent one.

She says she's bored with flat art.

We eat off plates made of fired clay.

Everything in Alex's house is art.

We bake squash stuffed with lemon and dates and mushrooms and garlic.

We drink the wine and I walk home in the clear, cold air. Sometimes you can see more in night air than you can in the day. Maybe it's the city lights.

11 Oliver talks of legal scandals. He's not the only lawyer to have left his wife for a paralegal student. He puts on his overcoat, a new coat for him. I say, Nice coat. He says that Maisie never liked it on him. That it's grubby. She's got something against second-hand clothes. It's okay if you have money. But for the poor, it marks you as poor.

I tell this to Maisie later. And I say, The coat is a bit grubby. Yes, she says. Fact is, it doesnt look good on him.

12 Max: When they were building the office tower, I didnt think it would ruin the view. At first, the scaffolding around the

infrastructure blocked only a little bit of the Narrows. It wasnt offensive. I thought I could live with that. Seemed a narrow building. Then I found out that was only the elevator shaft. So we grew trees in the backyard and now there's nothing.

13 I watch Craig Regular walking out of a restaurant carrying an Obusforme for his back. Tinker Bumbo at his side.

Craig holds the door. He is holding the door open for Lydia.

I follow them. I havent allowed myself to think that they really are an item.

They enter the Mighty White laundromat.

I stroke Tinker, who wags, blind, but his nose knows me. I think of the dog that saved Ernest Chafe. Chafe, lost in a storm, tied his sled dog to his wrist. The dog sniffed his way back to camp.

Craig is pushing detergent along the lid of a public washing machine, coaxing it down the crack in the lid. Wiping his hand over the lid to get all the blue detergent down. His money's worth.

Now, he's trying on a new shirt. I can tell that Lydia has bought the shirt. She tells him to try it on. Does she want to see if it will fit?

They get in Lydia's car. I follow in mine. They drive into the Battery. To Craig's house beyond the yellow rail.

I sit in the car and watch them through Craig's kitchen window. It is a beautiful window that looks back over St John's. His view is the reverse of my view.

There are two frozen salmon steaks hauled out to thaw. Their pink skin crystallizing to a hot white. Craig turns on a light and closes the curtains.

14 There is a warm wind blowing, a soft buttery moon. Max baked a brie with glazed crushed walnuts, a date on top. There is fresh-baked sourdough bread. We dip chunks into the melted brie and drink wine.

I ask Daphne what they did today.

Daphne: Max cooked a pheasant.

A pheasant?

Max: Daphne told me you can find pheasant in Sobeys and I imagined them hiding in behind the boxes of Cheerios, wild pheasant nesting in the rafters.

Pheasant is a good dish, Daphne says.

Max: I stuffed it with plums and quince and sewed it up.

He pronounces sewed like lewd.

Daphne: Then we sat down and ate it.

I walk home from Max's, a wind bouncing off the southside hills. It's on nights like this that things happen. It was a sinister wind. And the moon with fast wisps of cloud over it. Max raised a glass to Eugene Cernan, the last man to walk on the moon. On this very night.

15 Maisie launches her novel at the Ship Inn. She has a beautiful line where a character fires up her zipper. That's what I like about Maisie: she chooses the right word. There's more going

on in the story, but it's that word I remember.

Maisie's nervous at the Ship. She has no need to be nervous. The work is good.

16 I walk past Lydia's house. I look in through the front window. I see Craig passing two pills to Lydia's cupped hand. Then a glass of water. Tinker Bumbo stretched out on the couch. Craig holds the water in his right hand and Lydia takes the pills into her left hand. So there is a moment when their arms are crossed, in reception.

I remember Lydia asking, But what do you love about me? When I paused she said, Youre obsessed with my body. Yes, I said.

Youre obsessed with being in love, she said.

I am obsessed with being in love. I admit to this.

Lydia: You are weak alone.

I've never liked being alone, it's true.

17 When you describe an experience, what you are recounting is your memory of the act, not the act itself. Experiencing a moment is an inarticulate act. There are no words. It is in the sensory world. To recall it and to put words to it is to illustrate how one remembers the past, rather than actually experiencing the past. Keep this in mind as you read the words of others as they remember an incident.

18 Catholics rehearse their stories. They tell stories over and over. The same story, torquing it a little, realizing a certain

detail is not working, adding stuff. I've heard the same two dozen stories out of Lydia about thirty times. And then there are the daily stories. Events that happen that she recounts. She'll tell me, and then she'll call Daphne, and then her brother phones and she tells her brother. The thing I find interesting about this story-telling is that if you heard only one of these stories, you'd think she was telling it for the first time. The enthusiasm behind it. That's definitely a Catholic thing. Protestants tell a story once and it's over with. They feel self-conscious to tell the story again. They are aware of who has already heard the story. Protestants tell a story best the first time; Catholics, the last time.

This follows through into making up after arguments. Lydia wanted to list every point in the argument, make sure it was fleshed out, whereas I was happy enough to say, Okay, let's apologize and get on with it. It's as if there is some pleasure in recounting each moment of the fight, who said what when, and admitting to each wrong turn taken. Usually, of course, I had taken the wrong turns. I'm not sure if this is Catholic or not, but Lydia was convinced she knew my true motives, and I would be a bigger man if I could only admit to them. But by that time the entire fight would have evaporated into a mist with no detail or shape to me any more, and to admit to wrong-doing would be a lie. I admitted to nothing. I can be stubborn in this.

19 I watch ships coasting into harbour with bulk. Or are they empty. So slow. Ships seem arduous. Yet if you take your eye off

one, it has instantly docked or left harbour again.

I bought a crate of tangerines. This is the only export I have seen from Morocco.

Helmut has come for Christmas. He says, We should put candles on the tree.

Five months of sailing has made him thinner and ropey. He is like a coil of rope. He has tremendous strength in his grip.

He makes candle holders out of copper wire. He places twenty-six candles on the tree. We turn off the lamps as he touches the candles with a match. The candles offer light from below. The tinsel lifts in the updraft. It's a soft, uplifting light.

I watch Helmut in the kitchen, sharpening a knife on the back of a plate.

He gives me a stainless-steel spatula made in Sweden. It's wrapped and looks exactly like a spatula.

20 Wilf says his father used to sniff out fat fires. There was a man at bingo when his house burned down. They couldnt find any evidence of arson. It was a new house, properly inspected. So they gave him the insurance.

A couple of months later the police got a letter from the man with a cheque for the full amount, plus interest, and a confession to arson. The man had just found out he had terminal cancer.

People were visiting him and saying what an honest man he'd been all his life. He couldnt live with the guilt. Or better, die with it. Even his wife didnt know.

This is what he did: He crumpled newspapers and shoved

them under the couch cushions and chairs. He doused a couch with a forty-ouncer of gin. He lit the paper and went to bingo. If you want to commit arson, use alcohol. It leaves no residue.

The man had burned down his house so he could build a new one down by his daughter's place. He wanted to be close to his daughter and he knew he wouldnt be able to sell his house for what it was worth.

Because of the cancer, they didnt charge him.

One final note, Wilf says. If it was a fat fire, Dad had no compassion. He'd let photographers take pictures of the bodies.

21 I am drunk and sentimental. Can't believe what I've said to Lydia. I called and said let's get married for a year. It would help me, I could let you go more, knowing you were mine for a full year, and then we could renegotiate the terms.

And Lydia thought about it, then spoke about Oliver's voucher. You dont like it when I talk about the voucher, do you?

I think it would be disastrous, I say.

One bacchanalian night a year. You go home with someone and there are no questions or repercussions. It was meant as a fleeting proposition, but Lydia has latched onto it. There is a corner of her, a small pocket with a line of lint in it, and the lint agrees with this voucher idea.

But really the voucher is a ruse. She's attaching herself to Craig Regular. She has been hurt by me and is drifting to that smooth smart goofy guy. Who wouldnt.

22 I tell Max, There's nothing better than holding tight to the one person whose smell, whose taste, youve craved all day long.

Love is a savage thing, he says. Love is all to do with head, heart, and animal.

Daphne: You do the silliest things to make that one person laugh.

Max and Daphne are over for lunch. Max: I've been busier than a mink on a rabbit trail.

I ask Daphne what she did today and she says, and she's got this raspy voice, these sharp features, and a deep larynx like she's been shouting all night — she says she got up at noon and read Maisie's new book and then took Eli out Christmas shopping.

Max: I'm tired of buying things.

Me: So what do you think of the book?

Daphne: It's not my kind of thing.

Me: I dont persist in things that dont grab.

She laughs: I like that bit of you.

On several occasions she says, Oh no, Max, Gabriel wouldnt do that, because he no longer bothers with things he's not interested in.

23 I hear Max say: So are you and Craig seeing each other?

Lydia says nothing. Then she says, So how are things with Daphne? Is sex good?

Coming and going, Max says.

Lydia: Is it more coming or going?

24 I'm with Max, Maisie, Una, Daphne, and Wilf singing We Three Kings in front of the dark fire station. Three garage doors ascend and yellow headlights wink under the edge of the doors, then beam out. There are five silhouettes with arms crossed standing in front of the trucks, legs splayed, theyre wearing gaiters. We sing and the fire-engine lights flick on silently and strobe red. The men walk towards us in their gaiters. We see their faces. They are grinning. The kids stretch up tiptoe and break from the carollers. They see that the firemen have candy. We follow. That was wonderful, one fireman says. We were just collecting for one of the men who's in hospital.

They show us the thick chrome pole. And three men slide down, bending knees to absorb the landing, and peel away. The kids scream at this. Theyre allowed to jump onto running boards and look in at dashes and tremendous gear shifts.

25 Lydia calls me early on Christmas morning. To say Tinker Bumbo is dead.

Lydia: He started to cough up blood and I took him to the vet and the vet gave him an injection.

She's crying on the phone.

Are you alone?

Mom and Dad are here.

Do you want me to come down?

I walk down. The harbour is covered in new snow, and the morning light is pink on the snow. The water is bright. The shipyard is quiet.

Tinker Bumbo is lying on his cushion. He looks asleep. Except he's not noisy enough.

Lydia's father says, We should bury him.

Lydia: Out in the woods.

She calls Max and Daphne and they come by with Eli, and Maisie comes too and we drive out together to the barrens on the highway. Lydia's father has put Tinker Bumbo in a canvas sack and laid him on a plastic sled. We tow him, single file, into a group of spruce trees beside the mouth of a pond.

Under a big spruce we push away the moss. And Lydia and I pry out a big rock with a crowbar. The rock separates from the frost.

I lay his blue blanket in the hole. Then lay him gently on it. He's cuddled into his position. Lydia covers him in moss, and I trim a few boughs and lay them over him.

We cover Tinker with the crystallized soil. The sun is soft on the water. There'll be grouse here soon enough.

Lydia's father says Lydia and I should come back in the summer and paint the rock for Tinker.

26 Last night I walked to three different parties. At three in the morning I'm at Maisie's. I am on the couch with Alex Fleming. I have Alex's hand cupped in mine. We are drinking beer Maisie found in a cupboard. Tonight Alex is taking care of me. We are all wounded in ways that require temporary solace.

I say to her, I'm blowing this popsicle stand. This entire city. I'm leaving it. I'm gonna drive my trusty Jethro to Heart's Desire and never come back.

Alex asks if I need company.

I wouldnt be good company.

You'd be a useless article.

Precisely.

27 The snow comes when you arent looking. Snow as fresh as a new, sinister avocado leaf.

I'm in my bedroom with the space heater on blast. The Star of the Sea looks large. Alex, at midday, comes over for a cup of tea. She's wearing funky inner-city sneakers that look as fortified as skates. I'm still in my pajamas.

Alex: I can't stand people asking me what I'm up to.

Me: I've noticed people dont ask me that any more, because times are so hard. I have no job and I broke up with Lydia. I've given up on the novel. I'm drinking too much. They ask me where I'm at, that's all. They dont want to feel embarrassed.

When she leaves I go back to bed. I look at the city through binoculars. The Christmas lights make me forlorn. I look in the window where Oliver lives, but he's not in. But later, when I call about the Heart's Desire house, he says he was there. On his back on the floor, keyboard on his stomach. He says I can go out there any time I want.

I am focused on the last saltbox house in St John's. Then down to Craig's house in the Battery. Every spring the neighbours paint the rocks in his backyard white.

28 I wake up with a clenched, sore jaw. I drive out to Heart's Desire because Christmas in town is driving me to fury. It's so

cold. And I think of Bartlett's candle. So cold at the pole the flame could not melt the outside of the candle. Merely the wick and a narrow pool down the centre. I make a smoked-salmon pasta when the jannies come in. A barrel-chested fellow with a dress on, a crutch, and a large beige bra on over the dress. He's wearing a rubber Halloween mask and rubber boots and trigger mitts. A woman dressed as a man wiggles her behind, where a silver bauble dangles. A third janny quietly sits himself down and lights up a smoke. He has a green towel over his face, and he parts the folds to smoke.

Me: You'll be wanting a drink of rum.

And the one with the crutch says, We'll settle for that.

I put out the rum and some glasses and mix one with Pepsi and another straight.

Me: Now how am I going to guess you?

The crutch says, with an ingressive voice, Oh, you'll never guess us.

There is a scratching at the door then, and a little dog wags in. It's Josh's dog.

Oh, now there's a clue.

The dog barks then wags at the crutch man. Oh, he's a nice dog.

I guess them but it's not Josh and his parents. It's Toby and his mother and father. They are sweltering under their garb. They say, Come out with us now.

How come you have Josh's dog?

Oh, the Harnums moved to Alberta.

I wrap a quilt around my waist. Toby's mother takes down a

sheer curtain and I place the curtain over my head. I shove on a beanie and they say, Youre perfect. Grab your guitar and let's go down to the road.

We'll leave the dog in here.

We walk past Josh's house. The windows are boarded over. A For Sale sign below the mailbox. And then I notice a lot of the houses in Heart's are boarded over.

The guitar loses its tune in the cold. Toby raps on the screen door.

Any jannies in tonight?

And in we walk, banging our boots in the porch.

They take down a bottle of rum and some glasses and get the girls down to look at us, but the girls arent interested. They frown at us. And the missus holds under her arm a little cocker spaniel that barks. She doesnt tell the dog to stop, and she doesnt take it away. Just points it at us, barking.

I play I Can't Help It If I'm Still in Love with You, in falsetto. And they all sing along. The guitar has warmed up again.

But they can't guess us, and they look interrupted, so we leave, and Toby wants me to continue down the shore.

I say, I'm heading home. No one knows me.

Sure, look at the length of you. Who else could you be?

Well, they never twigged.

When I get back I remember Josh's dog. He spends the night, at the bottom of my bed. The only thing left of the Harnums.

29 I realize living in Heart's Desire is agony. When youre on your own, you can focus on your agony all day long. I decide to drive back to town and confront it. I shovel Lydia's front steps, salt her path. I make Egyptian lentil soup.

I've decided to attend Lydia's party.

She is making quiche and pear melba pies. There are casseroles of turkey soup. I've learned, from Lydia, to make pastry without touching it. Craig is arranging a bowl of marzipan apples. I notice he's put on weight and let his hair grow an inch. He has a softer look. His glasses are made of titanium, the hinge is one single wire bent and the temple pushed down through the coil.

Max, out of allegiance to me, says, Hey, Craig, nice glasses. They come in men's?

Craig: No. But I hear you do.

Craig has zippers on his front pockets. A quiet man.

Wilf is in a corner chanting to himself: Got to get through. January. Got to get through. February.

Pause.

Got to get through. January. Got to get through.

Craig corners me to confess a feeling for Lydia. So I pretend Lydia means nothing to me. That I highly recommend her.

He says, The human being can't live too long with uncertainty. It prefers failure to uncertainty.

Lydia says then, There are so many fucking mediocre artists in this country.

Then, to me: I suppose youre writing that down.

Max says to me, I can't believe how polite youre being.

What, should I start throwing furniture?

Cause a scene, man. This is your moment to shine.

Wilf comes over to me and says, So Tinker's gone, hey?

Yes.

Max: He was a dog especially loved for doggy acts.

Wilf: He was a dog's dog.

Wilf has strong forearms. And a willingness to try on a woman's pillbox hat.

Boyd Coady's television is still in the living room.

30 I wake up alone and open the blinds to the city. The harbour is frozen shut. Iris and Helmut have flown to Miami to study a sailboat. I'm the kind of man who craves to be alone, but once alone, I crave company. It's as though I'd prefer to live in a tough situation than to live in a vacuum. I'm thinking that I have to learn to live alone, but what I really need to learn is how to live with someone else. Happiness seems impossible.

I sing the saddest songs I know, Hank Williams songs. I cook some eggs and brew a pot of tea. Tea is far better for a hangover. I can feel the corners of my mouth drooping in sadness, and I laugh at my sadness. I can examine and appreciate my own emotional torment. Luckily, I'm not a man prone to moroseness. If it were not for my buoyant constitution I would slit my wrists in the bathtub. I would.

I have been reading writers who say, essentially, that we'll be food for worms soon enough, so make sure that what you are living you love. And it's true there was too much anguish and ruin with Lydia. And Lydia seems a far sight happier with that asshole. He's not an asshole. He's such a great guy he must be an asshole. No one can be that perfect. I bet he has a hole in his heart. I bet Craig is emotionally cold. Assholism is relative. It proves the theory of relativity.

I gotta leave this place. I gotta start over. I've used up everything here. I have to let the city go fallow.

31 It's the last party of the year and every one I love is in Max's house. The women are dancing in the kitchen. Wilf says, When women dance with women I get happy. I have to force myself to keep my eyes off Lydia and Craig. I ask her before midnight and she says yes she may be a little in love with Craig. Can she be in love with a chunky man with a little scar at his lip? Do I mind seeing her with him? I ask, Are you doing an Oliver Squires? and she says, Gabe. I never thought of Craig until it was over with you.

She has been going to his house to watch rented, subtitled movies. She did not want to watch foreign movies with me. She claimed they were too hard to follow on a TV. But it's the man, not the film you watch, who makes the difference. She is willing to concentrate for Craig. Fair enough.

I stand by a window and realize that love is not constant. Though I love Max and Maisie very much. I would kill myself to save them. I would do the same for Una and Eli.

Maisie says if you take care of the moment then regret will not creep into your past.

But always there is, circling around us, a sense of unfulfilled grasping. A moment winks like a black locomotive, harnessed fire, sitting impatiently on its haunches, forever primed to lurch and devour. And I'm getting older. My feet hurt, a wrinkle in my earlobe. When you are out of love you become disappointed with the weight of your body. Baths are good.

I've decided to leave St John's. I will head west and look for a desolate, foreign place. All that can happen to me here has happened.

Acknowledgements

The author would like to thank the writers in the Burning Rock fiction group for advice on many of these journal entries. I thank Claire Wilkshire, Larry Mathews, Mary Lewis, Jennifer Barclay, and John Metcalf for reading versions of this work. Mary Lewis deserves special thanks for reminding me of the importance of brevity, clarity, heart, and story.

I thank Anne McDermid for finding a home for this work, and offer much appreciation to Martha Sharpe at Anansi for taking a risk on me. I hope Martha gets a good return on her risk.

Much of *This All Happened* was written and edited during time funded by the Cabot 500 Year of the Arts program. May you all visit Newfoundland.

MICHAEL WINTER is the author of *The Big Why* (winner of the Drummer General's Award and a finalist for the Trillium Book Award and the Thomas Head Raddall Fiction Prize), *This All Happened* (winner of the Winterset Award and nominated for the Rogers Writers' Trust Fiction Prize), the short-story collection *One Last Good Look*, and more recently the novels *The Architects are Here* and *The Death of Donna Whalen*. He lives in Toronto.